NNEDIMMA OKOLI

I0587260

Torn between Homes

Between history and heartache
lies the truth of who we are.

Nnedimma Okoli

BRIDGES

For my mother,
the strong woman who has been the subtle inspiration
behind this novel.

AUTHOR'S NOTE

From childhood, I loved hearing little scraps and tales from my mother about her life in Germany, where I was born. These stories fascinated me over the years, and in November 2022, I finally listened to my inner heart and decided to weave them into a novel. I began gathering the threads of those tales, interviewing my mother during a visit, and taking notes late into the nights.

When my mother first travelled to Germany in 1993, she met a kind German woman who helped her settle in. This woman, whom my mother said had long passed, inspired the character of Zelda. Although she served as inspiration, the real woman bore no resemblance to Zelda. The character was entirely imagined and created to lend conflict and depth to the story.

That said, this novel remains a work of fiction. The characters are wholly imagined, though some events are drawn from real experiences. Even so, I have shaped and altered those events for narrative purpose, so that no plot unfolds exactly as it did in life. As novelists, we take liberties to mould truth into story.

Finally, if you are reading this book, know that I truly appreciate you. Every writer dream of being read, and without you, the years I spent creating this novel would mean nothing. Take your time to savour the words as you turn each page. Although every reader experiences a story differently, I hope you enjoy this journey as much as I enjoyed writing it.

For my mother,
the strong woman who has been the subtle inspiration
behind this novel.

AUTHOR'S NOTE

From childhood, I loved hearing little scraps and tales from my mother about her life in Germany, where I was born. These stories fascinated me over the years, and in November 2022, I finally listened to my inner heart and decided to weave them into a novel. I began gathering the threads of those tales, interviewing my mother during a visit, and taking notes late into the nights.

When my mother first travelled to Germany in 1993, she met a kind German woman who helped her settle in. This woman, whom my mother said had long passed, inspired the character of Zelda. Although she served as inspiration, the real woman bore no resemblance to Zelda. The character was entirely imagined and created to lend conflict and depth to the story.

That said, this novel remains a work of fiction. The characters are wholly imagined, though some events are drawn from real experiences. Even so, I have shaped and altered those events for narrative purpose, so that no plot unfolds exactly as it did in life. As novelists, we take liberties to mould truth into story.

Finally, if you are reading this book, know that I truly appreciate you. Every writer dream of being read, and without you, the years I spent creating this novel would mean nothing. Take your time to savour the words as you turn each page. Although every reader experiences a story differently, I hope you enjoy this journey as much as I enjoyed writing it.

Home. Home is where we belong;

...

Sometimes history is cruel, and in this moment,
I imagine that when you were moored in the Schooner York
heading to Dunbar by the sea,
The fishes that heard your wailings shocked at their fins and
pectorals;
Above the sea, the seagulls that flew past took to the sea waves
The horrible things they saw happening to you.
Even the wind itself bore witness. And Roswell King,
with his own eyes during the landing,
saw 75 bodies in the openings of history.

~ Chinua Ezenwa-Ohaeto

A JAPA STORY

PROLOGUE

Zelda Wolf walked into her office that morning, looking elegant. She had made heads turn on her way to the University, which had been her intention. It had taken her a little over thirty minutes to dress like an English woman, which was embedded as part of the study her second year students were to learn that morning, at the Department of English and Linguistics, University of Mainz, Germany.

She wore a well-tailored subtle-patterned navy blazer, with grey trousers to reflect the archetypal and timeless styles that were popular among the English women. Beneath the blazer was a high-quality cotton shirt. On her feet were low-heeled classic leather loafers. Simple gold stud earrings and a wristwatch of similar colour adorned her and complimented the dressing. Her lipstick was a soft, neutral shade; understated rather than bold. To bring it all together, her hair was styled in soft curls. She had made great efforts to look like the topic of that morning's lecture: Cultural Factors, Including Fashion and Dress, Indirectly Influence Language Use and Linguistic Behaviour.

Zelda saw the stack of mail neatly placed on her office table the moment she dropped her grey handbag. They were not there the previous day when she closed from work. Her office cleaner, whom she usually requested to grab her mails, must have brought them in that morning. She picked the first mail and ripped it open with the letter-opener she got from her desk drawer. The headline which read *Internal Memo* stared back at her as she unfolded it.

Scanning through it, Zelda realized it was an official notice appointing her as a member of the "Immigrants' Lecturers Welfare Committee," alongside five others. The committee would oversee the welfare of the immigrant lecturers resuming work at the university the following session, and she shuddered at the thought. She knew why she had been selected after going through the list; they had all lived outside of Germany at some point in their lives. By the time she got to the end of the memo, her face had acquired a deep frown. Her legs felt weak. She went around the table and sat down, the letter still in her hands. She felt a new heaviness in her forehead; an ache.

Hannah. She had neither seen nor spoken to her in close to two years. She was still angry and disappointed in her for marrying against her wish. Now she has been appointed to see to the settling down of some immigrants with high likelihood of having the same skin tone as the man her daughter married. She crumpled the memo in her hand and trashed it, making sure that the paper felt the heat of her anger. By the time she finished writing her rejection letter to the committee, it was almost time for her class to commence. She made a mental note to submit the letter after the day's lecture.

That night, the air within the house, which was surprisingly stifling enough that early spring, prompted Zelda to set out the table on the lawn in front of their home, which stood in a private, secluded area, away from the bustle of the city. While she and her husband, Stefan, sat eating with the soft, yellow glow of light bathing the table between them, she brought it up.

"I got appointed as a member of a new committee. I got the notice today." She was scooping her potatoes slower than she normally did.

"That's some great news, dear. What committee is that?" Stefan asked. The bright lantern light not far away from him gave his face a sheen, while the contents of his plate kept vanishing fast into his mouth.

"Some committee for immigrant lecturers. We are to ensure that the immigrants settle and fit in when they arrive for the next session. I'm sure some of them would look like that man Hannah fell for. *Was für eine Drecksarbeit!*" The disdain on her face could not be mistaken, even in the near darkness.

No answer.

"You're not saying anything, darling."

"Hannah gave birth to her baby last night. A boy."

"How did you know that?" Zelda jerked first before the words came, her voice an octave higher. The rustling of the leaves from the apple tree close by continued to whisper through the near darkness, playing a subtle melody.

"She called the house this morning. We have a grandchild, dear," Stefan announced. He belched and reclined into his chair. His plate lay empty before him.

Zelda's face fixed on her husband; her spoon dropped back into her plate with some potatoes still in it. The table began to shake a little, propelled by her shaking legs. "The pregnancy was already due?"

"Yes. Maybe you should accept the immigrants' appointment or whatever it is called. When the time comes, you might want to interact and engage in conversations with the immigrants to broaden your views. You could even learn a lot and get prepared to meet the man our Hannah chose to marry... and our grandchild. It's long overdue, dear." Stefan's huge frame straightened from the chair and moved into the house, stopping in front of the television in the sitting room. He released himself into the couch with the TV remote in his hand.

With the arrival of more darkness, the crickets' night chirping began; their rhythmic sounds resonating through the air.

PART ONE - 1993

CHAPTER ONE

29th September 1993

Earlier that day, in the quiet hours of that morning when she woke, Ifeoma Odogwu laid back on the bed, watching through the window as the sun crept over the horizon, slowly spreading daylight into the room. It seemed to her that the universe had conspired in her favour. And now, finally, the day she had long dreamt of was here, almost like any other one. It was a bright, beautiful day to leave the shores of her country.

She had had many dreams of travelling. In the dreams, she often saw herself making travel preparations, buying things and packing them. But the dreams always ended just as she was about to board the plane, or something vague would come up to delay the trip. Whenever she woke from these dreams, she would stare at the ceiling, wondering why waking always felt like stepping away from something just within reach. But she knew the answer; it was the way of dreams to take elements from one's innermost thoughts and begin to weave details around it.

In her university days, three to four years ago, when most of her friends talked about leaving the country after graduating, to some other place with better government and better opportunities, Ifeoma had simply listened to them talk. She had no such plans and thought nothing of leaving her home country. How could she have known then that her future husband would make it possible in a few years to come? How could she have known she would welcome it with all enthusiasm? Time and chance had brought it all her way. That was life. She had met and married a man who, just like her friends, wanted to leave his country. Somehow, she had gone along with the plans. She had loved every part of the preparations, especially the beam she saw on people's faces whenever she announced to them that she was leaving the country and heading to Germany. Their faces and words always synchronized into saying one thing; how lucky she was.

***

The September morning sun shone bright as usual at the Murtala Mohammed International Airport in Lagos, Nigeria. As they stepped out of the taxi into the airport parking area, the mix of faint jet fuel and exhaust fumes from private cars and taxis hit Ifeoma, and she immediately missed the crisp, clean air she'd left behind in Awka. Ifeoma and her mother, Ogechi, retrieved their luggage from the taxi's trunk, with Ifeoma holding her one-year-old son, Ikenna, by the hand.

A serene smile danced on Ifeoma's lips as they retrieved their luggage and began walking, thinking of times when she had imagined this day would never come. Her mother's voice pulled her from her thoughts.

"Did you remember to pack all the spices I left out under the sun to dry?"

For days, Ifeoma's mother had hammered on it, constantly reminding her daughter to make sure she didn't forget it. Ogechi was the kind of woman who thought about every little thing. Her head-tie hung loosely on her head, one side of the cloth more pointed than the others, creating an imbalance as if it were tied in a hurry. She had dressed hastily early that morning, for she didn't want her daughter and grandson to miss their flight, if she had settled in front of a mirror to tie the head-tie the way she normally would. There would be enough time for that in the future after they were gone.

"Yes, Mama. I packed them inside the smaller box with the other condiments," Ifeoma was smiling, exposing her well-arranged dentition. At twenty-seven, her oval face gleamed with shine, like a piece of ebony lying under the bright sun. Her legs stood straight and slender, which she knew was part of the many features that had attracted her husband, Ugochukwu, during their early courting days. She had caught him many times, lost, and staring at her legs. The stares hadn't stopped, even after the courtship was over and they were married.

Ogechi looked at her daughter. The expression on her face was that of a typical Nigerian mother who must have the final say with her child, no matter the age. "*Akam asikwa*! I would have sent you back to Awka to get them because you would be needing a lot of them when you finally put to bed."

Unsurprised, Ifeoma's expression remained unchanged as she listened to one of the familiar lines she had often heard in the past week. Her mother had been buying things she believed she would be needing in Germany, making unrealistic threats, and scolding unnecessarily. She remained calm, aware that her decision to leave her mother behind in Nigeria, without a clear return date, was silently weighing on her mother's mind. Ifeoma knew the separation was taking a subtle toll on her.

"Yes, Mama," she said simply.

Ogechi halted in her stride just a few steps to the airport security, as if something very important had occurred to her. She turned sideways to face her daughter. "How can you and your husband travel so far away? How would I care for your unborn child when you give birth? How can you both deny me this *omugwo*, *eh*? Did I deny my own mother any *omugwo* when I was having you and your siblings? I had you and your four brothers, Ifeoma, and I did not do that, but that is what you want to do to me!"

Ifeoma paused, biting back a sigh. Now? After weeks of silence. She looked at her mother, theatrically clutching the edge of the baggage she wheeled like it was a lifeline, and thought her mother putting on a bit of a show. She opened her mouth in a bid to explain that since her mother came for Ikenna's *omugwo*, she didn't deny her so much, but then thought better of it before closing her mouth. Her explanations would yield nothing. She had known her mother long enough to understand that she wouldn't win any argument with her. She looked at her mother and wondered if she was doing that on purpose. She had grown to know she had a way of getting whatever she wanted from her father. Maybe she was trying to play that trick on her now.

She remembered one such instance years ago, in late July, her mother was preparing to attend the Women's August Meeting in their village. She had wanted to buy very expensive shoes and clothes so as to show-off during the gathering. Her father had refused to give her the money for days, advising her mother to instead use the ones she had been buying non-stop over the years. Her mother had simply refused and started to drop comments around the house about *how some men could be selfish in doing only the things they wanted.* This went on for days till her father got tired of it all and gave her mother everything she wanted. Her young mind had observed each of those episodes as they unfolded while growing up, each having that same pattern. Was that the weapon her mother was trying to use on her now? Trying to play on her emotions like she did to her husband all those years? In a bid to hold herself from protesting, something sounding like "*ah*" escaped her mouth instead.

"It is okay, my child. I should not make you sad this morning that you're travelling. I should not burden you with my troubles."

"Ha, Mama! This is the first time you are indirectly admitting you will miss me," Ifeoma teased as her mother looked away. "But don't worry, Mama, we won't stay in Germany forever, we will be coming home to see you, I promise."

"That is good. It is not proper for a mother not to see the child she had birthed, nursed and raised for a long time. Your father and I will be praying for you. Everything you and Ugochukwu will lay your hands on shall prosper." Ogechi unwittingly slipped into prayer, a habit Ifeoma knew well.

"Amen!" she said.

***

Ifeoma grew up in an affluent family. Her father, Okwesilieze, was a famous well-to-do trader whose containers of car spare parts arrived six times every year through the Apapa port in Lagos. He controlled a significant share in the distribution of the car spare parts in Lagos State, as well as in the eastern part of Nigeria.

The story of her father's business talent had been told to Ifeoma countless times. While growing up in the village, rather than playing football with his peers, Okwesilieze had spent his free time creating toys for sale to other children. He would repurpose discarded materials like old tires and wood to craft his products. Occasionally, a parent would notice his creations and make a purchase. By the time he reached grade six, Okwesilieze had lost interest in formal education and announced his desire to pursue a career in entrepreneurship. While his mother initially disapproved, his father, who had multiple sons to support through school, was only too relieved. Eventually, Okwesilieze's mother gave her blessings and he embarked on his journey. And with time, Okwesilieze did succeed.

Growing up, Ifeoma lived with a number of male apprentices known as *umuboyi* in the house. These apprentices helped her father, Okwesilieze, in his numerous business outlets. Each apprentice usually lived with the family, in the boys' quarters, for about six to seven years, serving their 'master', Okwesilieze, and learning the trade from him at the same time. At the end of their apprenticeship period, her father would 'settle' the apprentice with a reasonable amount of money and some goods, so that the apprentice could start off on his own. That way, her father ended up 'settling' about twenty-one apprentices in thirty years who were currently independent and making their own money in their businesses.

Her father ran his household the same way he ran his businesses. If he pays your school fees, you have to reward him with good school results. If he shelters you, you must do house chores in return. Discipline was the order in the household from the time Ifeoma started cutting her teeth. There were always rules on how everything should be done in the house, the majority of which her father had made. The only person to whom the rules never seemed to apply was her mother, Ogechi. Such rules as what time to watch television or when to eat did not apply to her mother who seemed to rule her father instead. It was only her mother who could cajole her father into modifying any house rule he made. She saw this play out a lot whenever the schools were on holidays; her mother only had to ask her father to allow them extra hours to play around the house before going to bed.

***

Still a few steps to the airport security, Ogechi suddenly let out a chuckle. Seeing the surprised look on her daughter's face, she said, "Don't look at me like I'm mad, Ifeoma! It's really funny that when you and your siblings were little, I couldn't wait for all of you to grow up and leave the house for me, so I could have less responsibility. You started talking early and asked too many questions when you were little. 'Mama, why is this? Mama, why is that?' I even had to hide from you sometimes."

Ifeoma laughed.

"Yes *o*, I would hide so that you will take your questions to your father or anybody else, then I will come out from my hiding."

"I don't remember these things, Mama."

"You won't since you were little. I can't believe I wanted you all to leave."

Ifeoma noticed the pain on her mother's face; the corners of her eyes crinkled as she spoke. She had been more emotional in a single day than she'd known her to be in a whole year. She turned from her mother and walked on as gingerly as her pregnancy could allow her so as to quicken her mother's steps who seemed to be stalling on purpose.

Once they got inside and picked up their scanned bags, Ifeoma led her small group to the check-in counter, which were surrounded by piles of suitcases awaiting conveyors to convey them to their various storages for travel. She took out the two passports and tickets she would present.

CHAPTER TWO

29th September 1993

At the counter, Ifeoma met a queue of people. She found a space at the end of the line and stood there. After a short while, she felt her son tugging at her hand, trying to wriggle free. She'd been holding on tightly, knowing he would soon grow restless from standing still. Ikenna was predictable that way. If nothing was happening, he would find a way to make something happen. There were never any dull moments with him.

Turning to her mother, Ifeoma said, "Mama, you will have to find a seat somewhere to sit down *o*, it could take some time to get to our turn with this line. We will meet with you later after we have been checked-in."

"I will do that, my daughter. But be careful with the bags so you don't misplace any of them," Ogechi said and left in search of a seat.

A man stood in front of the line a while later, facing everyone, and began to speak to the people in the queue. "Please stand in a single line so we can attend to everyone." His hands were raised so everybody could see him. "Older persons above the age of fifty-five are now invited to proceed to the front of the queue for check-in. Expectant mothers can also proceed to the front. Please make way for them."

That was all Ifeoma needed to hear for a wide smile to appear on her face. It was a considerate thing to do. It wasn't that the line was moving too slowly, but this new development would save her some energy. With Ikenna, she never knew when the need to spend that energy would arise. Guiding her son, she walked to the front. It was just her and two elders. When her turn came, she presented the tickets and passports to be checked before she rolled her bags to the left where they would be searched. There were two custom officers in charge of the search.

One of the officers was a tall, broad-shouldered man with a stern expression. With just one glance, Ifeoma sensed there were two possible reasons for his seriousness: either the job meant a great deal to him, or it made him feel important. Whichever it was, he carried out his duties with unwavering intensity. His partner, a woman, looked smaller in comparison, and had a warm smile that put Ifeoma at ease. This was a balanced combination and it suited their role, Ifeoma reasoned. One appeared welcoming while the other looked the opposite.

The male officer spoke, "Hello, madam. May I ask where you are headed?"

"Hi," Ifeoma replied, looking from one officer to the other. "We are on our way to Germany, to meet my husband." She had finished speaking before she realized it: was that last piece of information even necessary?

"Oh. That is nice, madam," the second officer said. "Has it been long your husband travelled?"

"Not very long, just a few months ahead of us." The words rolled effortlessly off her mouth in response to the officer's smile.

"It is good you're going to join him over there. A man is not supposed to be left alone like that, my friend. I wouldn't allow my own husband to stay far from me," the female officer said and let out a little laugh. "You know men and how they are naturally, don't give them that chance."

What the female officer said about men and not giving them any chance did not sit so well with Ifeoma, but she felt it unwise to say anything to counter it. She looked instead at the male officer as he concluded the search on the first bag and proceeded to the second. In order to appear busy and avoid saying something awkward, she bent towards Ikenna, wiping a non-existent dirt from the corner of the boy's lips.

The officer continued when she didn't get a reaction from the woman. "You know this, *ba*?"

"Yes, I do know," Ifeoma concurred as she straightened up.

"You are a wise woman, madam," the female officer said and smiled. She had learned in this job that if she could put people at ease with small talk, they were more likely to let go of some money. Get them chatty and comfortable enough so that they could easily agree to the demand she would make at the end of their little chat. But the woman before her wasn't chatty enough. And prolonging the chat could get uncomfortable for both of them. She decided to go straight to the point; there would be better prospects after this woman had gone. "*Find us something before you leave us here o.*"

Ifeoma only smiled at her.

The male officer spoke next. "Our scan shows you might have some paper money wrapped in a corner in one of your boxes, is it naira or foreign currency?"

Ifeoma hesitated. Was it a crime to leave the country with naira notes? This wasn't a good time to be breaking any laws. "It is both, sir. But the naira isn't much, just some change. I can leave the money with my mother before boarding, if it's not allowed."

The male officer shook his head sideways and said, "No, no, it's totally fine. It is not against the law. But since you wouldn't be needing any of the naira notes where you are going, you can keep them with us here."

That was the first time Ifeoma saw something resembling a smile on the male officer's face; an expression better termed a smirk than a smile. "You are right, officer. I wouldn't be needing the naira notes over there." She then unzipped the inner side of the box in question and brought out a paper bag containing notes she had wrapped neatly the previous day. She had given her mother some of these naira notes that morning. The remaining was what she kept with her in case of any need at the airport. She separated the Deutsche Mark she had received from her husband (Ugochukwu had hidden some Deutsche Mark inside the gift box he last sent to her) from the few naira notes and handed the naira notes over. She noted that the smirk on the male officer's face increased before pocketing the money. He didn't even bother to check the amount.

"Thank you, madam. Have a safe flight," he said and waved Ifeoma on.

They found her mother seated somewhere close to an emergency exit and joined her, waiting for their flight to be announced for boarding. Thirty-two minutes later, the announcement came. There were movements around as people stood to say their goodbyes to loved ones. Ifeoma straightened, her belly standing out in front of her.

"Mama, it is time to board the plane," she said, looking down at her mother.

"Is it time?" Ogechi asked as she stood from her seat.

"Yes, they just made the first call," Ifeoma replied, wrapping one arm around her mother's back, while making sure that the other hand held her son.

Ogechi hugged her daughter. "You're finally leaving with my first grandchild," she said, staring blankly at the movements around them. "You still don't know when you will be back?"

Ifeoma closed her eyes, still leaning over her mother. "I don't know yet, but we will all come back to see you as soon as we can."

"Your father and I will miss you, all of you. You know he'd be here if the *Umunna* hadn't called an emergency meeting for the titled men in the village," Ogechi said, lifting Ifeoma's head from her shoulder, then bending down to Ikenna. "Take care of him very well, and the one you will soon give birth to."

"I will do that, Mama," Ifeoma answered. "I will miss you too."

"I know you will bring me over to America when you settle down."

"Mamaa!" Ifeoma strained the last syllable of the word. "We are not going to America, it is Germany."

"Hmm, anyone *biko*. Are they not all the same, *eh*? White man's land is white man's land. Anyway, do you remember Mama Nkechi?"

"The one that sells clothes at the end of your line at the market?" Ifeoma asked.

"Yes, that one. I went to her shop to inform her that you were going to America. Instead of her to be happy for me, she told me that her own daughter in America was planning to bring her over there soon for *omugwo*. Very boastful woman. I will go to America too."

"Mamaa..."

"Don't forget to send my greetings to your husband when you get there, let him know that I am not happy at all; he is taking you all far away from me," Ogechi said.

Ifeoma smiled. "I will deliver your message, Mama. Please send my greetings to Papa when he returns from his trip," she said, hugging her mother again. "Tell him I already miss him."

Ogechi waved at them, straining to look at the ceiling. She didn't want her daughter to see her tears now. She would allow the tears to flow freely later when they were gone.

Ifeoma took her son's hand and turned towards the gate. She knew that since her back was turned on her mother, she would likely stand there looking at them till they were out of her sight. She turned on her way and gave her mother one final goodbye with a wave of hand.

"Tell Big Mama bye-bye," Ifeoma urged Ikenna, but the boy only looked towards his grandmother and smiled.

***

The airplane was in view now; gigantic in size. The aircraft stood tall and long, stretching out like a giant metallic bird preparing to take flight. Was that not what it was? The more she looked at it, the more imposing it seemed to appear. It was a sight: dwarfing every structure and person close to it.

The iconic logo – LUFTHANSA AIRLINES – was boldly inscribed on its body in dark blue. Ifeoma's eyes widened as she looked on. She had seen lots of planes in the movies, in drawings, but never in real life. As she stood looking at it now, there was no doubt that the movies, pictures, and even her mind did a bad job in creating the real picture. None of them had presented the airplanes to be as huge as what stood before her now. Her eyes went briefly towards the sky and down to the airplane, and she wondered how such a mighty huge thing would fly up with all its metallic weight.

Soon, she settled in the plane after finding their seats. It was then that she recalled how this journey really started.

***

The three of them had travelled to Lagos from the eastern part of Nigeria the previous day, and had expected it to be an easy six-hour journey, but it turned out to be far from it. The white-coloured bus they had boarded had left the park at exactly 8:05 a.m. the previous day.

The stress started when they were all seated in the bus, waiting for the bus driver to start the journey. Instead, a bus preacher had emerged out of nowhere, hanging himself by the door. He started with singing praises which her mother and other passengers joined along. Or did they scream it? It felt more like they had screamed those songs. When the preacher began to preach, his loud voice worsened the headache she already felt.

Ifeoma heard the preacher, "Stretch your hands towards the west..." That was the direction of Lagos, their destination. "...command the roads to be safe. Command the tyres to keep away from the dangers of the road." Every other person had stretched their hands after the prayer point was declared. Who wouldn't do that when there were potholes glaring like shallow graves on the roads? Ifeoma thought. She only stretched her hands with the others when her eyes met her mother's glowering gaze. Her right hand had jerked forward quickly in front of her before she was conscious of it. Her mother never joked with prayers. Not even the prayers they said that morning before leaving the house were enough for her.

As they prayed, a train of four blind beggars approached the bus, circling it with singing and waving their musical *sekere* as their partially blind leader, who was in front, led the group. The noise from the musical instruments which all the beggars held soon drowned the voice of the preacher. The preacher's voice remained drowned till the beggars had gone round the bus stretching out their bowls and singing their blessings. Some of the passengers dropped money into their bowls. Ifeoma had seen the preacher's face twitch as he waited for the beggars to leave.

It was only when the preacher was done and had collected the offerings made to support his ministry that the bus driver appeared and they commenced their journey. The two acts were so synchronized that she suspected that the preachers and the bus drivers in the park worked hand-in-hand.

The bus hit the first of many potholes only five minutes into the road, jostling the bus back and forth. Unfortunately, her seat in the bus was situated at the back, directly on top of the rear tyre and as such, she felt every rough bump and pothole as the bus moved along. The journey had been that discomforting. Her mother sat beside her, offering words of comfort the best she could. *"Ndo, nwa m."* *"Nwayo o."* "We will soon get to Lagos."

Ikenna, on his part, slept soundly on his grandmother's laps for the greater part of the journey, blissfully unaware of the discomfort. Each time the bus hit a pothole, he would stir and turn, then get back to sleep again. He only woke up to urinate and eat midway when the driver stopped at Agbor for passengers to stretch their legs and get refreshed.

Many times, during the journey, the air had gotten thick with the smell of smoke whenever they got to a slow-moving traffic. There had been smoking cars, lorries, and trailers carrying goods, vehicles not supposed to be road-worthy due to the level of smoke they emitted. But those vehicles had been there, sharing the road with every other sound car. It had been those vehicles that filled the air with smoke and fumes during such traffic.

Towards afternoon, Ifeoma had felt the heat and humidity pressing down on their vehicle, making her feel suffocated. It was usually worse when the bus was not moving fast to let in enough breeze. This was bad for her since her pregnancy made her perceive even the faintest smell.

As they got closer to Ogun State (this was the last state before Lagos), she felt the pressure on her knees and legs begin to mount. She tried many times to shift her weight from one side of her buttocks to another to relieve the pressure, but it was of no use. Her legs eventually became very much swollen by the time they got to Lagos.

If her mother had experienced any discomfort, she neither showed it nor complained openly. Though Ifeoma was aware that her mother's mind was heavy with the impending thought that her only daughter and grandchild would be leaving Nigeria the following day with no clear date of return. That must have drowned any discomfort she felt.

Finally, at half past five, they arrived in Lagos. A supposed six-hour journey had turned to nine. Ifeoma was the last to stumble out of the bus, with shaky and unsteady legs. Her mother had helped her, supporting her as they left the bus park. Then another problem arose that grey evening when they tried to locate the home of the relative that would house them overnight.

Her mother had been given directions to the house of her relative days before that journey. They had been told that the house was within walking distance from the bus stop where they would stop, and so they started asking around for directions. They asked the driver of their own vehicle for the address, but soon realized that the directions he gave conflicted with the one given by two other drivers they later asked at the bus park. It took them over an hour to finally locate the house. It was the similarity of the street name to another street nearby that had confused the drivers.

Within an hour of entering the relative's house, Ifeoma had eaten, taken her bath and was soon snoring away, leaving her mother to take care of Ikenna and his needs.

***

Presently, Ifeoma looked at Ikenna who was a little calmer than usual in the plane. The boy watched people enter the plane and search for their seats, and the boy's eyes were very much engrossed with the movements around, she was grateful for this little favour.

CHAPTER THREE

29th September 1993

Ugochukwu Odogwu entered the one-bedroom apartment he had rented not far from the University of Mainz, Germany, where he worked. He had lived here for three months. He took the shopping bags he was carrying into the kitchen before returning to the room. The wall clock which read 11:09 p.m. reminded him of how late it was. He rubbed his face with both hands and yawned. He needed to rest.

He had been out trying to put final touches to getting the apartment ready in preparation for the arrival of his family the following day. He had finished work around five p.m. and returned to the apartment to put it in order before taking a bus into the city to do some more shopping. He hadn't seen his pregnant wife and son in the last three months but it felt like years. He had to make the apartment feel like a home when they arrived. Left for him, he would have elected to order his meals or eat outdoors. But he knew his wife well enough; he knew that the moment she arrived, cooking would be done daily in the apartment. She wasn't the type that liked to eat out often. Due to this, he had gone to an African store at the outskirts of the city to pick some foodstuff. He had selected things he thought were similar to the ones they shopped in Nigeria. He had to make this space feel home enough to her.

He pulled off his clothes and got into lighter ones before releasing himself into the bed. He hoped again that the decision to leave Nigeria and make out a whole new life from scratch here will be worth it. He sighed. It hadn't been easy leaving behind everything he had known from childhood to adulthood: his family, friends, and familiar surroundings to come here in search of greener pastures.

As an undergraduate student studying Literature in the University of Nigeria, Nsukka, he never thought he would be the kind of person who wanted to leave his home country. Back then, he had seen his future so clearly, his dreams laid out before him like a path he was certain to follow. He had thought of his future life to be straightforward and easy. He loved writing and had written poems and short stories whenever the muse came to him as an undergraduate. He had submitted to poetry contests he had seen advertised in newspapers and had emerged as one of the winners on three occasions, placing first in one and second in the other two. There had been no doubt as to where his life was headed. He would graduate and become a professional writer. That had been his calling.

Writing. It made him come alive. It drew out his emotions and feelings. He could even spend hours just thinking about this calling alone; writers could create realms that never existed, then go ahead to fill them up with beings never heard of in all the known realms, and make their readers think about those beings as if they were real. And the readers? They love to journey with the writers as they wove their tales, even if for a short time, just to somehow forget about the harsh reality of living. It was all he wanted to do with his life.

But fate had other plans. In those years when he believed he could get by in life with just his writing; he began submitting his writings to publishers. He did it the first year after graduation, did it again the second year, but each time, his manuscripts came back months later brimming with rejections. With time, he knew that he couldn't continue to hold onto that dream. His parents were also beginning to make the house uncomfortable for him. They kept telling him to man up and get a real job. His writings weren't going to feed and clothe him. By the beginning of the third year of submissions, he became convinced that his parents had been right. Writing wasn't going to feed and clothe him, maybe not yet.

He buried his nose in every newspaper he could find, scanning the job advertisement columns for work suited to him. Whenever he saw a job advert related to what he studied, he would fold a copy of his curriculum vitae, relevant certificates, and cover letter, and send them to the required address. It was in his second month of sending out applications that he found the advert for the position of Graduate Assistants at the Nnamdi Azikiwe University, Awka. Seven departments in the university were advertised including the department of English Language and Literature. Exactly his field. He applied, making sure to emphasize his literary awards and writings.

He got a letter the following month scheduling him for an interview at the university which he attended.

The letter offering him the job came back two months later requiring him to send some more documents, along with his letter of acceptance. Not long afterwards, he left his parents' house (much to their delight) and moved to Awka, into an apartment close to the university.

Five years later, he met the young lady he would later get married to. He used to watch her sit on the edge of one of the lecture benches. Her eyes looked straight at the lectern with resolve and interest while she scribbled down things. He always saw her in a group of three other students. A group he could best describe as a clique. And they always sat in the same position in class; with the young lady he had eyes for always sitting at one of the edges of the bench.

It was her legs that first got his attention that morning as she hurried into his class to take her usual seat in the final year class. They stood long, lean, and perfectly toned. He remembered her wearing a skirt that was slightly above her knees exposing a fluid elegance as she walked. It was only when she turned to apologize for her lateness that he realized he had stopped teaching and merely fixed his eyes on her.

He had recollected himself and simply asked for her name.

"Ifeoma, sir," she had said.

"Don't be late to my class again."

"Yes, sir."

Two weeks later, he had given the class a written test and withheld her script. It was all on purpose. His plan to draw her to his office worked and he didn't waste any time in asking her out, after assuring her that her script was safe. That had been the beginning of their friendship and courtship. They later got married not long after she graduated.

That first year of his year of marriage, he'd seen the advert for a fully funded Humboldt Research Fellowship in the newspaper, offered by the University of Mainz in Germany.

At Nnamdi Azikiwe University, where he was employed, the lecturers were on the verge of embarking on a strike to protest meagre salaries and subpar working conditions. Dissatisfaction and grievances pervaded the atmosphere, with staff meetings frequently convening to debate the pressing issue of whether or not to go on the proposed strike. It was in the midst of these troubles that he found his first motivation in the fellowship advertisement that he had come across in The Vanguard newspaper under the 'Classified Section,' contemplating a potential escape from the turmoil. He usually bought The Vanguard and The Punch newspapers on his way back from work and relaxed at the end of day to read them.

With a three-month deadline looming, he methodologically assembled the necessary documents for the fellowship application, including enrolling in a basic German language course and obtaining the certification. Having met all the requirements, he submitted his application and continued to hone his German-speaking skills over the next six months, completing the full language course. A year later, when he had almost given up hope, and assumed his application had been overlooked, he found an offer letter lying in his Staff Mailbox one Thursday afternoon. His heart rate increased when he saw the sender's name, and his joy knew no bounds when he opened it and his eyes settled over the first paragraph which read: 'Congratulations Mr. Odogwu'. It was indeed good news. Scanning through the offer letter, he saw that the first topic he had supplied during his application had been approved, and he was to explore 'the reception of Nigerian literature in the German-speaking world and its impact on literary theory.' Additionally, he would teach African literature at the University of Mainz's Department of English and Linguistics.

The news of his offer had been welcomed with celebration. That particular day would always remain indelible in his mind. He had returned that Thursday afternoon with the offer letter. His wife had finished her National Youth Service Corps (NYSC) programme months ago, which was the mandatory one-year service to their country, and he knew she would probably be home busy with writing and sending out job application letters. He just hoped that she wasn't stressing herself with combining the job applications with caring for their little one, Ikenna. It turned out that there wouldn't be any need for those applications after that day.

Ugochukwu knew that she wasn't expecting him home that early December afternoon as he parked his Mercedes 504 downstairs, since he had told her he would be home late due to the departmental internal defence that was ongoing at the university.

The wooden entrance door was unlocked when he tried it and walked into their three-bedroom apartment, holding the offer letter and an expensive wine. When he lifted the bottle of wine and turned three hundred and sixty degrees, her eyes widened as it rested on the wine bottle.

He remembered her asking, "Ugom, what are we celebrating?" but he let the suspense linger while he poured the wine, filling the two wine glasses he brought from the glass cabinet to the brim. Placing both glasses on a side stool, he handed the letter to her. He watched as she read it, and savoured the excitement that followed. His wife had danced round the sitting room countless times before she finally flung herself at him in an embrace. As he lifted her off the floor to swing her round, her leg hit the side stool where the wine glasses stood. But the sound of shattering glasses didn't matter to them at that moment.

When they later settled down to go over the details of the letter again, they felt joy flow through their bodies like a warm shower.

"So, you mean to tell me that I will go to Germany with you? Haa! We will leave Nigeria?"

And she had begun to dance all over again. Watching her hips move with the music of happiness, he had beamed with satisfaction.

Which sane man would want to leave his young family in a different country for years? It certainly wasn't him. If the offer had stated otherwise, he would have had lots of considerations to do. Yet he didn't take his family along immediately. He and Ifeoma had decided it would be best if he went alone and got a place ready for when his wife and son would later join him. To them, it was the best plan they could come up with since they knew no one in Germany who could accommodate them till they found their own accommodation. And on top of that, a child was involved.

The preparations began in earnest the following day when he prepared his acceptance letter and the other documents he would need. In late January, he wrote to Nnamdi Azikiwe University informing the school that he would be leaving his job behind in June.

He had travelled three months ahead of his pregnant wife and little son to rent a place, get acclimatized with the city before they joined him. He wanted to be sure he was settled before they arrived.

Maybe it wasn't all a mistake. Time would be kind enough to reveal this to him.

He yawned again and looked around the apartment. It wouldn't be just him occupying this space by the end of tomorrow. Soon enough, sleep claimed him.

***

Ifeoma looked around the plane, it was almost full except for a few unoccupied seats. Almost everyone was seated and only the airline crew were about. A look at Ikenna told her the boy was starting to get bored where he sat, he was attempting to get down from his seat. She pulled him back and fastened his seatbelt just as the announcements came for belts to be fastened. In no time, the plane began its movement through the runway, picked up speed and started to ascend.

Her nerves had been very much relaxed until the plane started to ascend. That was when she started to feel something different; like something in her head was trying to pull her backwards, down the plane. Her husband had asked her not to get scared in one of his letters. That was the last letter he had written from Germany before this flight. Inside it, he had described how she might feel. *Keep your eyes closed when the plane ascends, till it is balanced in the air. Occupy your mind with thoughts of things you like so you wouldn't think much of what is going on. Try to use the toilet before you settle down in the plane. The toilets could get busy and have a line in the middle of the flight, so don't forget.* But she hadn't taken that advice seriously. She should have.

And her husband had been right. She should have closed her eyes and filled her mind with thoughts of her favourite food: fried rice and chicken. That way, she wouldn't be passing through this now; this feeling of something trying to pull her down.

She felt her head growing large as her left hand gripped Ikenna's shoulder, without being aware that the boy stared at her with questioning eyes. Her right hand gripped her chair, in a way that could have cracked it if it were made of light plastic. Her heartbeat was racing as she shut her eyes, just like her husband had asked her to. After all, it's never too late if it can still be done.

Her eyes remained shut till she felt differently; no force was trying to pull her down anymore. Releasing the breath she held, she quickly became aware of movement underneath her fingers. She opened her eyes and saw Ikenna squirming to be rid of the hold she had on his shoulders. She dropped her fingers immediately and was sorry she didn't think of her son as they gained altitude.

Things were normal three hours into the flight. She had mostly kept herself busy with looking outside the window of the plane, watching as they passed all shades of cloud. She had kept her boy busy with snacks, but Ikenna was now tired of them. He started to make little noises as he squirmed in his seat. She saw the boy try again to pull at the edges of his seatbelt, in a bid to free himself from its grip.

Loosening her seatbelt and drawing herself closer to her son, she placed her hand on Ikenna's shoulder in an attempt to calm him down, but he pushed her hand away and threw his own hands and legs into the air, screaming as he did so. In the process of throwing his fists and legs around, they got Ifeoma on the stomach. It all happened fast, making Ifeoma let out a shrieking cry as the pain hit her abdomen.

Upon her loud and anguished reaction to the pain spread in her tummy, Ifeoma heard voices hovering around. People were murmuring, and she clearly heard one passenger ask if she was okay. But she couldn't answer with the pain stifling her ability to talk. Clutching her tummy, she spread out her legs in a desperate attempt at pain alleviation. She had known that Ikenna had strong bones as the boy grew from a baby into a toddler, and she had somehow ascribed it to the biscuit bones she had consumed almost daily while pregnant with him. When her son held onto something, it wasn't always easy prising it out of his hands.

"Hello ma'am, are you all right?" A voice asked.

Ifeoma saw the pair of female shoes first and knew immediately that it belonged to an air-hostess. She had noticed earlier how similar their clothes and shoes looked. Then the elegant legs appeared before the knee-length skirt, as she tried to look up while still holding her abdomen where the blow had landed. "Not really, my son is giving me a hard time." She managed to sit straight before she continued. By this time, the pain had subsided. "It is difficult to manage him in a small space."

"Sorry about that, ma'am. If you don't mind, we can help to look after him for a while so you can get some rest," the hostess offered.

She smiled at the offer, "I would appreciate that, please."

The hostess released Ikenna from his seat. As the boy walked beside the hostess, he appeared glad to be taken away from his detaining mother. He half-walked and half-jumped as he was led away. Ifeoma sighed, but she appreciated another capable hand handling Ikenna for a while. She got up and slowly walked towards the toilet to ease herself. Sure enough, there was a small line.

The pain from Ikenna's fist was completely gone by the time she returned to her seat, as if it never happened. She relaxed into the chair with thoughts of the place they were heading to. She had read a story from a novel during the long vacation after her second year in the University. The book was based on a true-life story and followed the lives of a couple who lived in Berlin during World War II in Nazi Germany. It told a sad story of how Hitler meted out harrowing persecutions to Jews and other certain minority groups through his Nazi party till 1945.

She hadn't known at that time that she would someday set foot in Germany. She would have read more of such books if she had known. Now, she had only the general knowledge of that story, but not the specifics of it. She was heading to Germany where the events in the story had occurred and she wondered whether time had changed things.

In her mind, she counted the decades since the end of Hitler's reign in Germany. It was close to five decades. Forty-eight years was time enough for the after-effects of Hitler's deeds in Germany to wear off. She hoped so, wondering why she suddenly felt uneasy. Besides, the present is more important than the past. She was living in the present and that should be the only focus.

Her mind became completely shut as she drifted away to sleep.

CHAPTER FOUR

29th September 1993

Something nudged her lap softly and her eyes slowly opened to see the happy face of her son. Ifeoma shut her eyes again for a while to recall where she was and the past events.

"Mama! Shee!" Ikenna said with stretched-out hands, showing his mother what he was holding. He held out two chocolate bars the size of two blacksmith's fingers put together. Two small toys were shooting out of his trouser pockets.

Ifeoma looked up, her eyes wilfully thanking the airhostess who had returned her child to her.

"Welcome to Belgium, ma'am," the hostess announced, spreading out her hands to further buttress her words.

Belgium? Ifeoma thought. Then she remembered she had a connecting flight to take. "Thank you, and thank you for taking care of him," she said, rubbing her hand over Ikenna's bushy hair. She had purposely left the boy's hair without barbering it since his birth, against her mother's wish. She had refused to go through the normal tradition of giving the boy a haircut immediately he clocked one year. When it was clear that they would be leaving Nigeria to a cold environment, Ifeoma found a stronger reason to give to everyone asking her to give Ikenna his first traditional haircut. *Germany's cold could get to his body from his head,* she always replied.

"You're welcome, ma'am. Hope you were able to get some rest?" the hostess asked.

"Yes, I rested really well," Ifeoma answered. "Was he much of a trouble?"

"Not at all, we just gave him some toys and space, and he had a good time."

Ifeoma smiled. "He doesn't joke with his space."

"We noticed that, and we loved having him around. That's one energetic child you've got, ma'am," the hostess commented.

"Yes, he's such a handful. Thank you so much, I do appreciate," Ifeoma said.

"It is nothing," the hostess acknowledged.

Ifeoma turned to her son. "Ikenna! Give the toys back and say 'thank you'." She'd rather ask her son to give the toys back himself than try to take them from him. She had no strength to struggle with him.

Ikenna stared briefly at his hands and at the toys shooting out from his pockets, he pushed the toys further down his pockets before putting the hands holding the chocolate bars behind his back, then moved slowly towards his mother, away from the hostess.

"He can keep them, really. It's a gift from us," the hostess said with smiles.

"That's nice of you, thank you for the chocolates too and for all the help," Ifeoma said. "Is there someone else I need to thank?"

"Not at all, its fine, ma'am," the hostess said. "Is Belgium your final stop, or do you have a connecting flight to take?"

"I will be taking a connecting flight to Germany."

"That means you will be heading to Terminal Four. You can go look around, stretch your legs, and get some fresh air. The boy needs it too," the hostess said. "But stay around and listen for the announcement."

"I will. The flight is in an hour's time," Ifeoma said, looking at her wrist watch. "Thank you so much."

"Not a problem," the hostess said and left.

Ifeoma stared at the young lady's retreating figure: young, slender, and neatly dressed, same as the first hostess that had taken Ikenna from her. Was that a major criterion for being employed as an air-hostess? It had to be. They all looked the same, had the same manner, spoke with the same rehearsed politeness. Perception could be the major reason for that. She got hold of Ikenna and started walking towards the door. The flight had lasted for over six hours from Nigeria.

At the terminal, she could see neon signs hanging around the place. They clearly read—Brussels Airport, Zaventem, Belgium. The air inside was a little chilly, but thanks to their jackets. She walked around for a while and soon spotted a chair with padded seats and backs. The chair also had an adjustable arm, exactly what she needed to stretch her bones out. As soon as she got comfortable in the chair, she placed Ikenna beside her and closed her eyes to get some more rest.

Slipping between drowsy consciousness and light sleep, a peculiar sensation jolted her back to her senses. Something had brushed against her thighs, rousing her from her restful state. Panic stiffened her body as she noticed that Ikenna was no longer by her side. She was on her feet before she knew it, angry at herself for abandoning all caution. She knew her son too well, too well to know he would do exactly what he had just done.

Ignoring the sudden heaviness she had begun to feel from her pregnancy, she began turning in every direction in search of him. And sure enough, there were tiny legs running not too far off.

She caught up with him just as he was about to run into the baggage carousel. Ifeoma simply scooped the protesting boy into her arms, holding him firmly. The boy's weight added to the weight of the pregnancy, but she couldn't be bothered with that at the moment.

On her way back to her seat, she grabbed and pulled a trolley that stood in her way as she walked back to the waiting area without thinking twice. Once they were back on the chair, she put Ikenna inside the trolley, and placed his toys in there with him. She opened one of the two chocolate bars he held and gave to him before collapsing into the chair again. Then, with one of her legs, pushed the trolley back and forth, while humming softly. She smiled to herself at her ingenuity. Ikenna would not find it easy to escape the trolley if he tried, and the slightest attempt would easily alert her. The toys the boy had with him would keep him busy. She just needed to rest a little while longer.

The announcement for the flight to Frankfurt, Germany came on and she gradually gathered herself. She carried Ikenna out of the trolley and they began making their way to the gate.

CHAPTER FIVE

29th September 1993

The immigration and customs process didn't take her long to complete at Frankfurt International Airport, Germany. The officers had asked for their passports and visas, asked questions about her husband, where he works, and the address they would be staying at. She concluded the process within an hour before heading to the baggage-claim area.

When they got to the waiting area, Ikenna started to rub his eyes with the back of his hands. He had slowed down his play and merely looked around now, watching as people walked about. One look at him was enough to see that the long flight had exhausted him. His eyes were beginning to droop as he stared wide around him.

It wasn't the first time her boy had tried to fight sleep. He basically preferred to be active doing something. To him, the world needed to be explored and sleeping when there were chairs to be jumped on, toys to be played with, or places he could run to, wasn't worth it.

The sight of him struggling with sleep made Ifeoma reach into one of the bags, pulling out a folded rectangular-patterned-cotton-fabric. It was a *lappa* she could use to tie him to her back.

She lifted the boy, swinging him behind her. Then stooped a little low before gently placing him at the centre of her back, making sure he was well balanced. She was still bent to prevent him from slipping off as she spread out the *lappa* behind her. Bringing it up to Ikenna's neck level, she made sure his hands were tucked inside the *lappa* so he wouldn't have the liberty to move his body so much. To conclude the process, she straightened and knotted the upper part of the *lappa* to her chest, just above her breasts, before lifting the boy's legs and packing the lower part of the *lappa* under him for more support. She knotted it firmly below her tummy.

She started to pace around in circles where she stood. Pacing would get him to sleep faster. Bearing the double weight of the pregnancy and Ikenna's wasn't easy, but it was the easier way to get him to sleep off faster. She paced, circling the small space in front of her. Engrossed with getting the boy comfortable enough to sleep, she only noticed the stares when she looked around.

The lingering looks from people milling around the waiting area got her transfixed to a spot for a moment. She circled again and some pairs of eyes followed her, watching her movements. She quickly turned her head away, mentally picking apart everything about her appearance and wondering if her outfit looked out of place. Was she doing anything wrong? She felt Ikenna's head drop on her back, indicating that the boy had stopped fighting sleep and surrendered to it.

In the distance, Ifeoma could see a smartly dressed middle-aged woman looking fixedly in her direction and approaching.

From the dressing, there was no doubt in her mind what she was. Gripped by a brief surge of panic, she did a quick mental scan of all her activities since she arrived at the airport. The only significant thing she seemed to have done, after presenting their passports and visas, was to tie Ikenna behind her. Wasn't it?

Her attention stayed on the police officer's uniform as she approached, with a greater part of her strength channelled towards appearing normal and less scared than she really was. The officer looked smart in her uniform, like a well-polished machine. Ifeoma couldn't deny the allure of the crisp, navy-blue tunic and trousers she wore. One part of her attire stood out before Ifeoma's eyes; the pair of black leather gloves she wore. Why was the police officer wearing hand gloves? It made her look like a bride in front of the altar, ready to wed.

When the officer got within an arm's length of her, she said with a smile, "Good evening, *Frau*."

"Hello, officer," Ifeoma answered in one breath, relieved that the police woman had spoken English. Her mind was spinning as she recalled a parting advice from one of her neighbours: *Be careful in that Germany, Ifeoma, those people are very rigid with laws and rules.*

"Is everything okay with you?" the officer asked, looking intently at her.

Ifeoma forced a smile, wanting so much to scream; as if there was anything that seemed odd with her. Why, it seemed as though people were staring at her like she was some clown performing in a circus. Or maybe she was actually performing for everyone at the airport without knowing it. "Everything is fine," she heard herself say instead.

"That is good to know. Do you need help with something, *Frau?*"

Of course I need help with everything! Or don't you have eyes? Ifeoma's mind screamed. "*Erm*, I do need some help, officer. We are currently waiting for my husband; he was supposed to be here when we arrived. But I can't find him anywhere." She was looking around, as if this one more scan around the airport waiting area would produce Ugochukwu.

"Well, we got two concerning reports from people around here. They were worried by how you were handling your child. So, we looked into your details and then placed a call to your husband's home and office phone. He is currently on his way to pick you and your child," the officer announced. "In the meantime, you can follow me to make yourself comfortable, while you wait for him, *Frau*." The officer grabbed the two bags and made to push them along.

Ifeoma looked surprised. Reports of how she was handling her child? The child she currently had tied safely behind her? There were enough questions just waiting to escape her lips, but she decided to ask this one. "Wait, you mean you know my husband?"

"Not personally, *Frau*, but we have his records with us," she answered while leading the way.

"And you have phoned him?" she asked again to be certain.

The officer turned towards her. "*Ja, Frau*, we looked up his details." Then turned and continued walking, a little faster now.

The officer led her to a part of the airport that looked like a lounge, then into a small room, inside the same lounge. The room had a sizeable bed. A drawer stood beside the bed, with a reading lamp on it. There were a reading table and a chair at the other end of the room with a few books on it. A small door stood not far from the bed which Ifeoma guessed to be the rest room. A window stood high up on the wall. It was unlike most window levels she had seen. But she was glad for the degree of warmth in the room.

"You can rest on the bed while you wait for him," the officer offered.

"Thank you."

"Your child," the officer pointed behind her. "Why is he tied up?"

"Tied?" Ifeoma asked. It was the way the officer asked her the question that conveyed a whole new meaning to it. At that moment, it clicked for her. They had thought that the way she tied up her son was wrong, not knowing she did it to convey him easily as he slept. She rushed to explain to the officer: "I'm only carrying him in a convenient way so he can sleep."

Ifeoma watched as the officer's brows drew together, and then gradually began to relax as she loosened the *lappa* to release Ikenna. To show that everything was normal, and that she had done the act several times in the past, she swung the boy to her front and gently placed him on the bed, being aware all the while that the keen eyes of the officer watched her every move.

Another police officer entered the room, carrying a small tray with a teacup. Placing it on the reading table, he pointed Ifeoma to it without speaking. Then turned to the first officer and said something in German before turning to leave.

"The tea is for you, *Frau*, to help you keep warm," the officer said.

"Thank you, officer," Ifeoma said and watched as she too left the room. She was alone with her sleeping son now. She liked the hospitality, but secretly prayed that the service being rendered to her was free. She had no intention of incurring expenses for her husband.

Once she was done with the tea, she opened the door leading out of the room and placed the tray just outside it, away from Ikenna's reach in case he wakes while she's asleep. She then dragged herself into the bed to join the boy.

***

Ikenna was playing with the wheel of one of the luggage when a tap on the door woke Ifeoma from her little nap. The officer's voice followed, informing her of her husband's arrival.

Outside the lounge, Ifeoma spotted her husband easily where he stood. Ugochukwu was strongly built. Walking a short distance from the lounge to the main waiting area afforded her a full view of his stature which was about five feet and eleven inches tall. He wore a brown long-sleeved shirt, black trousers, and matching shoes. He had that charming smile on those lips she had always known. His large transparent eye-glasses, which had earned him the nickname 'Professor' by his students, back in Nigeria, was there sitting squarely on his face.

His hair looked just the way she expected it to be; grown and bushy. Her husband hardly got himself a haircut and often gave the excuse of not having the time for it. It always sounded funny to her. In the past, she had succeeded in cajoling him into getting a monthly haircut since she married him. Without being around in the past months, she knew he would not bother with a steady haircut.

Seeing his family approach and escorted by a police officer, Ugochukwu walked briskly to get to them. He hugged his wife first before stooping to face his son.

Ikenna peered at the face of the man in front of him, looking unsure on how to react. Then he walked away from him, trying to hide behind his mother's legs. He circled his hands round her legs until his mother laughed.

"He has forgotten you, Ugom," she said to her husband.

"Ikenna *m*: my father's strength! You're bigger now, looking much more like my father," Ugochukwu said to his boy and then hummed a tune he used to hum to him in the past.

But Ikenna said nothing. Only more stares from behind his mother.

"See him looking gentle as if he didn't stress me out on this trip," Ifeoma shook her head.

Ugochukwu stood up. "Let him be. I know how to get to him later." He faced his wife, "I have been counting down to this day, Ify, marking each day off as it passes."

Ifeoma smiled wearily. "And we are finally here."

"Yes, my dear. You look worn out. Sorry for not being here when you arrived; a meeting at the faculty lingered longer than usual," he explained.

"Well, that gave me time to do some acrobatics with your son," she said and they laughed.

Ugochukwu turned to the officer who had been standing with the luggage she helped to wheel. The police officer had been content just standing and staring at them, as if she was there to check out or confirm something for herself. "I am grateful to you for taking care of them in my absence."

"It is my pleasure, *Herr* Ogoo-choo-kwo," the officer said with some difficulty before turning to walk away.

"Let's get to the taxi, the meter has been running since it dropped me," Ugochukwu announced and took the luggage.

"Won't you tip the lady officer? She helped a lot in making us comfortable," Ifeoma requested.

"I don't think that the police officers here appreciate tips," Ugochukwu replied.

As they approached a cab, the driver pushed his head out of the car and half screamed… "*Bereit*?!"

"*Ja*," Ugochukwu answered.

Soon, the taxi zoomed away with the family.

CHAPTER SIX

29th September 1993

The taxi came to a stop in front of a large building, and a magnificent structure stood tall before Ifeoma; the type she had only imagined before.

"This is your new home," Ugochukwu announced, pointing to the building.

Ifeoma stared at the large three-storey building. "You mean we will live in there?" she asked, taking her time to survey the surroundings. The building loomed over her with neatly trimmed hedges encircling it, so perfectly shaped that they looked almost artificial.

"Yes, our apartment is just inside, on the first floor." He was looking at her. "You don't like this place?"

"Not that. Can't you see? The building is too large for a residential house," she said. She glanced at the flowers planted around the place, and at the brick exterior that seemed to be darkened by the years of exposure to the elements but still looked well maintained. "It looks like a big hotel."

He laughed. "It really does look like the hotels we have back home, but this is just a building housing apartments."

A young couple walked out of the building hand in hand. From their looks, Ifeoma could tell they were of Asian descent. Stopping just past them, what the couple did next surprised her. "God!" Ifeoma said. "Those two are kissing in public."

Ugochukwu followed her eyes and saw what she had seen. "Let's get inside, Ify." He nudged her forward, leading them into the building. "You will get used to such scenes, don't worry about them."

"People kiss anywhere they feel like here? Don't they corrupt the little children?" she had a puzzled expression on her face.

"Parents kiss their kids on the streets at the slightest opportunity. Even adults kiss each other anywhere here. It's very normal."

"*Hia!*" she exclaimed.

"Just don't bother about that, you need to get some rest after the long flight."

They took the stairs to the first floor. The hallway was lined with doors, each leading to an apartment that left Ifeoma wondering if she might get lost searching for theirs someday. Only the large numbers artistically placed above each door made all the difference.

Ugochukwu unlocked and pushed open one of the doors in the hallway, stepping in after his wife.

Ifeoma shut her eyes and opened them again before taking in the sight of the one-bedroom space. The walls were painted white and appeared bright. There were four doors on each corner of the four walls. The first was the entrance door they came in through. She tried the second and saw it led to the kitchen. Although it was a space she would rather term a kitchenette due to its compact size, she liked how the little space was utilized. Cupboards were lined within arm's reach of the walls where items could be stored. The cooker placed directly under one of the lined cupboards had four burners of different sizes; it was more than she would need. Apart from the small standing space the kitchen provided, the rest of the space were countertops which housed even more cupboards beneath them. It wasn't bad.

She opened the third door. "Oh," she said, staring into the white-tiled bathroom. She was about to try the last door when her husband spoke.

"That door is always locked. It leads to the next apartment."

The apartment looked vastly different in size compared to the three-bedroom apartment she lived with her husband back in Nigeria. The room was sizeable enough, but it looked a little smaller when compared to the very large room she had shared with her husband.

"What are those things?" Ifeoma asked, pointing to openings situated low on the walls.

"The heating vents. They provide warm air during winter."

"That explains a lot."

Although Ifeoma loved how the window was spread out, taking almost the whole side wall by the left side of the room, she didn't like the size.

The windows were on one side of the room. When she opened the brown-coloured window blinds covering them, it revealed a clear window glass adorned with simple white frames, and despite their modest appearance, they were wide enough to occupy three-fourths of the space beside the bed. From there, she could see the houses across the road. A playground for children was close by and she could see part of it. Few children were in the park swinging and running around under the watchful eyes of their parents and guardians.

"I hope you like our little home," Ugochukwu said. It sounded more like a statement than a question. He then took the traveling bags further into the room. "The laundry room is at the end of the corridor, everyone on this floor does their laundry there. I'll show you around tomorrow."

Another quick glance round the room and Ifeoma's eyes rested on the wall clock hanging on the wall, just above the reading table holding a stack of neatly arranged newspapers and magazines placed against the wall. This brought a smile to her face. The clock's design did not surprise her. She'd known her husband to love artistic wall clocks, and this one was made to look like an Ostrich. The wall clock in their apartment back home was designed like an eagle, with a sharp eye that looked to monitor everything going on in the sitting-room.

Turning around one more time, she took in the space; it wasn't exactly what she had expected. She had known they would be managing a one-bedroom apartment, but she had imagined it to be widely spaced like in some of the foreign movies she had seen. Sadly, there was no door in sight leading to a veranda where they could sit out and get some fresh air. Weren't all apartments supposed to have at least one veranda? Theirs in Awka had three. That was the normal way she'd known houses to be built all her life.

"Is this how all the other apartments look?" Ifeoma asked.

"Most of the other one-bedroom apartments look just like ours and similarly spaced, except for the apartment occupied by the Weaver couple situated on the ground floor. They own this place. I think theirs is quite large, can't say the actual number of rooms they have there." He had dropped the bags at one corner of the room.

"They could have at least made it more spacious. With this small space, this building must be housing a lot of people."

"It actually does. Most people living here are immigrants," he said, laughing. "I think it's because it is cheaper than most apartments around. We are all here managing and searching for a better life."

"We better find that better life fast," she said, crashing into a chair.

"So, we have to manage the space for now, until we can get a bigger apartment. The building is owned by Julia and Walter Weaver. They have a little cleaning firm managing the whole place, and the firm is responsible for keeping the environment clean. We will go over to meet them later when you've rested well. You might like their dog and cat when we get to their apartment." Ugochukwu said, putting things in place while he talked.

"Hmm. You sound like they live with the animals inside their house."

"They do. In fact, people live with their animals here as pets," Ugochukwu explained.

Her eyes widened. "If they don't build separate houses for their animals outside their homes, how do they manage their droppings?"

"My dear, that is something you need not bother yourself with. They have their own way of handling their pets."

That night, they both talked long after they had eaten pasta and Ikenna had been settled and gone to sleep. They recounted things that had happened during the last three months they were apart from each other, finally dozing off past midnight.

***

It was Thursday evening, the following day, when the Odogwus appeared at the door of the Weavers' apartment on the ground floor. Before the door was answered, Ifeoma noticed that the Weavers had no doorbell installed on their door, unlike the other tenant apartments in the building. There was instead a metal door knocker which made a loud noise when her husband lifted and allowed it to fall on the door. She pushed her hands on her earlobes to block away the noise the door knocker made. Didn't door knockers give way to the more fashionable door bells some decades ago? But she didn't think long about it.

Julia, who had been a schoolteacher in her active years and had taught in three of the local schools in the city of Mainz, was as welcoming as she appeared when she opened the door to them that evening. Even with her hair almost all white, her almost non-existent breasts, and a few wrinkles, her face lit up with a warm smile. She was of average height, about five feet and eight inches, had a slender figure and an air of easy grace about her. One could easily guess that she was once a charming youth by looking at her. These distinct features were not lost to Ifeoma as they were welcomed into the spacious apartment.

In Ifeoma's eyes, the dining room alone seemed to be the exact size of the room in their apartment. The Weavers had taken enough care not to spare any space for themselves. The sitting room itself looked double the size of the dining area, with a fireplace directly under the large television, opposite the cushions where they sat. She couldn't determine the number of kids the Weavers had from the pictures that adorned the walls. There were kids in different stages of their lives with the same faces and hair colour, but she could distinguish that they had at least a male and a female child. There was no doubt that at least one of the Weavers liked flowers; there was enough evidence of it around the place, from the entrance of the house to the four corners of the sitting room.

Before taking her seat, Ifeoma had discreetly inspected the sofa. She believed that dog or cat poop could be lying around anywhere. Anything was possible with people that would live in the same house with their animals. Soon enough, she spied a big cat and a German shepherd at opposite ends of the dining table feasting on their meals from their eating plates. It had taken enough self-control not to burst out laughing. A dog and a cat eating in the dining room, in their own separate dining spaces, was the weirdest thing she had seen in a long time.

Mr. Walter Weaver, at eighty-four, walked with a stick and seemed a little bent, but still stood tall at six feet when managing to stand straight on his walking stick. He spoke German at first to his visitors but reverted to English laced with a strong German accent, with heavy pronunciations and elongated syllables, when he noticed that Ifeoma was lost in the conversation. The old man never got tired of bringing up points into the conversation. He talked about football and how he played in his younger days. He talked about the one time he visited the United Kingdom and how the buildings looked older compared to the ones standing in Germany. Mr. Walter chatted mostly with her husband while she merely observed, grateful for Ikenna's hyperactive nature which came in handy. Ifeoma busied herself by engaging with him and keeping him calm. The passionate way the old man spoke made her conclude that he needed a talking companion whose role his wife probably wasn't filling in well.

Walter barely had enough skin supply clinging to his bones, Ifeoma noticed. Because of this, his face had taken the shape of a bare skeleton. He might look scary at first to a child, which was the case with Ikenna, but his chit-chat and laughter made him lovable, especially if one did not pay close attention to his face. Age had also left a few striking dark spots on his fair face.

By the time the Odogwus were ready to leave, Ifeoma was satisfied with the sweet snacks they had been served. The Black Forest Cake which Julia had called *Schwarzwälder Kirschtorte* had been a delight. It had been accompanied with a tasty apple juice. Ifeoma decided that she would be friendly with the lovely Weaver couple.

***

The days that followed after Ifeoma's first arrival in Mainz revealed how different living in the country was from her previous life experience.

Even after many days had passed, she kept asking her husband why no neighbour had knocked on their door to welcome them. Not even the Chinese woman living next door with whom they shared an adjoining door, and definitely not the middle-aged man whose entrance door stood opposite theirs. That alone seemed strange to her. The last time she had asked her husband about it, one evening after he returned from work, he had merely shrugged his shoulders as if it was nothing and said, "People keep to themselves here." That was when it dawned on her that she might not be going to another young mother's apartment to gossip about their husbands and children.

CHAPTER SEVEN

23rd October 1993

Ifeoma met Zelda during her first week in Mainz who lectured in the same department as her husband. According to Ugochukwu, Zelda had been assigned by the university to help them get settled in Mainz. She was their main contact for questions about the city and would guide them as they found their footing in their new environment.

Ifeoma's first impression of Zelda was one of curiosity. She didn't understand the woman at first, just as she suspected the woman didn't understand her as well. Zelda had acted cold the first day they met. It had been awkward too. It wasn't just the constant request of 'can you repeat that?' from Zelda that bothered her the day she showed up at their apartment, it was also the obvious lack of effort on her part to pay attention to what she was saying. Ifeoma had gladly obliged the first time the request came, obliged the second time, but by the third time, she felt like her visitor's mind was elsewhere, instead of the little conversation they were having.

When Zelda came to the apartment again the following weekend to check on them, while her husband was out to buy a few things they had run out of, things were slightly different. The encounter had been better than that first day they met. Zelda had broken into a warm smile the moment she opened the door, which contradicted her facial expression during their first meeting. Zelda must have noticed how wary she was of her, and how short she kept her replies, because she soon apologized for that first day and explained that she had been under some kind of stress. Out of courtesy, Ifeoma had simply asked her not to apologize for something beyond her control. Then Zelda had explained that she wasn't supposed to have been back to visit them so soon, but that her husband, Stefan, had thought it wise to check on them again just to make sure that they're settling in fine.

After that exchange, Ifeoma had offered her some light snacks and a drink and the two of them fell into an easier conversation as if they had known each other for long. It was during this second meeting with Zelda that Ifeoma felt comfortable enough to ask her questions about the city of Mainz. When she asked for the best places to get certain items, Zelda had produced a map of the city from her handbag containing bus stops and their schedules as if she had anticipated the request. She had left her with the city map.

Of all the pieces of advice Zelda had given her, one stood out: to go shopping with her own shopping bags as they were not free at the stores. Then Zelda had asked her how prepared she was for the coming winter and she had listed a number of thick clothes she had brought along with her from Nigeria.

But Ifeoma had noticed something else during that second visit which bothered her a little. She was well aware that she wasn't in the same age group as Zelda who looked to be in her middle to late forties, but that couldn't be the reason why Zelda seemed to draw away from her each time they both seemed to be physically getting close. She had first noticed Zelda's hands flinch away when she stretched her hands towards her to receive the city map; it happened again when she unconsciously touched her while talking. Was Zelda wilfully trying to avoid her touch? Ifeoma wasn't sure whether or not to take this to heart or to drop it as each episode happened. There was also the likelihood that she was overthinking and imagining things that were not there.

***

Weeks after first arriving in Mainz, Ifeoma was in the kitchen preparing *oha* soup. She had craved this delicacy for days; she knew she had to prepare it, so it would stop occupying most of her thoughts. The rich aroma of local spices, which had been meticulously sun-dried and ground into powder by her mother before she left Nigeria, filled the kitchen. Ifeoma had all the ingredients she needed, except for one crucial thing that was lacking.

She had visited two nearby grocery stores she had located from the city map earlier in search of any vegetable that could replace the *oha* leaves for the soup, but couldn't find something suitable. Zelda had suggested going to one African store at the outskirts of the city when she phoned her, but the long distance discouraged her. She wouldn't want to take the city bus for such a long distance with Ikenna, only to buy some leaves. She finally settled for some frozen spinach in one of the grocery stores nearby. It surprised her that a leafy vegetable could be frozen in order to be preserved. What happened to just keeping it refrigerated, instead of frozen, to preserve its freshness?

The spinach was the only leafy vegetable close enough in comparison to the *oha* leaves she had searched for. Even though she will not be enjoying the taste of *oha* as she knew it, adding the spinach was better than having a naked soup.

The spinach, meant to replace the *oha* leaves, was supposed to be the last item to enter the soup to avoid being overcooked. So, as the soup boiled and thickened, she turned her attention to the spinach, intending to pick and shred the leaves. But one look at the wilted spinach made her heart sink. It had looked good enough when she brought it out from the freezer. Now that it had defrosted, it looked like a gathering of dark-green slimy pile in a sorry state. There was no way she could use a vegetable in that condition to cook, it would simply spoil her soup. She lifted the spinach, and as soon as she trashed them, the doorbell rang out. The soup will have to do without the vegetables.

Thinking it must be her husband, "Come in, the door is open."

The door swung open and Zelda appeared, holding a large shopping bag. "Hello, Ifeoma, how are you today?" It amused her whenever Zelda pronounced her name: *ee-feh-oh-mah*. Zelda was swinging her left hand, a habit Ifeoma had noticed the first time they met. She had assumed it indicated that Zelda was nervous in her presence, but she doubted that now that the act continued into their third encounter.

"I'm good. Good afternoon," Ifeoma answered, beckoning her to a chair close to the reading table.

"Yeah, it's a nice afternoon. The weather is cool. How about your husband?" Zelda asked, following Ifeoma's gestures to the direction of the chair, but didn't sit on it.

"He should be on his way back by now," she answered.

Zelda kept looking round the room and occasionally running her hand over her nose. "And what about your son? There's an awful smell in here, not exactly like poop, but I think he might have pooped on himself."

Ifeoma stood close to the door leading to the kitchen watching Zelda. She tried sniffing the air for the offensive smell since Zelda made it obvious that she was perceiving a foul smell. "Ikenna is taking a nap. Even if he pooped on himself, I doubt you would smell it from there?"

"Well, the smell is strong. Can you not perceive it?" Zelda asked still covering her nose and swinging her left hand.

"I cannot, and I would have known if he pooped on himself. Ikenna is sleeping," Ifeoma replied.

Ifeoma had divided their apartment into two; the living space/dining and the sleeping area using a thick silky curtain she purchased at a household store, hanging from mid-air to the floor, so a visitor would only see the outer part of the room. She had also added a single-seater cushion to one corner of the living space. The outer half of the room currently had the table, a cushion, the refrigerator and a couple of chairs for visitors. Ikenna was asleep behind the curtain on the bed while Zelda visited with her in the 'living room'.

Zelda's right hand remained on her nose, forming a barrier to the offensive smell. "I'm sorry to insist, but there is a bad smell in here. I could be wrong, but can you please go and check him?"

"I will check him now," Ifeoma said and walked into the 'bedroom' with her mind racing with confusion, all the while wondering if her sense of smell had suddenly vanished or if something was seriously wrong with Zelda. Bending over her son, she sniffed, trying to catch any hint of an odour. Nothing. Absolutely no bad smell. She gently felt him with her hand, confirming that the boy was dry and clean. She sat down on the bed, her mind spinning as she tried to make sense of the situation.

Then it hit her like a slap in the face. She began to smile as she made her way back to the living room.

"He did poop, right?" Zelda asked, pulling a face similar to that of a child asked to swallow some bitter medicine.

"No, he didn't." Ifeoma continued to smile.

"What then is this smell?"

"It is from the kitchen. One of the local spices I use in making the soup smells badly, though not like poop, of course," Ifeoma explained.

Zelda looked at her, eyes wide with either surprise or distain. "Oh, why does it have this foul smell?"

Ifeoma laughed some more. "It's just a local spice we call *ogiri* in my language, made from castor oil seeds and left to ferment before it can be used in cooking. It gets the bad smell from the fermentation process." She was amused by the look on Zelda's face.

"Oh, that is strange. I've never known a spice with this smell," she said, finally moving her hand away from her nose. "It will surely make your neighbours uncomfortable."

Ifeoma smiled again.

"Can we step outside for a while?" Zelda asked, with her eyes appearing to join in the pleading.

"Of course, we can do that," Ifeoma accepted, entering the kitchen to make sure that the cooker was turned off, then proceeding to check whether Ikenna was comfortable enough before leaving the apartment to meet Zelda in the long corridor.

"I brought some things you would be needing soon. My husband asked me to get them for you after I mentioned the little talk we've had," Zelda started once they were outside.

"What are they?"

"Well, from the list of winter clothing you mentioned you had the other day, I noticed you didn't travel with all the right clothes you would need for the coming winter, so I got you these," Zelda said, handing the shopping bag over. "They would serve you better during winter, and you can buy more of them if you want. There are toys in there for your son as well."

"That's kind of you," Ifeoma said, accepting the large bag. She opened it. There were toys like Zelda mentioned, a black heavy wool coat, two winter scarves, two head warmers, and two pairs of black and white leather gloves. Ifeoma smiled. "I didn't know that I would be needing all of these things."

"Trust me. You surely will."

"You look out for us, thank you," Ifeoma said.

"It's my pleasure. My husband also insisted that I do this," she acknowledged.

"You and your husband have been very kind to us, we do appreciate the kindness," Ifeoma stated and thought of how wrong she had been about the doubts tugging at her mind concerning Zelda. She really cared.

"I should be on my way now," Zelda announced.

"All right. Would you like to have some soup before you leave?" Ifeoma asked, blinking her eyes and trying hard to keep a neutral face. "You will enjoy it."

"No! No, please. Maybe next time," Zelda replied, taking two steps backwards and waving her hands frantically to further show her refusal.

Ifeoma let out a little laugh.

"Have a pleasant evening, Ifeoma."

"And you too, ma." Ifeoma added the 'ma' as a form of respect, even though Zelda had asked her to drop it because it sounded too formal.

Zelda spoke now as if she had forgotten something. "One more thing, I would like to invite your family over to dinner next Saturday evening. My husband, Stefan, would really love to meet all of you."

Ifeoma didn't know how to react to the request at first. She thought of telling Zelda she would inform her husband first to know if he had other plans for Saturday, then she thought of how kind Zelda's husband had been by insisting that his wife check on them to ensure that they were settling well. Lastly, she remembered that she had had communication problems at some of the grocery stores because some of the cashiers couldn't speak and understand English, so she ignored all the other questions on her mind and asked instead, "Can he speak English?"

"He can. My husband and our three children can all speak English. We lived in the United States for many years before coming back here." She gave a reassuring smile. "Don't worry, he's fun to talk with, just come prepared to laugh and be entertained."

"What time?" Ifeoma asked, suddenly becoming interested in seeing how the older woman lived and what her husband looked like.

"4:00 p.m."

CHAPTER EIGHT

30th October 1993

I t was finally one of the two Saturdays Zelda dreaded. Today, she would host one of the two families assigned to her by the Immigrants' Welfare Committee. She had first been assigned to an African from Nigeria. Another had been assigned to her two weeks later. This time, he was a Mexican. While the African was one of the fellows of the Humboldt Scholarship program, the Mexican was part of the International Academic Exchange Program in the university.

She had invited the African family first; it would be easier to deal with the more challenging of the two. And Stefan was more interested in the African family. That did not surprise her at all. Not in the least. He always wanted to sit and talk with Africans ever since Hannah disappeared from their lives. But to what end? It wouldn't restore the broken relationship she had with Hannah. It could not! Just what would Stefan achieve by putting her through this?

Did he think this would help her in any way? That was the reason he kept telling her. *Get familiar with them. Talk with them some more. It would help you get past some hidden anger. It would help you to be more accepting and relaxed when you finally meet your son-in-law.* That was absurd but she finally gave in. As if merely sitting and chatting with this family could restore her relationship with Hannah to how it was before Hannah's heart was stolen.

Discharging her role as a member of the Immigrants' Welfare Committee had come with some difficulties. For weeks, she had been going through it with all the smiles and warmth she could muster. It had been most difficult the first day she met her colleague's wife, Ifeoma. She had gone to their apartment to welcome the woman to the city but had ended up feeling quite uncomfortable while at it. The family was cramped in a one-bedroom apartment. A family of three, with another one on the way! And those Africans bred like rabbits. Was that how they lived where they were coming from? She had almost asked the woman why she would leave her own country to be where she was. But that would have been unprofessional. Besides, she herself had relocated once and worked in someone else's country before returning back to Germany.

Her mind had been far away that day, wondering what her own daughter found in the man she settled for. She had ended up making that first meeting awkward. It didn't bother her much since she had dropped her house phone number with the woman in case she had questions about settling down in the city, but Stefan had cajoled her into returning the following week to know how they were faring. It had led to a prolonged argument. For days Stefan had told her it would be best to be friendly with the couple. *To what end?* She had asked him. She had scorned the idea at first. Then with almost all their conversations leading back to that family cramped in a one-bedroom apartment, she had accepted to go, just to satisfy Stefan. Few days before she paid them that second visit, she got the idea to try to use that opportunity to get her emotions under control. She needed to if she still had any hopes of reconciling with Hannah.

Hannah. This pain could have been less if her daughter had married a Mexican. Maybe it would have been bearable. Where had she gone wrong? Was it when she relocated with Stefan all those years ago and had her three children in the United States? She shouldn't have accepted that job offer in the first place. See what it ended up costing her in the long run.

She had just been fresh out of the university when that job offer came from Ryan who had been a visiting lecturer from a university in America to the University of Mainz where she had completed her first-degree program. Ryan's sabbatical at the University of Mainz had ended at the same time she had graduated from there and Ryan had returned to the States. She had been friends with Ryan and she had once told him of her desire to teach. Not knowing that Ryan still remembered that little talk she had with him, she had received a mail from him informing her of an opening for the position of a graduate assistant in the Department of English in University of Vermont, Burlington. Zelda had applied and gotten the job and then convinced her husband, whom she had married a few months before, to relocate with her.

They had been a young couple when they left, just like those Africans, although she had put off getting pregnant until a few more years into their marriage. It was in the United States that they had their three kids: Hannah, Max, and Felix. They had raised them there. All was fine, until years later when Hannah, her first child, announced that she would be getting married to a Black man three years after Zelda applied to continue lecturing in the University of Mainz and got the job, and the family had returned to Germany to continue their lives. Hannah was twenty-one at the time and in her final year in the university. That must be what corrupted her daughter; spending all those years raising her in the United States where the people there unrealistically thought that it was a free country. Hannah had even tried to placate her by saying that the Black man who had stolen her away was born and raised in the United States, as if that made any difference. The system there must have made her daughter think that anything was just possible.

It had been a huge blow on them, particularly on her. Her only daughter! Her baby girl in love with a Black man! They had tried to dissuade Hannah from such a foolhardy venture. Her pure German blood was going to be polluted if Hannah didn't listen to reason. And she had pooled all her anger and efforts into making sure that Hannah was dissuaded.

She had threatened, cajoled, sweet-talked, even tried to match her up with some of her friends' handsome sons, but all those efforts only served to drive a wedge between them. Hannah took after her in that way; she knew her mind and once it was made up, there was no changing it. At one point, she banned Hannah from their home if she went on with the wedding. That was the last day she'd seen her daughter. When Hannah vanished, the whole implications of her actions slowly dawned on her.

Hannah had a son now with the Black man; her grandchild whom she hadn't seen physically since he was born. It was a mistake she now regretted; one that left her with only knowing the name of her grandson, without knowing if she would ever meet the boy. Zelda's two sons were now at the University of Vermont and rarely came home. The last time Felix was home last Christmas, he complained that his mother had become withdrawn, sad, and easily annoyed. Before he left for school after the holidays, her son had made it clear that he wasn't looking forward to coming home soon. Zelda didn't know how long the 'soon' meant.

The desire to get back the relationship she had with her daughter had driven her. It was why she had later accepted to be a member of the Immigrants' Welfare Committee despite her initial misgivings. It was also why she had tried to be friendly with Ifeoma and was putting an effort into making this dinner a success. If she could pull this off, she could stomach the reconciliation process with her daughter and the man she had chosen.

Her life was sad.

Zelda stood up. Time was ticking away and she had to put finishing touches to the food. She stretched her hand and smoothed the edges of the fresh, grey tablecloth as it settled softly over the brown oak of the dining table in the front porch which was spacious enough to accommodate a table for six to be hurdled comfortably in the corner, away from the staircase and the main door. The fragrance from her garden mingled with the aroma of roasted chicken and potatoes sifting from the kitchen window.

She sighed, remembering how her daughter had always wanted to set the table with her as a child. A lot had changed in all this time.

***

They arrived at the Wolf's residence a few minutes before 4:00 p.m. Ugochukwu had started the preparations an hour earlier, explaining that keeping to appointments in time was a culture they had to seriously imbibe. The African time syndrome they were plagued with, where one would not keep to the time slated for an event, but would arrive much later with the excuse that the event could not have started at the stipulated time, was alien to the culture here.

When the cab pulled up in front of the address Zelda had given them, Ifeoma became tensed thinking about the family they were meeting. What if the meeting turned out to be an uncomfortable one? Was Zelda's husband like his wife? What if Zelda's husband stared her bone marrows out of her skin like some people did while walking on the streets and in the grocery stores? She was already getting uncomfortable with the stares she got, especially from children.

The house stood on a serene spot, surrounded by flowers and a few trees to the north and west corners of the plot, casting a cool shade on the house. When Zelda took them round the exterior part of the house, she mentioned that the trees helped to keep the house cool during summer. Zelda showed them the little garden she cultivated behind the house, which was apart from the one encircling the house. It looked beautiful.

Everything from the front view of the house to the back where the garden was, appeared well planned and maintained that Ifeoma felt like she had stepped into a carefully curated gallery. Every detail around the house seemed to reverberate intentionality. All the same, none of these attractions were as magnetic as the apple tree flanked by two other trees bearing fruits she hadn't seen before, giving shade to the house.

When they finished making the rounds, Zelda left her visitors at the table set on the porch, while Ifeoma's eyes rested on the fat, red apples placed in a glass bowl, obviously plucked from the apple tree they had seen. Her attention was still on the apples when an unusual man emerged from the house, wearing a welcoming broad smile. The man was so tall, taller than Zelda, that the first thought Ifeoma had was what the two would look like if they stood side by side in a family photo.

But it wasn't his height that drew her attention the most, it was the man's facial features. He had large ears which could probably flap around if the wind was strong enough. The face was large, and at the centre stood a big nose that appeared to be slightly bent at the tip.

The man carried a large tray of roasted chicken and smiled all the more when he noticed her unease; a clear sign that he often got that reaction from people seeing him for the first time. Ifeoma reverted her eyes and tried to inhale the aroma from the chicken, which had immediately spread around the table.

"Welcome to our home," the man bellowed, placing the roasted chicken on the table. He stretched his hand to Ugochukwu who shook it firmly. "Sorry you couldn't meet the kids; they are all grown and out in search of their own lives. Now, it's just us and the cat."

He bowed a little towards Ifeoma in greeting, still wearing a huge grin on his face. He then tried to touch the little boy who was seated on his mother's laps, but the lad was gone before his hand could get to him. Ikenna jumped down from his mother's legs and raced behind her, refusing to look at the man. Stefan took the seat at the table head before speaking. "I often get this reaction from kids; they are scared of my nose." He laughed loudly as he sat on his seat.

"Thank you for having us, Mr. Wolf." If Ugochukwu had any reaction to the long nose and strange face before him, he didn't show it. He appeared rather composed.

To Ifeoma, however, the man hosting them appeared at first glance like something straight out of a comedy show; something unreal. Except that those features were very much real, sitting at the head of the table. One thought stuck to her head as she stole glances at the man, especially in comparison to his wife: the Beauty and the Beast cartoon. She wondered at how two people looking completely different could have met and gotten married: Zelda who was beautiful and could still turn heads at her age, and then Stefan whom no one would accuse of being handsome. Love, indeed, is blind, she mused.

Zelda returned with a bowl of potatoes on one hand and a tray filled with salad on the other hand, to go with the roasted chicken that Stefan had brought with him. "Ugochukwu, Ifeoma, you must have met my husband, Stefan. I'm sure he has made you laugh already. I told you he's fun to talk with." She motioned her hand toward each person as she mentioned their names, after placing the bowl and tray on the table.

Surprisingly, even to herself, Ifeoma laughed. "Yes, he's really fun to be with." She hoped that the sarcasm in her voice would be lost to their host. All she could think about Stefan was his long nose that appeared to be slightly bent at the tip, like that of a Green Goblin in a Walt Disney cartoon. When Stefan turned his sky-blue eyes to look at her, they seemed beautiful on their own, but a bad combination with the nose and fanny ears. In spite of his features, she loved Stefan's hair. He kept the curly black hair short and neatly trimmed. She could move her eyes away from his face and focus on his hair. That way, her mind might not wander away as she talked to him.

"You seem to know something about me already, *Frau*," Stefan grinned, heaping food onto his plate and beckoning his guests to do the same. "Time to get to know you both as well, so how has it been for the family in our little city, have you been adjusting well?"

Ifeoma opened her mouth to reply but Ugochukwu beat her to it.

"We are trying to adjust. The city is beautiful and I easily get carried away with the beauty when riding in a car or *Stadtbus*," Ugochukwu said.

"Mainz is indeed a beautiful city, no doubt. And I am glad you like the views. What about you, *Frau*?" Stefan asked, looking at Ifeoma who sat to his right.

"Mainz is a beautiful city, and the landscape makes it even more charming. But the major difficulty for me here is the language. I cannot speak German, although I understand a little, like why you addressed me as *'Frau'*; it's a title for women here and I've gotten used to it. Also, the food is a little challenge for me. I can't seem to get some of them past my mouth. Maybe it's the pregnancy, because I've vomited after eating some of the food."

"That's a pity. But these are things you get used to with time." A forkful of chicken was halfway into his mouth. "We took English lessons before moving to the United States after we got married. You may not believe it, but we spoke very little English at the time. So just give it time."

Ifeoma nodded.

"So, what else is different here?" Stefan asked with his eyes still fixed on Ifeoma.

As her husband spoke, Zelda kept her eyes on her plate, reminding herself that she didn't dislike her guests, that her feelings could not totally be termed dislike. She remembered how her own mother had once spoken, saying that Black people looked like apes. It had been a single comment made to a friend, something she overheard, but the words had lodged in her mind from that day and never left. The United States had somehow changed her psyche to be more accepting. It was in America that she saw a lot of Black people living normal lives for the first time. But then, being more accepting doesn't mean that her daughter could choose one of them as a life partner. Her eyes studied her colleague as he spoke and scooped potatoes into his spoon. The man had pronounced dark lips. Lips were supposed to be pink or light brown, but not dark. Remembering that her daughter fell for one was heart-breaking enough. Now, there's a tainted grandson somewhere with her blood running in his veins. Maybe more would follow.

The best she could do so as not to show her discomfort was keep calm and allow Stefan to be the host. After all, he had been the one pushing for this dinner. He should keep it going.

"*Erm*, the stares. I should have mentioned that first. Some people here stare right into me and sometimes make no effort to disguise it," Ifeoma said, and watched as the man's smiles grew wider. Smiling seemed so easy to him.

"Yes, we do get stares. Not everyone stares, but a lot of people do it. It doesn't bother me much, though," Ugochukwu said, hoping that his wife would feel the same.

"Oh, I must say that this part is interesting," Stefan laughed. "I am the grandmaster when it comes to being stared at. I've been getting long stares since I was a child."

Ifeoma knew exactly what he meant. Her eyes shifted from Stefan and she caught Zelda staring at her food with a forkful of potatoes on her plate. Zelda's mind seemed to be far away and she hadn't said much while they ate.

"Truth is, you wouldn't be getting the stares if you were somewhere else like America. Black people are everywhere there, it's not the same here. But you can always choose how you respond to the stares. Just like you don't allow it to bother you, I always ignore them and smile instead."

As he spoke, Ifeoma felt a slight brush on her legs below the table. It was a tickling brush and she jumped away from the table in reaction, startling Ikenna. Just as Ugochukwu sprang to his feet to hold her, they saw a cat jump in surprise too, with its fur standing up straight on its back as it ran towards the corner of the house. Why do they like to keep animals around?

"Sorry about that, *Frau*, Cleo can be sneaky sometimes," Stefan apologized and waited for them to settle back into their chairs. "So, I guess you've never seen snow in Africa?"

"Africa is a large continent. But you guessed right, we have never seen it in my country, Nigeria," Ugochukwu said, shoving the last scoop of food into his mouth.

"Right, Nigeria. I've seen snow all my life, both here and in America. I don't like summer so much because the sun is usually too hot and I sweat a lot. I love cold weathers when it's mild enough."

"That sounds like something I would not like," Ifeoma laughed and only stopped when Stefan's mouth quaked his nose. She was surprised by the look.

Then the table fell silent.

"Excuse me a moment," Stefan said and went into the house.

When Stefan stood up, Zelda jerked too and began to clear the table. Ifeoma offered to help, but she declined stating that it wasn't much to do. It took Zelda two trips to the kitchen to completely clear the table.

Stefan returned later with a photo album when Zelda was away on her second trip to the kitchen and handed the album to Ifeoma who immediately got busy with it.

The first page she turned to had pictures of three little kids, smiling to the camera. "Your kids are beautiful, and the boys got your ear."

Stefan laughed. "Only Hannah escaped my ears, she took after her mother."

As Ifeoma got engrossed with the pictures of the family, Stefan and Ugochukwu got to discussing wrestling matches, their work, and their coping mechanisms, their voices flowing and ebbing.

***

One thing Zelda hadn't revealed to her guests was the motive behind this invitation. She had returned from doing the dishes and sat there at the table watching her husband laugh with their guests and she envied him. He talked with so much ease. He laughed easily too as though nothing worried him. She was sure Stefan had been pained when Hannah broke the news of her plans to them. He had sat their daughter down to explain that nobody in the history of their lineage had ever been married to a Black person and it shouldn't start with his own family. They had both tried to convince her not to go along with it. But as soon as their Hannah was gone from their lives, leaving home and headed to America to her man, Stefan's reservations left him like it was never there. He stopped caring about whomever their daughter chose to be with, and cared more that he was in his daughter's life. It was so easy for him; to forget something and laugh it off. It wasn't the same for her; to easily forget the hurt Hannah's revelation brought to her, to think that Hannah couldn't settle for any other fair-skinned man in the whole of Germany and the United States. For this reason, Hannah would sometimes call the house when she knew that her mother would not be home. And she never left a call back number.

She knew that she wasn't being a good host. Though she had spent time preparing the food and setting the table, there was still the job of engaging the guests in conversation. But something weighed on her, blocking away reason. Thoughts of Hannah overwhelmed her.

***

It was a little past seven in the evening when he felt a quick kick under the table from his wife. He knew exactly what it meant. It was time to leave.

"Thank you for the delicious meal," Ugochukwu said while carrying Ikenna up into his arms. Then he turned to Zelda. "We appreciate everything, especially how you've helped us settle down easily here."

"You are welcome. Thank you for honouring our invitation," Zelda replied and extended the little bag she held on her hand to Ifeoma. "Here are some apples I got from the apple tree. I know that you like them."

"I do," Ifeoma admitted, beaming with smiles and accepting the bag. "Thank you."

"Remember you can always phone the house if you need guidance on anything."

"Yes, I will."

Outside the house, they hailed a cab across the street and went home.

CHAPTER NINE

30th October 1993

Zelda sank her head into her hands, taking solace in them as she released her body into the kitchen chair after putting everything in order. The day's activity had drained her both physically and emotionally. Her thoughts were filled with her daughter when Stefan walked into the kitchen.

"Let's go to bed, dear. It is almost ten p.m.," Stefan said, stretching himself to show his tiredness.

Zelda placed her hands on the table and looked up at him. "Are you satisfied now that they've come and gone?"

He was aware and wary of the frown plastered on her face as she spoke. "It's a step we have to take, dear," Stefan said as he approached her. "And the dinner was a success."

"Yes!" she banged her hand on the table as the word came out. "It was a success for you, not for me! I couldn't even engage well with them because all I could think about was Hannah. I am going through all of this because of Hannah."

Seeing that her emotions were rising, he began to rub her back to soothe her. "You are right, dear. Hannah is the reason we are doing this, and thinking of her throughout the day is also good. Trust me, we will get through this together. I don't want you thinking that today wasn't a success because it was. We talked and ate with them in our home and they enjoyed it. That makes it a success. We will dine and talk with the second family when they also come here next weekend and you'll see that it will be so much easier."

Her shoulders slowly slumped. "For Hannah, I hope so."

"No need to worry," he said and made to lift her to her feet. "Let's go to bed, dear. We have a morning church service to attend tomorrow."

Zelda stood up and followed him upstairs to the bedroom.

CHAPTER TEN

10th November 1993

Lukas Hoffmann sat in class skimming through his notes as he waited for the clock to chime the hour of nine a.m. for his first lecture to begin. He knew that his handwriting was bad, but not being able to read some of his own words written in haste during lectures was worse. He read through a sentence and tried to make sense of what it meant but gave up after several attempts. Finally, he looked up from his notebook and his eyes met Vanessa's, his course mate and friend. He greeted her and requested for her notes on the last lecture on African Literature and she obliged him.

Vanessa stared at him for a while after handing her notebook over and hoped that she didn't look as lanky and unkempt as Lukas. "You know, I keep wondering why you don't take enough time to look at yourself in the mirror before leaving your room. It's just the same with your writing; both appear to be done in a hurry," Vanessa said, not being able to hold back her thoughts any longer.

Lukas smiled. "It's why we are friends. You are there to tell me these things. Maybe your words will have effect someday.

She snorted.

They had been friends since their first year in the university and he knew that Vanessa never meant ill with her words. She had been the first friend he made the first day he found himself in the university premises standing in a line to get his student identity card. Vanessa had been the last person on the queue when he joined. And as soon as he found out that they both were in the same department, he had kept close to her. He liked her for many reasons, but the top on the list was how every cloth Vanessa wore clung to her tall and slim figure. It had kept him attracted to her.

"I don't see the reason why this university would employ someone whose words we cannot understand," Lukas complained to Vanessa as his fingers combed through his yellow hair and straightened his shirt. He was aware that he had forgotten to run a comb over his overgrown hair again. Being in Vanessa's presence was one of the very few things capable of reminding him of the things he should have done better. He often overlooked things, including being conscious of his looks whenever his mind was burdened, which happened most of the time.

"As if this course is not hard enough on its own already. Why do we have to struggle with understanding the man's words?" Vanessa asked. Her blonde hair was pushed up in a ponytail. She was slim, with a lean face. Despite this, her full figure, hazel eyes, and full lips made her look pretty.

"They should have, at least, made this course an elective," Lukas said. "I mean, what's the point? It's not like we will ever use what we learn in this course for any purposeful thing in life."

"Exactly! What is really the connection between The Department of English and Linguistics with a course like African Literature?" Vanessa asked, taking a bite from the chocolate bar she had pulled out from her shirt pocket.

"*Alter*! I don't see the deep connection, I know that I like to learn technical things but this one seems like a waste of time," Lukas agreed, waving his hands in the air in front of him for emphasis.

"I don't think it's a total waste of time," Maria said, wearing a thoughtful expression. She had entered the lecture room and taken the empty seat on Lukas's left while the two were talking. She hung her backpack behind her seat and sat looking at Lucas and Vanessa. As though coming to a conclusion in her mind, she spoke: "Don't you think getting to know other cultures makes it easier for people to get along and see where others are coming from. All the same, that is just my own opinion and I like the man."

As Maria spoke, Lukas thought back to when he had a fall out with his father after announcing that he was going to study English and Linguistics in the university. "Other cultures? Get along? In an English and Linguistics class? *Krass*! We are here for English, not for your different cultures, Maria." His father had sneered at him in disdain when he made the revelation, accusing him of always looking for an easy way out of life, and asked what he was going to do after wasting his time and years studying the course. His father had called him names suggesting that he was weak, but they were nothing new to him. It hurt him the way his father seemed to find any excuse to quarrel about him and the choices he made. He had lived with the hurt over the years, and with time, he started to believe that maybe something was wrong with his father instead, and not him. It seemed to him that Hoffmann Senior's actions were a way to express the anger and hurt of losing his wife and leaving him to raise two boys alone.

Lukas wasn't certain about what his future would look like, but he was certain that he didn't want to study the courses his father wanted him to. The man had said one time that he wasn't sure his brain capacity was enough to handle any of the good courses like Medicine, Law, and Engineering. Maybe his father was right. What he wasn't going to do was go on to prove him so. He had looked at all the courses available in the university and had chosen English and Linguistics; a course his father would never have dreamt of him studying. That was enough for him at the moment, although he was still plagued with making good grades. He had to make the grades because his fees and allowances still came from his father.

"Good for you and your Africa!" Lukas stated, then turned to Vanessa, "Maybe I should write a complaint to the department on our behalf and see if they would make the course an elective. I might fail this course with the way it is going and that would displease my father a great deal."

"That's a good idea, Lukas, instead of getting low grades. We should push for that," Vanessa supported.

"They wouldn't heed to your request," Maria said, laughing. "Guess how I know?"

"How?" came two demanding voices.

"My cousin took this as a minor from his department. One of his course mates wrote a letter to the faculty complaining about the course and how it served no purpose to him. He got a reply. A four-paged typed reply explaining the benefits of the course and how it was related to his study."

"That is terrible," Vanessa sighed.

"Here he comes," Lukas whispered and sat straight. He wasn't very good at getting the best grades but he wasn't going to fail and give his father a reason to drastically reduce or withdraw his sponsorship. How he hated that brother of his. Leon could take glory in all the praises he got from their father but it wouldn't be forever. Nothing lasts forever, not even grades. He had never been as free as he felt now, away from his father and his disapproving ways, and Leon, the golden child, who could do no wrong in his father's eyes because Leon always came home with the best grades. His brother would soon be in the university next fall and if he made good grades, his father would start comparing the grades he had in his first year with that of his brother.

The lecturer walked into the class, heading straight to the podium. When he got to the front of the class, he looked up and ran his gaze across the length of the hall, his eyes stopping at the lanky young man whose hair made him think of the yellow *oka* his mother planted during the rainy season to make *akamu* with. The young man was a torn in his flesh. On some days, he hoped that the young man would somehow get caught up with traffic during his classes. Or maybe develop a running stomach that would keep him away from his class.

He dropped his bag on the table in front of the class. "Good morning, everyone," he said in an authoritative voice. "Today, we will be discussing some of the most important works in African literature."

As the lecturer spoke, Lukas's mind reverted back to his younger brother, Leon. Their father had always taken pride in his brother and often boasted of how much smarter Leon was. Lukas was two years older but their father always addressed him without any regard in front of Leon. This usually angered him, but he bottled it all up. It was better to bottle it up. If he showed that he was angry at his father's words, Hoffmann Senior would say more hurtful words. All their father did since they were little boys, after their mother died from cancer, was compare them both. His old man often compared their intelligence in his own weird way.

His father had never acknowledged that he was good at detecting what was wrong with faulty electronic appliances which his brother, Leon, wasn't good at. Detecting the issues with electronics, and possibly fixing them, however, didn't count as being smart enough to their father who didn't attend a university. Only school grades did. He had fixed their faulty television when he was only twelve and didn't get a single praise from their father. He had repaired the fan and the air conditioner with no acknowledgement from his old man.

The lecturer reached into his bag and pulled out a book, then held it up for everyone to see. "This is a novel: *Things Fall Apart* written by Chinua Achebe. This book is considered to be one of the most important novels in African Literature. In summary, it tells the story of a man named Okonkwo, a respected Igbo warrior, and the impact of British colonialism and Christian missionaries on his traditional way of life. It is a powerful exploration of cultural clash, identity..."

The lecturer's loud voice brought Lukas out of his thoughts and into the present. He had missed jotting down some of the things that the lecturer had said, so he left some vacant space on top of his notebook and continued jotting from there. He would make it up with Vanessa's notebook later. Lukas scribbled a few sentences, stopped, and dropped his pen. "He talks very fast with his terrible accent. I can hardly follow everything he is saying," he whispered to his friends. He knew that his father would not accept excuses, and he had given the man enough for a lifetime. Not even the excuse of a Black lecturer's accent would be legitimate enough to fail the course.

"Same here," replied Vanessa, stifling a giggle. "It's like he sometimes drifts to a different language."

"I can understand what the man is saying perfectly. Just pay a little more attention and follow the movement of his lips," Maria whispered back, but stopped at the last word when she noticed that her friends were glaring at her.

"Oh no! *Läuft gar nicht*! I can't afford to fail this course," Lukas declared. He started to raise his hand.

***

Fatigue registered on Ugochukwu's face as he walked into the apartment that afternoon. He went through his usual routine of pulling his shoes and placing them on the shoe rack by the door, shoving the door close with his foot, then removing his bag from his shoulder and putting it on a hanger before proceeding to wash his hands.

"How was your day, Ify?" he asked, using the fond name he called her.

"Same as usual. At least Ikenna wasn't much of a disturbance today," Ifeoma stated.

"Mine was bad," Ugochukwu sighed, sending himself flying into the cushion.

Ifeoma sensed his exhaustion. "Why don't you go have your bath? I made something delicious for you, then we can talk about it."

"Hmm," he heaved. "Sounds like a wonderful idea. Honestly, if I were a woman, I might be in tears right now."

"It must have been very bad," she said.

After he had taken a bath and eaten a plate of *garri* and *ogbono* soup, Ifeoma asked him to tell her what had happened.

"I talked a lot today. Most of my energy actually went into talking," he began.

Ifeoma smiled. "Is that not the basis of your work? To stand and talk to the students." She was careful to make it sound like a tease.

"Yes, but this is different. A few students were having problems with my accent while teaching them. I had to repeat myself many times upon their request. It was worse with one particular boy with ruffled yellow hair asking questions that were time consuming. But then I asked him to see me after class because we needed to understand each other. After we spoke about the issue, I permitted him to start using a tape recorder for the next classes so he could listen to the tape in his free time."

"And he accepted?"

"He agreed. I hope I don't have any interruptions next time. The other students are starting to take a cue from him. I can feel he's setting the tone for the whole class."

"Don't worry yourself too much. I'm sure that is a normal thing to expect," Ifeoma consoled. "Having trouble with the accent is not out of place, and things should normalize with time."

"You're right. It's not like there's much I can do anyway."

"Dada!"

Ikenna walked out from the inner part of the room rubbing his eyes. Then walked into his father's arms. He had picked the name 'daddy' from his mother. Ifeoma sometimes addressed her husband as 'daddy' in Ikenna's presence so that the boy could learn. He nudged his father to carry him on his laps and he did.

"I need to get to the store to pick a few things we will be needing this week," Ifeoma announced.

"All right, when do you plan to go?" Ugochukwu asked.

"Right now. I've been waiting for you to return," she replied.

"Okay, get me a shaving stick please," he begged.

"I will add it to my list," Ifeoma answered.

"Are you taking Ikenna with you?" he asked.

"I wasn't going to, but I will take him now. You need to get some rest."

"Okay then. Take five!" he called out to his son, raising his right hand in the air. Ikenna clapped his right hand into his father's, laughing. "See you both soon."

Ifeoma dressed the boy in a warm jacket, thick trousers, and a beanie before taking a piece of paper held in-between a magazine on the table and left. The piece of paper was a list she'd been making for days containing items they needed in the apartment. Anytime a need came up, she rushed to put it on the list before it slipped from her mind.

Since there were no shops very close to the apartment, and no verandas to run out to and shout at the street hawkers to bring their wares to the apartment where she could haggle and buy commodities for a price, Ifeoma had to build the list till it was enough for a trip to the store.

CHAPTER ELEVEN

19th November 1993

Rosemart remained Ifeoma's first shopping spot since she spotted the store from the city map that Zelda had left with her. She stood with Ikenna outside the Mart that evening looking at the name hung on the top of the building, each letter coloured green and written in different fonts, as if they were arguing on which of them stood out best. Before she knew about this place, she had mapped out two different stores where she could get food and household items separately, until Rosemart came into the picture. Here, she could shop for both categories in one location.

Approaching the entrance door, she caught a glimpse of her and Ikenna's images in the one-way mirror glass used to adorn the building. She turned and peered directly at her reflection, aware that they would be visible to anyone inside the store looking in their direction. Her hand went over her tummy, rubbing her belly gently. She could see the changes in her looks. Her bloated body had looked the same way when she was pregnant with Ikenna. Her stomach was firmer now, but her fingers were swollen, and her face looked like someone had pummelled her with several punches. She frowned briefly at what stood before her and only smiled after she concluded that the image must be in her mind's eye. There was no way the swollen, grotesque looking woman staring back at her from the mirror was her.

Inside the store, she greeted the lady storekeeper out of habit. That was how she had been raised; to greet people as a way to show either regard or respect. But instead of a response or an acknowledgement, she often noticed a slight twitch of the eye and an inquisitive expression on the face of the storekeeper, who kept putting candies on the small stand close by, as if to say she couldn't be bothered. Ifeoma ignored her and went to pick the items on her list.

She looked around briefly and her eyes caught some shoppers. As expected, there weren't too many millings around. It was why she preferred shopping here in the mornings or during the weekdays when fewer people were about. Shopping here during the weekends wasn't an attractive option. She had tried it once and didn't like the outcome. The intensity of the gazes she felt that day had been enough to shatter her confidence, leaving her exposed.

Presently, she began to walk around the aisles, picking out the items on her list and adding them to her basket, at the same time struggling to prevent Ikenna from putting everything his hands could reach on the shelves into the basket. The boy kept himself busy by picking up every attractive and colourful thing he could reach, and when she got tired of placing the items back at the exact places that he picked them from, she allowed him.

The stares from the few shoppers around were beginning to burn into her awareness, however, she tried to pretend she didn't notice them. She had attempted to return their stares the first time she was here, but it only resulted in some shoppers pretending to look elsewhere, then resumed staring the moment she looked away. The people at the store today were not doing anything different from what she'd experienced.

Ignoring them was the only way she could concentrate on her shopping. They can stare all they want since their eyes belonged to them. But could she totally ignore them even when she wanted to?

It wasn't difficult for her to notice that, as before, people were reluctant to leave the store. As usual, she and Ikenna were the only persons with a different skin colour in the store. Curious pairs of eyes surrounded them. Maybe they wanted to see how she shopped, whether she picked the things a normal human would need, or maybe picked things like bananas that a Chimpanzee would prefer. She smiled to herself at the thought as she trudged to the fruit section and added some bananas and apples to her basket. She had to give them something to wonder about or there wouldn't be any fun in all of this.

Done shopping, she wheeled the basket to the storekeeper and proceeded to take out the items one after the other, placing them on the counter.

While the storekeeper was packaging her items into a large bag, Ifeoma sensed the stares behind her again. There had been no lines when she first came to the counter, but shoppers now stood behind her. She immediately turned in reflex, and as expected, people were staring. A small line had emerged behind her, with the next person giving her more than the usual distance in a queue.

Dear Lord, she prayed. These people must think that they were looking at something spectacular. Certainly, they must believe that they were staring at something different from a human being. They seemed to be waiting in anticipation of something.

As she counted out some money to give to the shopkeeper, a crazy thought crept into her head. What if she grabbed an item and ran out of the store, then dashed back inside, after pulling some King Kong-style stunts? She would love to see the reaction she would get from these people looking at her from the corner of their eyes.

She could imagine those stuck-up ladies behind her dropping their groceries and screaming while pointing for others to get hold of her. She chuckled and dropped the money into the waiting hands of the storekeeper who looked at her with wide eyes.

She caught Ikenna's hand and walked out into the chilly evening, but just before moving out of sight of the store, she turned back and gave a cheery wave. Though she could not see what was going on inside, she could bet that they were all peering at her from the inside. What she wouldn't give to see their reactions.

CHAPTER TWELVE

23rd December 1993

Ifeoma sat by the window that early morning looking out on the day's brightness. She inhaled the chilly air which seemed to stay put by the window, not venturing into the apartment's warmth, as she watched the slow snowfall descend from the sky in tiny flakes, adding to the pile on the ground.

Watching from the window and seeing the vacant white street, a distant memory came to her of children in the streets back home running about and throwing stones at lizards, jumping around and laughing, their clothes and bodies dusty. Children throwing sticks and stones into trees to bring down their fruits which were mostly unripened. She had been one of those kids. Carefree, with no worries burdening her heart except for how to get a few coins from her father to buy sweets and biscuits. Today, she could only watch the snow covering up spaces, with only a few people braving the weather for one reason or the other.

She sat there, admiring the unfolding of nature, and her mind went back to the first time she witnessed snowfall a few weeks ago in early December. She had woken up that morning noticing the unusual chill in the air. Rubbing sleep from her eyes, she walked to the closed window to see a white blanket of nature's softest crystals spreading over everything.

The sight had been fascinating to her. The excitement had kept building up until she couldn't keep it to herself any longer. She had woken her husband to witness it as well.

His arm was flung over his face in a defensive way as he slept, as if to block the morning rays from finding him. It made her smile before she tapped him and spoke in a low tone, not wanting to wake Ikenna. "Wake up, Ugom. Get up. You have to see this."

He groggily sat up in bed. "What is it, Ify?" he asked, still half asleep.

"Just come and take a look outside the window!" she said with all the excitement she could muster and pulled him out of bed.

"The air is a little chilly," he complained, wrapping his hands around his body.

"Yes, come and see why."

He followed her to the window and looked out through the curtains she had parted. "Oh, it is snowing. I wasn't expecting this till, maybe, December ending."

"Neither was I. I remember Zelda mentioned that we would likely witness the first snowfall in late December, but it actually came earlier than she predicted," Ifeoma said.

After a short while of watching the mild snowfall with her, he had left her at the window and gone back to bed. But she kept her watch that very first day till she had had her fill of the sight. Later that day, she had bundled up herself and Ikenna in the thickest winter clothes she could find and had gone outside to teach and watch Ikenna make a snow angel.

Presently, she shifted to a more comfortable position by the window as she cherished the memories. A sweet, flowery and earthy smell hanging in the air brought her thoughts back to the present. Her husband had been busy with the coffee machine and the smell meant that the coffee had been brewed. She stood up and headed to the table where he had placed a mug of coffee for her. "You now behave like the Germans, always drinking coffee and tea," Ifeoma laughed.

"I don't think it's a German thing. People living in cold regions have a habit of trying to keep warm. The hot coffee and tea give them that." Ugochukwu got himself comfortable beside her. "You seem to love watching the weather lately."

"Yes, you know I get more uncomfortable these days with the weight of the baby, and watching the weather helps me escape from my reality," Ifeoma explained.

A sound came from the bedside. Ikenna had woken up from sleep and walked slowly towards his father who cuddled him before placing him on the floor with his train toys in front of him.

"How do you feel today?" Ugochukwu asked, diverting their attention from the boy.

"Heavy, like a bloated balloon waiting to explode. My tummy is bigger than it was when I was about to have Ikenna."

"I noticed that. With Ikenna, people started to notice you were pregnant when you were already six months gone. But this one, they all noticed it earlier, that's a big difference."

"A huge difference. My body has already been stretched with the first pregnancy, as they said." She was staring at her stomach while she spoke.

"Your due date is close by. January third, and it's barely two weeks away. Please, always let me know if you feel anything strange," he said with his eyes pleading alongside.

"For me, I can't wait to put to bed and get back my shape. Just look at me, Ugom, looking like an elephant. Even to walk is now very difficult and slow. Plus, everything irritates me," Ifeoma complained.

He was laughing. "I'm not complaining of the way you look, it is normal for you to look the way you do. You are pregnant. In fact, I think it is your hormones that is talking right now, not you."

"Who said I'm complaining because of the way you see me, I'm complaining of what I see when I look at myself in the mirror, I know how ugly I look."

"Now, you are trying to be funny, everyone looking at you knows that you are pregnant and that is what they see when they look at you, nothing more."

Done with the coffee, she walked back to the window and sat in her usual position. "If you say so."

"Well, at least we know it will be over soon," Ugochukwu assured, walking to her and rubbing her back.

"You're right, it won't take long now," she accepted.

"I am glad you still have appetite to take something."

"I should. I can't starve the baby. I have to eat even when I don't feel like it," she said.

"That reminds me, what about the German language classes we discussed some time ago. Do you plan to start it after you've put to bed and gotten back on your feet?"

"German classes? *Hmm*. About that, to be honest with you, that's the last thing on my mind right now, Ugom. I just want to deliver safely. I will let you know when I am ready. Besides, I haven't really felt a welcoming atmosphere since I got here, and I keep having reasons to believe that the people here don't really want us to be here," she said. There was an unmistakable frown creased over her forehead, mirroring her heart's displeasure at that moment.

Ugochukwu dropped the magazine he had grabbed from the table earlier and faced his wife. "What do you mean you don't think that the people want us to be here? Has anyone bothered you or Ikenna when I wasn't around? *Eh*?"

She was quiet.

"Say something."

"It's just what I've been complaining to you about, they stare too much at us. I'm sure they stare at you too even though you wouldn't complain to me about it. I go to the stores to buy things and I keep noticing people's eyes following everything I do. Don't people here travel out? Don't they know that the world has people of different shades? I am not so enthusiastic about learning any language belonging to people like this!"

"Is that why you get moody sometimes when you return from the stores? I ask you why you become withdrawn some of the times that you go out but you keep telling me that it is the pregnancy. I should have known," Ugochukwu said in a more subtle tone.

"Sometimes, the pain of those experiences tends to be minimal by the time I get back home, but I do talk about it more than you do," she said.

He hugged her from the side. "Don't worry about those things. I experience them too but I just ignore it, what you don't pay attention to does not exist. All the same, you won't be going out by yourself anymore till the baby arrives. I won't have you getting moody because of how others act."

"I have heard you. For now, I need to concentrate on our coming baby," Ifeoma said, stroking her belly as the frown on her forehead straightened out.

He held her hand. "For sure, you and the baby are the major concern now."

CHAPTER THIRTEEN

26th December 1993

It was the evening of Boxing Day. Ifeoma lay on her back, spread out on the bed. She stared at the wall clock, admiring its design, and at the same time getting worried about her husband and child. They were supposed to have been back home from their outing. For days, her husband had been very excited and talked about little else, except the World Wrestling Tournament. He had been a huge fan of wrestling ever since she got to know him. He couldn't contain his excitement when Timo, his German friend and colleague at the university, informed him that there would be a live wrestling match right there in Mainz. Her husband had bought the tickets for himself and Ikenna when she stated that she wouldn't be going with them.

It was not difficult to notice that her husband was a huge fan of wrestling the first day she visited his apartment in Awka. He had video cassettes of wrestling matches neatly piled and arranged in small cartons in his sitting room. Out of the five cartons she had seen that first day, two were filled with cassettes of wrestling matches alone. Hanging on the wall just opposite the eagle wall clock was a wallpaper held to the wall with office glue. It was a picture of Hulk Hogan and Bret Hart squaring off in a wrestling stance, with the referee standing between them, holding the championship belt high for the crowd to see the prize. She only had to comment on the numerous collections of wrestling cassettes before her then fiancé prattled on; launching into a lively commentary of the wrestling matches he had seen. Even though she found it boring, she nodded and made the appropriate sounds so it wouldn't be obvious.

That particular week in Mainz, her husband had talked endlessly about Red Tyler, Bam Bam Bigelow, Razor Ramon, Earthquake, and the likes. She now knew the names of most of the wrestlers by heart. She had tried to appear interested, since it made him happy, as she listened to his stories about the wrestlers' exploits, all the while gazing at her husband blankly, lost in her own thoughts and at the same time giving him an occasional nod and "oh."

Her husband had dutifully woken up early that morning to do some shopping and prepare what she would be needing the whole day. While at his chores, he had jokingly warned her to make sure to avoid going into labour that particular day.

"You are important, Ify. But some things are more important on some days," he had said.

On the other hand, she was glad that she could have a whole day to herself; a day she didn't have to listen to her husband ramble endlessly about his wrestlers, and a day she didn't have to deal with her son and his troubles. She was glad when Timo arrived in his car and left with the two early that afternoon.

She was still in bed later in the evening wondering if she should call Timo's home phone and enquire about her husband and son when the doorbell rang. It drifted her back to reality. She slowly carried her body to the door and unlocked it. Ikenna's voice came first when the door opened, sounding very excited as he uttered words only he could understand. The boy had obviously enjoyed himself.

No sooner had her husband entered the apartment than he started narrating how the day's wrestling matches went. Putting up an interested look, she kept smiles plastered on her face as she went back to the bed.

"This is the best match in the history of wrestling, Ify," he said, as though it wasn't the first time he was attending a live wrestling match.

"Really?" Ifeoma asked.

"Yes *o*. It started with Yokozuna and Bret Hart. They were so unevenly matched because of Yokozuna's weight. I felt pity for Bret. Yokozuna had simply sat on his head and won the match, forcing Bret to give in. That was the shortest match we witnessed today."

"That is sad," Ifeoma added.

"It is. Then, Doink the Clown and Reno Riggins came into the ring. This pair lasted the longest. Doink, being mischievous, showed up in his colourful outfit and beat Reno with his usual funny tricks. Funny enough, he'd pulled most of those tricks on Reno earlier in the match without success, but it worked at last."

"That is smart."

"Then the most dramatic set came into the ring next. Hulk Hogan and my favourite, the Undertaker. As soon as he came out, we all went crazy. The Undertaker was brought to the ring in a casket, and when they opened it, smoke just poured out. Then, once it cleared, he stepped out. Typical Undertaker."

Ugochukwu trailed off when he heard quiet snores coming from the direction of his wife.

"Ify! Can you hear me?"

Silence.

"Mama! Maamaaa!" Ikenna called out in his tiny voice in a bid to help his father.

"*Shh*, mummy is sleeping. She needs to rest," he said to his son.

He went to where she laid and raised the duvet to her neck. Looking at her snoring away made him realize how tired he felt. He too needed to rest. The wall clock read 9:42 p.m.

Soon, no sound came from the apartment.

***

The following day seemed more promising. The afternoon weather felt pleasant. The snow of the previous day had almost melted away and the temperature felt manageable. Ugochukwu had gone out, needing to pick some files from his office at the university.

Ifeoma, considering the weather, stepped out with Ikenna to get some exercise and possibly exhaust his energy by wearing him out with play. They both headed to the playground just across the building.

She had seen kids playing in there from the window of their apartment. Like many other days, she already knew the choice was between keeping her son indoors and having him bounce around in the small apartment creating havoc as he moved, or going to the park where he had more space to run around and expend his energy. She chose the latter. That aside, her gynaecologist had advised her to make it an intentional daily routine to walk around, especially now that she was close to her due date. She left a note for her husband on the table before leaving.

The warmth Ikenna received at the park was surprising. As soon as they arrived, about four children ran to their direction, wanting to play with him. Ifeoma stood there and watched. One particular little girl of about three kept shouting, "*Komm, kleiner Mann!*" "*Komm, kleiner Mann!*"—Come on, little man! —as she tried to get Ikenna's attention.

She hadn't known how popular her boy was since her husband had been the one taking him to the playground some evenings after work, and on weekends. Enjoying the attention he was receiving, Ikenna tore his hands from her hold and ran towards the children who immediately dragged him to whatever they were doing.

She found an empty bench and sat down, watching her son. Not far from where she relaxed, a young man was teaching a boy of about five how to ride a bicycle, he was one of the few male adults present at the park. His boy was catching on quite well from the encouraging words he was throwing at him.

"*Du musst schneller treten, sonst fällst du um!*"—You have to pedal faster, or you'll fall!

"*Ich trete schnell, Papa!*"—I'm peddling fast, dad!

"*Super, du hast es fast geschafft!*"—Great, you've almost got it!

The little boy smiled, revealing two missing front teeth each time he got praises from doing the exact thing the man wanted him to.

114

About thirty minutes had passed when Ifeoma heard a shout.

"*Mama, hilf mir!*"—Mother, help me! A little girl's voice rang out.

A middle-aged woman sitting on a bench and reading a magazine not far from her immediately scrambled towards the little girl who had screamed. She was the same three-year-old that had hailed her son when they first arrived at the park. To her surprise, Ikenna was standing very close to the girl. He hadn't been at that spot the last time she looked up few moments ago.

She found herself walking quickly towards them, the much her weight could allow. Then the girl, in a teary voice, started speaking to her mother.

"*Mama, er war es!*" she said, pointing at Ikenna. "*Er hat immer wieder Sand auf mein Haar geschüttet. Er wollte einfach nicht aufhören, Mama.*"—Mummy, it was him! He kept scooping and pouring the sand on my hair. He wouldn't stop doing it, mummy.

Ikenna stood there, oblivious of the problem his actions had caused. He tried to run off to find another activity to engage himself with when he saw the mother of the girl peering down at him, her forehead forming burrows. Ifeoma grabbed Ikenna's arm before he could think about running off, then started to apologize.

"I'm very sorry for this," Ifeoma said, trying to help the other woman clean out some of the hidden sand in the little girl's hair. But it was hopeless; some of the sand had embedded in the silky roots of the little girl's hair. She apologized again and glared at her son, but the boy's attention was focused on separating his hand from his mother's. "You know they are just little kids playing," Ifeoma said to the woman.

The woman, after taking in Ifeoma and her protruding stomach, did not respond to her apologies but turned her back to her instead, moved her daughter to her side, and continued patting the sand off her daughter's face, hands and clothes, cursing inaudibly under her breath.

Holding her daughter's hand when she was done, the woman said, "Lasst uns von hier weggehen."—Let's get away from here.

Ifeoma let out a sigh as the mother and child walked away. So much for trying to get Ikenna to expend his energy.

"Listen, Ikenna! You don't pour sand on someone's hair, do you understand?" she said, in what she hoped was her sternest voice, as they headed to the playground exit.

The boy merely nodded.

CHAPTER FOURTEEN

31st December 1993

The city was abuzz with festive activities.

Inside the apartment, Ugochukwu finished from the kitchen, turned off the gas and opened the pot to reveal his signature dish of pasta. They would wash it down with a soft drink. His wife lay on the bed, no longer able to do much. Recently, he had taken over the cooking duties and while he preferred not to cook if he could help it, he didn't mind doing it till his wife could get back on her feet.

He set the dishes on the table, then placed Ikenna's food on his eating chair and proceeded to lock him in. At his age, he could at least eat half of his plate's contents, with the rest scattered around him. Ugochukwu, in particular, let him do it because eating by himself kept him busy and concentrated on the task of getting the food from his plate to his mouth.

"Ify, food is ready," Ugochukwu called out.

"You're finally done? Do you know you spend double the usual time I spend preparing a meal?" There was some laughter. "I will soon be there," Ifeoma replied.

Ifeoma took her time to stand. She had started using adult diapers the previous day as her frequent urination came calling at every half hour interval. Having the diapers on had eased her stress of always dragging herself to the toilet especially when the amount of urine was too little to be worth the effort. She gradually walked to the table, being extra careful with her steps, and pulled out a chair to sit down.

"I think that the baby might come today," she blurted out.

Ugochukwu's eyes widened into large saucers at her announcement and he pulled out a chair for himself to sit adjacent to her, his eyes never leaving her face. When his wife's time was nearing during her first pregnancy, he had asked Ifeoma's mother to come around in case he was at work when the labour started. And that was what had happened. He had been at work when the music started to play. "Really, Ify? Are you in labour right now?"

"Not yet, but I feel it won't be long." She was scooping the pasta with her fork, but not eating it.

"All right, let me know when it's time to call the hospital, you know I'm still confused as to how to manage the situation when it actually starts. I will need to call them early." His tone was laced with a touch of anxiety as he reached for her hands, squeezing them in his.

"I will let you know the moment it starts." She smiled as she saw his unease. She picked her fork and dug into her food, slowly devouring her meal as he watched her. She was aware of being watched and liked the attention. When she took the last spoon, she said: "You're a good cook. But you've been hiding your talent for a long time."

"*Ah*! I'm really not that great at it. You know I don't like cooking, and I usually panic that it won't turn out right," Ugochukwu said in-between laughter.

"But it always turns out fine, sometimes even better than my own cooking *sef*."

"No, that is not true, you're exaggerating it."

"Well, we will be taking turns when I'm ready to resume cooking, I enjoy your food a lot."

He stared at her, but she pretended not to notice the stare. Looking for a distraction, she diverted her attention to Ikenna who had food all over his face, on his eating table, and on the floor. The boy had dropped his fork and started eating with his hands. It seemed that the fork wasn't grabbing as much food as he wanted it to.

"Your boy is creating more chores for you, Ugom. Look at him."

"That is a minor chore compared to cooking. He can do whatever he pleases with his food," he said.

"Okay then. I need to get some exercise, I haven't had my usual walk in two days," Ifeoma said.

"Are you sure you can carry your weight around?"

"I have to. The doctor said I should move around daily, and try to get some fresh air."

"Do you need us to come with you? Since you feel the baby might come today."

"Not at all. Though, the recent news on the radio has me worried. I'm afraid to go out in case I become the next to disappear since so many persons have been reported missing. If people that grew up here, stayed here all their lives could go missing in this weather, then I could get lost before I even know it."

Ugochukwu looked at her and tried so hard to suppress his laughter. "Those are the elderly people and it is basically due to their old age. I'm sure you also heard the age range of those missing persons, Ify. They sometimes forget the path to their houses because of the piles of snow covering them, but they eventually get found. Some of them even go to other people's houses to knock, seeking for direction, which they get. So, you don't need to worry about getting lost, as long as you don't walk too far."

"One of the missing persons was in her forties."

"Really? Did the news say why it happened?"

"They did mention that she had genetic dementia."

"You see? Those cases have their peculiar reasons. Just keep to the familiar paths."

"If you say so. My legs really need some stretching."

"Remember not to go far, just walk around this vicinity and come back."

"I will."

It was very bright that afternoon when she stepped outside. There were already fireworks going up and brightening the sky, marking the end of the year's celebrations. But then, it wasn't steady. It was as though some people were testing theirs out, making sure that it wouldn't disappoint them when the hour of New Year finally comes.

She was on the sidewalks now, dragging her body along and thinking she had gone far enough to turn around. But she decided to walk a little further to make up for the last two days she hadn't exercised. An elderly man coming from the opposite side, walking towards her waved a hand and muttered something she couldn't understand.

"Pardon?" Ifeoma asked and spread her hands to indicate that she didn't understand the man.

"*Einen guten Silvester,*"—have a good New Year's Eve, the old man repeated in a good cheer.

Not knowing what to say in return, Ifeoma merely nodded, smiled, and walked past him.

When she heard the word *Silvester* voiced out again as a greeting, she started to think about it. Two persons cannot possibly assume she is named *Silvester*, she reasoned. Was it not a male given name? Or could it be a new kind of greeting? She had occasionally heard her husband say different greetings over the phone in German, and none of them had *Silvester* in it. She made a mental note to ask him about it when she got home.

She had reached the bus stop now which was just seven minutes' walk from their apartment. Six persons stood nearby waiting for a bus. She decided she had gone far enough. Besides, that was the end of the snow-covered familiar paths.

Having turned her first leg in a bid to make a U-turn, she found her leg slipping on the slightly-covered and slightly-elevated pavement of the bus stop that shone with black ice. She let out a high-pitched cry as she fell, managing to twist her body midway in the air. Her efforts redirected her fall, and she landed on her side with her leather-gloved hands smacking the ground first and giving the rest of her body a soft landing. More surprised than dazed, she lowered herself fully and lay there for a moment trying to catch her breath.

When she looked up naturally expecting someone to be beside her, offering a hand, she was met with a vacant space. She had seen people standing nearby, didn't she? She was sure of that. Hadn't they seen her fall? They were close enough to hear when she screamed. She looked and saw that people were still there, but with diverted eyes.

There was something strange about the whole thing unfolding before her. For a minute, she absorbed it all before attempting to stand and straighten herself out with some dignity. She had expected a hand to be waiting, or at least someone running towards her. Wasn't that the most natural thing to expect?

Six people! She looked with anger in their direction after getting up. Raw shock followed closely after. But seeing that her anger served no purpose, she suppressed it. There was nothing she could gain from being angry. She could not control their actions but she could control her feelings.

Those six could have been anyone. They could have been the Jews whose citizenships were striped during the era of Nazi Germany under Hitler. Or the Aryans; the group for whom Hitler brought so many policies in force, so they could be the superior race. They could have even been some of those minority groups like the Romani people or the homosexuals that were severely persecuted. They all looked the same to her.

Thinking these thoughts, she felt like crying. The feeling was there, but the desire was absent. Crying would mean she was giving in, and she didn't know herself for such emotions in such situations. She straightened more and kept walking. When she turned briefly, she saw that they still stood there waiting for the bus as if nothing had occurred, as if a heavily pregnant woman hadn't slipped and fallen before them. She jammed her fists into the pockets of her winter jacket.

Midway as she walked home, something occurred to her. She looked down at her feet and instantly felt like laughing at herself. She had taken her sneakers instead of her winter shoes, and it had cost her a fall. Zelda had warned her about this.

CHAPTER FIFTEEN

31st December 1993

Every New Year's Eve, the Weavers hosted a party for all the occupants of the building. As the Odogwus came to know, this was a yearly ritual. It had been Julia's idea and it was intended to create a sense of community amongst the diverse occupants of the building who were mostly foreigners. The invitations issued were stamped with each individual apartment number.

Despite the Weavers' efforts, many apartments in the building usually turned out empty at this time of the year, with their occupants having travelled to celebrate the holidays elsewhere. However, for those who had no families nearby or were far from their homeland, this invitation served its purpose and was welcomed with festive warmth.

Ifeoma and her husband, having received the invitation days ago, concluded they would be attending. But for the most part of that evening, they had argued whether or not to honour the invitation. She, in particular, was reluctant. For she still felt raw from the incident of that afternoon: her fall.

"What is the point, Ugom? I don't have any strength left to meet any more Germans today. I've had enough of them in one day," she had stated.

"How many of the Germans live in this building apart from the Weavers, *eh*? And those two have been kind to us, you know that, Ify. We have to, at least, honour this one invitation, *biko*."

She sat down to think about it when he wouldn't relent in giving her more reasons why they needed to go. Finally, she said, "Once I feel uncomfortable, or sense any strange look, we are leaving. Do we agree on that?"

"It's a deal."

The family left for the party around nine p.m. that night, curious about the event taking place at the basement of the building. They hadn't known that the basement existed before the invite came. They made their way down the brightly lit hallway. Down the staircase. When they got to the ground floor, they knew they had to make enquiries. Someone was walking towards them and Ifeoma recognized her instantly. She was the same woman of Asian descent she had seen kissing her partner in front of the building the day she arrived. The memory brought a faint smile to her lips.

"Excuse me, please," Ifeoma called.

"Hi," the woman stopped and smiled, with her straight, long hair looking almost dark blue under the white fluorescence.

"Sorry to bother you," Ugochukwu took over. "We are trying to find our way down to the basement for the party, can you point us in the right direction?" He spoke slowly and carefully, picking out his words one at a time, so the understanding could flow easily.

"Then you go wrong way," the woman said, pointing behind them. "Go out to back of house, a door to left in middle of building, see stairs and go down."

Ugochukwu nodded as she spoke. Something in the way the woman spoke showed either she learnt English as an adult or her accent was affecting her words. "You know, we have a saying where I come from that a person who asks for directions never misses the way."

"We also say like that in my country," she said, exposing her teeth.

"Then we have something in common."

"Yes. Happy to meet you," she said.

"Thanks again for helping," Ifeoma appreciated.

"Will you be coming to the party?" Ugochukwu asked.

"No, no, no, I not come party," she said emphatically, shaking her head sideways. "We celebrate New Year later in my country."

Ifeoma stared at her in disbelief. "I don't understand."

She smiled as she explained, "New Year in China is not the same here. This coming year is year of dog starting February."

Ifeoma stared at her and was about to ask why the Chinese have a different New Year but her husband beat her to it, thanking the woman instead as they parted ways. He knew how curious his wife could be, and if he didn't step in, they could be there all night.

As they retraced their steps in search of the basement entrance, Ugochukwu explained, "The Chinese operate the Lunar Calendar which is different from our own Calendar."

"I haven't heard of that in my entire life," Ifeoma admitted.

"We learn new things every day," he said.

***

Soft music emanated from the entrance leading down to the basement. As they descended the stairs, the melody grew clearer, and they could hear the murmur of conversation blending harmoniously with the tunes. The inside was well-spaced, with only a few tables left unoccupied. There were hooks jutting out from the walls, holding an assortment of coats and jackets.

Ugochukwu pulled off their coats and carefully placed them on one of the hangers. The temperature inside was warm, made possible by the heating vents at every corner of the room. Carrying Ikenna into his arms, he scanned the room for Julia and Walter and found Julia sitting at the front, just before the make-shift stage. They walked over.

Julia stood from her chair and gave Ifeoma a side-hug. "Oh my!" she exclaimed, while staring at Ifeoma's tummy. "Looks like the baby would be here soon."

Ifeoma smiled. "Yes, any day now."

Ugochukwu extended his hand for a handshake which Julia accepted before patting Ikenna on his back.

"Walter is playing the piano, he enjoyed playing it since his youth." As Julia spoke, she nodded to one side of the stage where Walter sat in front of a grand piano releasing tunes from his fingers which blended with the soft tunes playing in the background. "I hope you enjoy yourselves."

"We will, thank you for this invitation," Ugochukwu said and led his family to seats at the end of a dimmed corner, which offered a good view of the make-shift stage.

When they got comfortable in their chairs, one of the servers approached them with a tray of snacks, placing three small plates of it on their table. Ifeoma reached for the snack and nibbled on it, savouring the crisp outer layer that gave way to the soft interior of the freshly baked pretzel dipped in cheese sauce.

Soon, the tunes changed and a man climbed the stage, introduced himself as a Vietnamese living on the third floor of the building before announcing that he would be singing a song in his native language.

"He's talented," Ifeoma said, her head swaying to the rhythm of the song, though she couldn't understand the meaning in it.

He leaned towards her so his words would not be lost to the noise. "You're a wonder, Ify. I expended much energy trying to convince you to come here, and now, look at you. You're enjoying this more than I am."

She ignored him with an unwavering focus on the stage singer.

Just before eleven p.m., Julia took to the stage and announced that the next performance would be just for laughs. The lights dimmed further as she left, and the room fell silent as two beloved cartoon characters, Tom and Jerry, appeared on the stage. Tom, a big cat costume, was worn by a person whose exaggerated movements brought the character to life, while Jerry, the smaller rat costume, seemed to house a shorter person. Probably a teenager.

The performance began with the familiar antics of Tom chasing Jerry. The cat's clumsy attempts to catch the clever rat were met with laughter and cheers from the audience. Jerry played tricks and outsmarted Tom at every turn, much to the delight of the crowd. By the end of each act, Jerry always emerged victorious, earning more applause.

Ikenna was completely taken with the characters and couldn't contain his excitement. The boy kept jumping from where he sat on his father's laps, following the movements on the stage. After a while, his boundless energy proved too much for his father who placed him on the floor so he could jump as freely as he pleased.

He soon noticed that Ikenna was no longer by his side. He then saw him running towards the stage. Before he could react, Ikenna had reached Tom, wrapping his small arms tightly around the cat's leg. Tom the cat carried the boy up, playing along. He swung him around as an act ended, as though swinging the boy were part of the whole show. Ikenna got the loudest cheer by the time he was placed back on the floor, just before his father reached for him. Back in his seat, Ugochukwu knew better not to leave him on the floor unguarded.

At fifteen minutes before twelve, Julia took to the stage again and made an announcement, "Hello everyone, it is time for the general dance. After this, we would all do a count-down to welcome the New Year together."

There were positive reactions as the stage was cleared of its make-shift stage to create more space for the dance.

"You will have to dance without me," Ifeoma said. "I just can't carry my weight around tonight."

"You shouldn't, and I don't feel like it either. The dance here would be a slow one, not the type we are used to," Ugochukwu said.

"*Ah ah*! But you like to dance all kinds of dance."

"No. Not with this kind of slow music."

"In that case, we might be the only ones sitting while the others dance," she said. "That would look awkward."

"Maybe, maybe not."

"We better leave before anyone notices."

"Good idea, let's go now."

When the lights dimmed further for the dance to begin, they grabbed their coats and strolled outside. Loud pops and booms of fireworks were already on display in the sky.

A lamp post stood just outside the building, casting a warm golden-yellow glow over the nearby flowers, set against the stunning display unfolding in the sky. They settled down on the pavement, in the shadow of the lamp post, to watch the fireworks. Some of them soared into the air, leaving a trail of smoke behind. Each burst of colour painted the night sky with displays of colourful sparks, illuminating their faces with fleeting hues of red, green, blue, and gold.

One particular type of firework beat the others in the competition. It shot into the sky like a rocket, and as it exploded, it wrote the words for a few magical seconds: 'FROHES NEUES JAHR 1994' or sometimes 'WILLKOMMEN 1994' bright and bold against the night sky. Happy shouts came from the party they just left. Happier, distant shouts echoed from the surrounding neighbourhood, adding to the collective celebration. It was a new year.

"I have never seen such a display of fireworks," Ifeoma declared.

"It is so beautiful to watch. The Germans really know how to celebrate," he agreed.

"It is surely beautiful," Ifeoma concurred as her eyes kept glued to the sky. "And it is kind of different from the ones back home."

He laughed as he adjusted a sleeping Ikenna on his shoulders. "You like to compare everything, Ify."

"Yes *o*, that's how I get to know which to appreciate more. I could stay out here for hours watching the sky, except that the air is beginning to get filled with sulphur." She was running one of her hands across her nose, as if doing so would take away the smell.

"Sulphur?" Ugochukwu asked, making an effort to smell the air. "How do you even know how sulphur smells?"

"Don't make me laugh, *biko*," she said laughing. "It's just the same smell released when fuel is burned. I once read somewhere that fireworks smell like sulphur."

"You did? Oh, I think I can smell it now. I have always associated this smell with fireworks and nothing else."

It was nineteen past twelve a.m. when they got into their apartment. Ugochukwu placed Ikenna on the bed gently before getting some warm water. With a towel, he gently cleaned his son's sticky fingers and face. Tomorrow, the boy would have a full bath.

No need to disturb his sleep now.

PART TWO - 1994

CHAPTER SIXTEEN

1st January 1994

She must have drifted off to sleep a second time because when she cracked her eyes open again, the brilliant rays of the sun shone so brightly through the window, making her shut her eyes immediately. Winter wind had been blowing earlier when she first cracked her eyes open for a short while. She felt well rested now, a sure sign that she had slept really well, but her body remained weak and heavy. She shifted from one end of the bed to the other before looking at the wall clock which read 1:01 p.m. Her eyes lingered on it, admiring its ostrich-looking design. She looked around the room, wondering how it was possible that she slept until the afternoon. She must have been more tired than she thought from attending the party last night.

Sleeping through the morning of a New Year's Day was indeed a first for her. When she was growing up, her mother would be up at five o'clock in the morning to begin preparations for the assorted meals that they usually prepared for the New Year. The food was always cooked in large pots because there were lots of mouths to feed, including the apprentices living in the household at the time. Her father, Okwesilieze, usually slaughtered a goat or cow to provide the meat for the large number of people in his house and to share with visitors and neighbours for the occasion.

They would be at it all morning, chopping the ingredients, the vegetables for the salad, and the meat to sizable portions, steaming and frying the meat, and cooking the rice and soups, till the dishes were ready. The more strenuous chores such as pounding the yam and the *fufu* that would be eaten with the soup, was left to the *umuboyi* in her father's employ. This had always been the norm in her father's house every New Year, and somehow, she carried on this tradition when she got married, this year being different because of her condition and location. A sense of nostalgia hit her. She would not partake in the frenzy of activities she was sure was currently taking place in her father's house and she missed it.

Lying on her back, she shifted to the edge of the bed in a bid to sit up. Her back was half way up when a moan escaped her mouth instead. Just below her abdomen, a sensation gripped her. She waited while the wave of pain subsided and then tried to sit up again. But the pain came back more intense than the first. This time it was no longer a moan, she screamed as her muscles tensed.

She heard a dull thud as her husband emerged from the kitchen, his right hand cradling his left elbow with a grimace on his face.

Ugochukwu dropped both hands and immediately rushed to her when he took in the scene from the kitchen door. "Ify, is it the baby? Is she coming? Should I call the hospital now?"

Silence. She stayed still, very still on the bed so that the pain could ease.

He left her side and ran towards the phone. His hands moved frantically around the table where the phone was, lifting papers and letting them fly about the room, in search of the phone directory. Hearing another moan from his wife, he turned and ran back to her, barely avoiding a collision with Ikenna who had stopped playing with his toys and was staring at the unfolding situation. Again, he turned and raced back to the phone.

Then he saw the phone directory lying leisurely on the same table beside the phone. There was no time to wonder why he hadn't seen it the first time. Grabbing the phone receiver and clutching it to his ears, he frantically turned the pages of the directory, stopping at where he had marked a particular number with a red marker so he could identify it easily. He dialled... Click. He spoke German.

"Hello!" he said impatiently. "Can you hear me?"

"Hello. This is Robert Johannes Hospital. How may we help you?" a female voice came.

"My wife! She's... she's in labour! Hurry!" he blurted out. He was breathing fast.

"Okay. Listen. You have to calm down," the voice said. "You will need to answer some questions clearly and we would be there soon."

"Okay! Okay!" He was pacing around the table as he spoke, conscious of the extent the phone wire could go.

"What is her name and address?"

"Ifeoma Odogwu."

"Can you spell it out please?"

"First name is I-F-E-O-M-A. Last name is O-D-O-G-W-U."

"Got it. And the address?"

"Blumenstraße 120, 55120. Apartment number is nineteen."

"Good, the team will be there as soon as possible."

The line went dead.

"They will soon be here," he announced as soon as he got back to her side.

"This is not the same way my labour pains started when I had Ikenna," Ifeoma said.

"It's not always the same, I guess."

"Listen, I need you to get some things together before they get here. Get the hospital bag, then get my nightgown from the closet..."

***

Ugochukwu was putting final touches to the packed hospital bag when siren sounds became audible. It couldn't have been more than eleven minutes since he called the hospital.

"They are here," he announced. "Anything else you need me to do?"

Ifeoma sat up immediately, momentarily ignoring the pains that shot up her spine as she moved. She was holding her breath when she asked, "Ugom, what did you tell them on the phone?"

"That you are in labour."

"That I am in labour?" she asked.

"You are in labour, Ify. Shouldn't I have told them?" he asked with concern.

"Don't look at me like that. That sounds like an ambulance. I am still alive!" she said, her voice stressing the last two words.

"Ify, the ambulance is used for emergencies, not for dead people."

"What are you talking about? An ambulance is used for transporting dead people to the mortuary, church, or to where they will be buried, isn't it?"

"They use it here for medical emergencies. Any person needing urgent medical attention here would get an ambulance. What they use to transport dead people here is a hearse."

Her face relaxed then. With nothing else to say, she gently and slowly stood up from the bed just as the doorbell rang.

"Thank you for coming so quickly," Ugochukwu said when he opened the door admitting two men.

"No worry, it is what we do." One of the paramedics said. He spoke slowly, as though he thought of each word before voicing them out. "Where *Frau*?"

Ifeoma emerged from the bedroom, quickly exchanging a look with her husband.

When the paramedic spoke again, Ifeoma recalled the request she had made during her antenatal to have at least one English-speaking medical personnel attend to her in the delivery room. The hospital had put up no objections to the request, but they had also given her no assurances.

The paramedic stood before her. "You can walk or we help you?"

"I can manage," she answered.

"Good. We take ambulance now, bring you hospital." He gesticulated with his hands as he spoke. Turning to Ugochukwu, "Mr. oh-doh-goo, you have hospital bag?"

"Yes, let me grab it," Ugochukwu answered. Any other day, he might have smiled and given some thought to the way the man pronounced his name, but this was not one of those days.

A stretcher lay by the ambulance waiting when they got downstairs. With some help, Ifeoma was placed on it and strapped, carefully positioned on her side. A foetal monitor was attached to her before she was wheeled in, just as Ugochukwu assured her that everything would be fine and that he would be at the hospital soon. Within a minute, she was alone at the back of the ambulance with the two paramedic men as the car started to move.

"You feel something? Like push?"

"Not yet, only the contractions." It was his gesticulations that helped her understand what he asked. Her temperature, pulse, blood pressure, and respiration rate were checked. The edges of her stomach were felt.

"Your water break?"

"Not yet." She saw him note her answers on a notepad.

"You tell us when feel need to push," the paramedic said.

Before he could finish speaking, a scream tore from her mouth following another contraction. The questions ceased then.

The ambulance was quiet now except for the movement of the car. As the contractions subsided, Ifeoma allowed her mind to drift from the situation at hand. She had been six months pregnant when she arrived in Mainz and had registered at a clinic attached to the hospital, for ante-natal care. The encounter she had on that first day she went to the clinic had been indelible on her mind.

After waiting for a while, she had been sent in to see the obstetrician-gynaecologist. The doctor had examined her body to be certain that the baby was well positioned. After the examination, her doctor had washed his hands in the basin by the corner of the office, and sat across from her on the table and began asking a series of questions. He had asked her if she was on any pills and she had unwrapped the pills given to her by her gynaecologist back home and extended it to the doctor.

The doctor had taken the pills from her, examined it, and trashed them afterwards. She had stared at him, lost for words.

"You are healthy and don't need any pills," he had stated. His English was heavily accented and she had to strain her ears to hear all that he was saying. "Pills are meant for patients with identified issues."

She had never forgotten his words. He had given her a small bottle instead; a blood builder, to be taken once a day.

"Would you prefer to have a C-section or a vaginal birth?" the doctor had asked.

At this, she had looked at him in confusion and asked, "Doctor, is there a problem with the baby? Why do I have to be operated on?"

"There's no problem but it's a choice if you prefer to have a C-section," the doctor had replied.

In that moment, she could not believe a doctor had asked that of a pregnant woman. No self-respecting woman would want to give birth by cutting open her womb without a good reason. No! She would give birth the way normal women did, just like her mother did before her. God forbid her doing it any other way.

Nodding emphatically, she turned to the doctor, "Vaginal birth," she had muttered.

On another occasion, when she and her husband had visited the clinic two weeks ago to find out the sex of their unborn child so they could know what baby clothes to buy, she had been asked to lay down on a bed situated at the corner of the doctor's office, pulling up her clothes and leaving her stomach bare. Then came the cold and thick transparent gel that the doctor applied on her stomach. "This is to aid us see the inside of your stomach," the doctor explained. It wasn't the gel on her stomach that made her cringe; it was its coldness.

There was a screen monitor beside her like a television, where the contents of her stomach were displayed. The doctor placed a device on her tummy, connected to the monitor beside her.

Moving his hands and explaining the position of the baby, the doctor revealed that everything appeared normal. Ifeoma kept looking at the screen, not being able to make out anything from the black and white shapes and lines before her.

The ultrasound probe kept on moving on her as if trying to penetrate a particular spot on her skin, searching. At last, the expected words came, "As far as I can tell, you are having a baby girl."

"How sure are you?" Ugochukwu had asked.

"Your wife is advanced. At this stage, I am ninety-five percent sure," the doctor replied flatly.

A smile appeared on Ifeoma's face. It was exactly what she wanted to hear. "Thank you, doctor." She said it as if it was the doctor that had determined the sex of the baby.

Presently, she felt the ambulance come to a halt and the door opened. The contractions had come three times during the ride.

Another team, which seemed as though they were already on stand-by took over and wheeled her into the hospital.

The fluorescent lights overhead, with the combination of the white walls, made the view too bright for her eyes. It was her first time being here.

CHAPTER SEVENTEEN

1st January 1994

The pains were getting intense as the minutes lingered slowly like hours. *Oh, God.* Ifeoma could feel her body burning. Subsequent child births were said to be easier than the previous births, but she wasn't so sure of that now. It was past nine p.m. and she still danced to the music her body was playing for her. Although this was a solo dance, she wished she had her husband on stage with her. After all, it takes two to tango, but why did she have to face the music alone? Why did she have to be subjected to this blinding pain, screaming her lungs out while the doctor or midwife looked over charts discussing her with the nurses or midwives as though she were a specimen under a microscope?

She sat on the hospital bed with one hand rubbing her waist in a bid to ease the pain. Her husband and son had been at the hospital earlier during the day, but had to leave when Ikenna became restless with sleep. It was because of her son's presence that she had muzzled up some of the screams that were on her lips during the contractions, begging to be let out.

She hadn't wanted to scare the boy into thinking that something out of place was happening to her.

She had thought her ordeal would be over by now, that by the time evening came, she'd be holding her baby in her arms. But the nurses, midwives, or whoever they were, kept saying she hasn't dilated enough. They kept saying words that meant the next time they checked, it would all be over. Their job was simple; to bring the baby out of her. To stop her misery. To stop the pains! Night had descended without any thought to her plight. They never kept to their words. They were liars, the whole lot of them! No, she shouldn't be saying such curse words. She was bringing a new life to this world. An innocent one shouldn't be born with curse words on her mother's mind. But the nurses were not making this any easier.

It wasn't just their words that never seemed to come true, at least not yet, that bothered her. She had noticed a certain kind of look in some of the nurses' eyes as they interacted with her. She couldn't explain it, but it seemed like their eyes watched her every move with a certain level of intensity. Almost as though they were expecting a supernatural phenomenon, other than a childbirth, to take place. She couldn't tell if their scrutiny was genuine concern. Although, she could be overanalysing some things in her present condition. She could be imagining things that weren't there. Each time the nurses or midwives came into the room, they seem to want to check more than they were supposed to. They had lingered each time they checked the baby's heartbeat, lingered each time they checked her dilation, as though hoping to catch a glimpse of something out of the ordinary.

Maybe it was all in her head. Just maybe. She screamed as another burning contraction hit her.

Two nurses or midwives on duty kept checking on her. One of them could speak English which settled her a little. At least she would have some semblance of familiarity as she pushed this child into this world. Her whole body burned, with sweat forming on the brows of her forehead. She wiped her face with the back of her palm, not because the room was hot; the temperature was enough to keep her cool, but because of the restlessness she was feeling.

Ursula, the nurse that could speak English, left the room and came back a few minutes later, carrying a large black ball. She had that smile that seemed to have been cemented on her face all evening, like it was part of the necessary requirements to keep her job at the hospital.

Ifeoma breathed deeply in reply. Her gaze shifted to the ball in Ursula's hands as she wondered what it was for.

Ursula explained, having seen the question in her eyes. "I brought you this. It should help ease your pain and improve the movement of the baby."

A ball? A sport ball to ease her pain? Then she remembered she had read about birthing balls in a magazine for expectant mothers while waiting to be attended to by her doctor in one of her ante-natal visits. "Is that a birthing ball?" Ifeoma asked.

"Yes," Ursula replied.

"Oh, I've read about it," Ifeoma said.

Ursula nodded. "You just place it under you and roll any direction you want. You can also sit on it and move around in circles."

Ifeoma stood up and managed to drag her body to sit on the ball while Ursula stood and watched as she rolled it underneath her. It wasn't just because she stood there looking at her, it was the way the nurse stared at her, following everything she did without another input. She felt like she was under scrutiny again. That her movements were being analysed and stored somewhere in the nurse's brain. To be retrieved and used like a computer data when needed.

"You learn fast," Ursula said.

***

Ugochukwu came to the hospital the second time without his son. It hadn't been easy on his end. After the ambulance took his wife away, he had stayed behind in the apartment pacing about. He had tried to control his anxiety by talking to Ikenna about the incoming baby, though he knew from the way the boy ignored him that he cared less for all the things he said. When he couldn't pace any longer, he took the boy and went to the hospital. He had stayed with his wife, encouraging her as she gyrated. He had been there, voicing all the available soothing words in his vocabulary, even the ones he didn't believe. Ifeoma had shouted at him once when one of the contractions hit, accusing him of being heartless in putting her through the situation. He knew she didn't mean what she said, he had only been concerned that Ikenna was there. If only his mother-in-law was not so far away, she would have known how best to comfort Ifeoma having had the experience herself. All the same, his wife wasn't wrong to have screamed at him, since he had actually put her in that condition.

It might have been different if he had been at the hospital when she birthed Ikenna, but he hadn't been there. He had been at work when she went into labour. If he had seen what she passed through for Ikenna, maybe, just maybe, they might have waited a couple more years before having a second child. It was traumatizing for him to watch, for Ikenna to see. So, when the boy showed the first signs of sleep in less than an hour that they'd been at the hospital, yawning and stretching, he took the opportunity to take him home.

But he didn't go home straight away. He had done a little shopping, buying some of the things Ifeoma had already bought. It wasn't every day that a person gets to become a father again. He had gone home afterwards and called the hospital to know how his wife was faring. He then arranged the house, fed Ikenna who hadn't slept in spite of his tiredness, and called the hospital again to inquire if the ordeal was over for his wife.

He had called his friend, Timo, asking if he knew of any night carers available for Ikenna. He wouldn't want to carry a sleeping boy to the hospital. Timo had offered to look after the boy till the following morning. What were friends for? He had three kids of his own, the last being the same age as Ikenna. That solved one of his current problems. He then set up the baby's cot in the small space left at the corner of the bed.

He had dropped a sleeping Ikenna at Timo's place on his way to the hospital.

It was just before midnight when he got back to the hospital. A midwife had medical gloves on, hovering over his wife's open legs. It was a different room from where his wife had been placed earlier. How he wished that the baby was here now. He didn't like seeing his wife looking all miserable, as if the whole world was crashing on her. Or maybe it was. Her next scream came and it shattered his heart. There was just too much pain involved with bringing forth life. It shouldn't be that way. Why was nature so complicated? Surely, he wouldn't have the heart to put his wife through this ordeal again.

He stood there in hospital scrubs, surgical cap, and mask, which he had been given to wear, trying to block half of his sight away with the mask. He kept pulling the surgical mask over his glasses, only to push it down again moments later. Yet, he didn't want to give the impression that he didn't care. He couldn't look in between those legs like the midwife was doing. Not in these circumstances.

By past one a.m., the midwife pressed a button and a nurse with a name tag: Ursula, walked in holding a stainless bowl filled with medical supplies.

That was when the midwife turned to him and spoke, "Ich brauche Ihre Zustimmung, ihr eine kleine Menge Morphin zu injizieren."—I need your consent to inject her with a little quantity of morphine.

"Was wird es mit ihr machen?"—What will it do to her? Ugochukwu asked.

"Das Medikament wird ihr helfen, weniger Schmerzen in dieser letzten Phase des Pressens zu spüren, während das Baby herauskommt."—The drug will help her feel less pain at this last stage of pushing out the baby.

"Natürlich, geben Sie es ihr,"—Certainly, give her. He consented.

He saw the effects of the morphine on her in less than a minute after it was injected. The veins jutting out from her face began to relax. A second nurse had joined the team by then, getting ready for what was coming.

When this second nurse entered the room, he noticed there was something about her. She had walked in a fast stride as if she was missing something. But she only walked up to the others, looking all over his wife like something was not going on as it should. This piqued his interest. Something cannot be wrong at this stage, he prayed. Not now, not ever. Then he heard her whisper to Ursula who stood at the side ready to hand the midwife whatever supply was needed. Why was she whispering like things weren't progressing as they should? he wondered. Because he stood at a distance not far from Ursula, the whispers coming from the nurses were audible enough to him.

"Heute werde ich sehen, wie sie ihre Babys zur Welt bringen,"—Today, I will see how they give birth to their babies, the second nurse said.

Ursula giggled. "Es sollte auf normalem Weg geschehen. Was erwarten Sie."—It should be through the normal process. What were you expecting?

That reply got him confused. Surely, one of the nurses was aware he could understand German. Or was he wrong? One of them had been present when he gave the midwife his consent for the morphine to be administered. Or wasn't she listening to the conversation?

"Vielleicht nicht, sie sind so anders. Irgendetwas muss anders sein,"—it may not, they are so different. Something must be different, he heard the second nurse say again.

Being less-informed and less-travelled surely had its consequences.

The three-person medical team now gathered around his wife's open legs like hungry vultures. His wife screamed again as she pushed, it was as though the morphine no longer had a strong grip on her now. He found himself slowly moving to the extreme corner of the room.

In the midst of her screams, they were telling her to keep pushing. Everyone present in the room was absorbed with what was happening except him. But he kept looking, he couldn't bear to look away and be thought insensitive.

He saw his wife gather what seemed to be all the strength she could muster to give a push. They were now telling her that the baby's head was coming, telling her to keep at it. Then he saw her do the unthinkable. Just as the baby's head popped out, his wife grabbed the nearest thing her hands could reach as her upper body jerked forward. She held tightly to one of the nurse's hairs and dragged the nurse closer to herself as she laid back. This was the second nurse who had whispered things about his wife. She had stood apart from the other two, but very close to where his wife's stomach was, bending a little, not wanting to miss out on the action taking place.

His wife pulled the nurse closer to her chest by reflex as she screamed and brought forth the new life. She still held the nurse's hair tightly as the rest of the baby came through. All the while, the poor nurse struggled to free her hair. Suddenly, the nurse was more concerned with getting away from his wife than with anything else she was inquisitive about. But the grip on her was strong. It was funny to watch, yet nothing about the situation was funny. Surely, his wife couldn't have known what the nurse had said earlier. She couldn't have known that she had deprived her of seeing something she very much wanted to. What did they say again about the inquisitive monkey? It got a bullet to the head.

His wife released the nurse as his baby's cry filled the room. His baby was here. It was all over.

Ursula held the tender being, oblivious of the magnitude of what her colleague just went through, "Es ist auf die gleiche Weise, genau auf die gleiche Weise."—It's the same way, exactly the same way.

But the second nurse only jumped away from his wife immediately she was freed, slightly coughing and massaging her head and neck. She moved away from the new mother as quickly as she could manage, and as far away as she could get.

Ursula gently clamped the umbilical cord with two devices and severed the cord at the middle, before taking the baby away.

CHAPTER EIGHTEEN

2nd January 1994

T he sound of two faint voices coming from outside her hospital room woke her. When the voices ceased and the door opened, a nurse walked in carrying a tray which held her breakfast containing some bread, cheese, a boiled egg, and a cup of tea. Except for the cheese, Ifeoma gulped down every other thing on the tray not realizing how hungry she was.

She was glad when she learnt that she didn't have to worry about food while at the hospital. Her husband would not have to heat up the assorted food she had prepared and stored in the freezer to bring to her. Her mother, Ogechi, had called every Saturday in the last four weeks from the NITEL office where people stood in line waiting for their turn to make a call. She had asked her to prepare the delicacies and store them in the freezer for when the baby would arrive. With every call, her mother had drummed into her ears the benefits of pepper soup and *ofe nsala* for a woman who just birthed. How it would help to wash away any remaining bad blood in her system. How it would aid her in recovering faster. Now, the soups would be in her freezer waiting for her to get back home. All the same, nothing was lost.

For the nth time that day, she looked at her baby closely to make sure she was still breathing. The rise and fall of her chest assured her that all was well. Although, the room was clean and comfortable with a large window that let in light, something crucial was still missing and she knew exactly what it was. Her mother. Just like every new maternal grandmother of her people, she was tasked with caring for her daughter and grandchild the moment the daughter puts to bed. Before the baby arrived, the new grandmother would have made preparations, buying native spices to prepare soups such as *ofe nsala, ofe oha,* and pepper soup. This was to ensure that she ate the right foods to regain her strength and to stimulate milk production. As soon as the news breaks about the baby's birth, the new grandmother would arrive at her son-in-law's house to help out with the chores, cook meals, and help with the baby so that the new mother can make a speedy recovery. She would stay with them until the baby is at least three months old. Some even stayed till the baby was half a year old.

She remembered how helpful her mother had been when she had Ikenna and she greatly appreciated the *omugwo* tradition. Her mother had been the one who stayed awake at night to rock Ikenna to sleep, especially after he had been breastfed. Her mother bathed him, holding his small, slippery body with experienced hands as she watched, fascinated while holding a towel to wrap him in after his bath. It had been her mother who went to the market to get foodstuffs and to buy bigger clothes after Ikenna outgrew the tiny, baby clothes she had bought for him in just a month. Her mother was the one that held Ikenna during his vaccinations since she could not bear to hold her baby as they pricked him with the syringe. Her mother had tended to Ikenna's circumcision wounds and found out after a week that the plastic attached to the boy's penis that was meant to fall off on its own was healing into his skin. Her mother had been her backbone and support and she realized now how much it meant to her now. This was what the traditional *omugwo* was all about. But with her mother separated from her by endless miles, she would be on her own this time. The thought made her feel more alone and it mentally exhausted just by thinking of all that she had to do to care for her baby.

It wasn't that her husband would not naturally be supportive, but he had his limitations. He wouldn't know how to prepare the native meals she needed for her recovery after the ones stored away in the freezer finished. He would not be able to hold the baby for long hours at night since he would need to leave for work the following morning.

She tried to shake off her worries and focus on the present situation. She stared at her daughter, wrapped in a soft white blanket with her tiny hands curled up. The baby's face was still scrunched up and her features were not yet distinguishable. She could hardly tell whom the baby resembled.

The low snores from the other side of the room, coming from her roommate who had robbed her of sleep, bored into her awareness. Last night hadn't been smooth for her after her husband left the hospital early that morning around three to get some sleep himself. Remembering the events and sighing, she turned to where her roommate lay sleeping soundly with her own baby beside her.

Melanie (that was the name she heard her roommate's husband call her) had been brought into the room barely an hour after she herself was placed there to get some rest. They both had their babies that early morning of January, the second. A nurse had drawn a curtain in the middle of the room, separating it into two halves to give each of them their privacy.

Melanie's husband had arrived at the hospital room a few minutes after her own husband left. The couple had talked, joked, and laughed so loudly for about two hours that she wondered if Melanie actually just put to bed through the same excruciating process as hers. With what had happened in the room in the early hours of the morning, Melanie might as well have vomited her child, wiping her mouth like it was a small hiccup.

It wasn't just the noise they made that had disturbed her, Melanie's husband had arrived at the hospital room with cans of beer and they had both consumed the drinks that early morning without care.

She hadn't been more shocked in her whole life. She had laid on her bed holding her baby, and watched the shadows of the two of them that the almost transparent curtain provided. The sight had stunned her. That was a woman who just had a baby. Did they want to intentionally harm their child? Did they want the baby to start off having alcohol in the system? Maybe Melanie had dozen other children at home and could afford to be careless with this one. But, even at that!

What about Melanie herself? Pouring alcohol into her system when she hadn't yet recovered from her childbirth ordeal. The thought scared her and she thought of reporting the situation, for the sake of the new child. But other things stopped her. She could have a problem communicating with any staff she might meet.

Around four a.m., after tossing and turning for what seemed a long time, she could not take it anymore, so she went to their side of the room. She asked them to reduce their voices but they had only stared back at her without uttering a word. That had been embarrassing. Then she tried again using gestures, asking that they kept their voices low. She even pointed to Melanie's baby and mimed sleeping, then pointed to herself and repeated her actions. At this, she got a smile and a nod from them which had been encouraging.

But as soon as she got back to her bed, they continued their loud chat, as though she had been just a passing mosquito that had disturbed their picnic. She had also noticed something; she never heard their new born baby cry, not once. Hers had cried at intervals.

She had stayed up on her bed nursing, tired, and sleepy. It was only around five in the early morning hours that her body was able to succumb to sleep. And the sleep had been deep.

At the moment, Melanie's husband was no longer in the room with them. Ifeoma watched her baby as she lay awake smacking her lips. The tiny sound emanating from her tiny lip-smacking was almost comical. She knew that her baby was asking for something. She got a towel from the bathroom, ran it under warm water before wiping her breasts with it, focusing on her nipple where the baby's lips would be placed. That had been part of her ante-natal lessons.

As she breastfed the baby, the door opened and a doctor walked in. He took a brief look at Melanie's side and walked up to Ifeoma. The doctor stood tall with greying hair and he had a friendly face. Carrying a stethoscope hung across his shoulders which dangled from his neck, he held four files in one hand and a bowl containing medical supplies in the other. He greeted her and she smiled in return.

"You look good." His voice was soft.

She noted that his German accent didn't much affect his English speaking. He wasn't stressing the first syllables of his words and his 'you' didn't sound like 'ju'. "I am better, except I didn't sleep well last night," Ifeoma said as she suckled the baby.

The door opened a second time and her husband walked in with her son. Ugochukwu had that beam every new father had on their faces, the day their kids were born. The kind of beam that made one forget the troubles of life for a while.

"Mama! Mama!" Ikenna screamed as he ran to his mother.

"My active boy," Ifeoma said the moment the boy got to her side. Ikenna tried to climb up the bed but he could not bring his hands to boost himself up. Ugochukwu chuckled and carried him to sit next to his mother.

"Hello, doctor," Ugochukwu greeted.

"Hello," the doctor said in reply.

"How are you doing little one?" The doctor patted Ikenna on his head.

The boy looked up at him, smiled, and dangled his legs from the bed.

"So, *Frau*," the doctor turned back to her. "You complained about something. Why couldn't you sleep well?" As he talked, he looked at the names written on the files in his hand and brought out one from the middle to the top.

"The woman sleeping over there, she was too loud with her husband last night," she pointed with her chin as she spoke. On a second thought, she no longer wanted to report about the drinking. It wasn't her business. If the city had taught her anything, it was that people here minded their own business. It wasn't in her place to interfere in the affairs of others. "I don't think I can survive another night in this room if the husband returns."

"Sorry to hear that," the doctor apologized. He looked to Melanie's direction and returned his attention to Ifeoma. "We don't usually allow visitors outside of visiting hours. The man you saw was let in as an exception since his wife had just given birth, like you. But don't worry, it's not something that happens often."

"Thank you, but I would like to be moved to a room where I can stay alone with my baby," Ifeoma requested. "My head would be heavy from lack of rest if her husband comes back to visit her."

"I completely understand your concerns. But then, a single room might not be possible today because they're in high demand and usually fill up quickly. I can still put in a request for you, just in case something opens up. In the meantime, we could arrange for a different roommate if that would help. We should be able to move you this afternoon."

"Hmm," Ifeoma sighed. "I would be taking another risk since I may still get myself in a similar situation with another roommate." The baby was sleepy now. Her mouth lay open, no longer clasped to her nipple. Ifeoma quickly adjusted her dress, covering her exposed chest. She leaned the baby forward over her arm while her other hand rubbed her back to burp her. When a tiny belch came from her mouth, she placed her back in the cot. She turned and stared at her husband, communicating her wish to leave the hospital with her eyes and an imperceptible shake of her head.

"I will see what I can do," the doctor said with finality. "Please sit straight so I can examine you." He proceeded to check her body temperature, blood pressure, and finally informed her that a phlebotomist would come later to draw her blood and send to the lab for more tests. "We need to make sure everything is as it should be."

"Is it possible to get discharged today?" Ifeoma asked, noticing a small tightening of the doctor's jaw, as if steeling himself. But she needed to make sure that something would be done about her situation that very day.

"It's possible, but I wouldn't recommend it. After everything you've been through, you're supposed to stay for close monitoring for at least four days. It's really important for your recovery."

"You mean I have another three days to put up with this?" she gesticulated her hands around the room.

"Yes, just three more days left to monitor you closely."

"Since leaving is an option, I would prefer to be discharged today," she stated. It was the lesser of the two evils facing her. At least, no one would be there in their apartment laughing, chatting, and drinking in the middle of the night. "I feel strong and I can take care of myself."

"Are you sure about this, Ify?" Ugochukwu asked. He knew the answer to his question. He also knew that the decision wasn't for him to make. He very well knew the meaning of that face his wife had made in his direction, telling him to support her decision. But he had to try to sway her mind. The four days policy was in her best interest. "Won't you wait a little longer to think this through?"

Ifeoma faced her husband and spoke in Igbo, conscious of the doctor's eyes on her. "I have thought it through already. I stayed two days at the hospital when I had Ikenna and everything was okay. Staying four days here is not necessary."

"If you say so." Ugochukwu turned to the doctor. "I agree with whatever she decides."

"All right, we'll proceed with her discharge today since that's what you both want. Before that, I'll need you to sign a form acknowledging that the hospital won't be held liable if anything goes wrong after she leaves," the doctor said, looking at Ugochukwu and hoping this would change his mind.

Ugochukwu nodded and swallowed.

The doctor turned his attention to the baby, bending over her cot and checking her over, starting from her eyes. "She is perfectly healthy," he announced. "You're both doing great." He then started a little lecture on what diet to eat, how to properly exercise, and how to care for the new baby.

When he was done, the doctor turned to Ugochukwu. "I will request the administration to bring the necessary waiver documents for your signature. The hospital bill will be sent to your address when it is ready."

Ifeoma would later see a picture of her baby hanging on the wall at the right-hand corner of the hospital's reception room after being discharged that late evening, with these words written under it: *DAS ERSTE SCHWARZE BABY*—The First Black Baby. The word '*schwarz*' or 'Black', after her husband interpreted the meaning, would make her cringe for a second, but she would shrug it off. Her baby had made history in this hospital.

CHAPTER NINETEEN

21st January 1994

Zelda and Stefan were relaxing in their sitting room that Friday evening after dinner. The sound of the television program was low when the phone rang.

"I'll get it," Zelda declared and stood up. "Hello, Wolf's Residence." She waited. "Hello? Can you hear me?" Another pause. "Is this Hannah?" She sighed, set the receiver back in its cradle, and went back to the sitting room.

"It is probably Hannah still refusing to speak to you," Stefan declared.

"Haven't I tried enough? What else can I do to show her that everything is in the past now?" She meant it as a rhetorical question, though she knew that her husband would give a reply.

"Just give her some more time, Hannah would come around eventually."

"It's been over two years and she wouldn't still speak to me. Over two years of not seeing my own child and counting...." The phone began to ring again and they both knew it was best Stefan picked it up.

"Hello Hannah," Stefan breathed into the phone receiver immediately he picked it up.

Zelda heard him laugh at intervals. Near the end of the call, she heard him ask if Hannah wanted to speak to her mother. Zelda already knew Hannah would decline again, and the thought burned inside her.

"She wanted to know if we were okay," Stefan said as he returned to his seat. "That's all she cared to know. Give her a little more time and she will come around."

"You keep saying that. You made me host two immigrant families months ago, hoping I would someday host Hannah's husband too. So much for the effort."

"Two years is a long time, but I promise you'll forget about them when she finally comes around. Just give it more time, dear."

"Time," she murmured. "It's such a vague, far-reaching thing."

"That's all I ask for, my dear," Stefan said.

CHAPTER TWENTY

23rd January 1994

A slight wind was blowing. The trees looked gloomy as though mourning the loss of something that had given meaning to their existence. They stood naked in the snow, lying in wait for a time to bloom again.

In the apartment, Ifeoma held her daughter, admiring the little bundle of goodness. As the saying goes, when one desires something deeply, the universe conspires to grant it. She had desired so deeply for a daughter. She had asked and prayed for this, and the universe heard her. Again, virtue has been said to lie in the middle. And when one gets a table, the next natural desire would be to get a chair. It creates balance. Not that she would have rejected another male child if that was what came through for her, but it wasn't what she desired. She was certain that her son's hyperactive nature was due to the boy's sex. That must be it. Boys were known to act like boys. But girls, they were softer in nature. She wouldn't want a second version of her son.

It had been three weeks since the discharge from the hospital. She sat on a chair breastfeeding the baby. Her husband sat opposite her reading a newspaper and occasionally lowering it to check on Ikenna who was driving his trains on a train track. He often ensured that their boy had something to keep him occupied or he would simply find something to do himself, which usually meant the possibility of spoiling or scattering things. A technician from a refrigerator repair company was in their apartment, diligently working to fix the freezer that had stopped functioning two days ago.

The phone started to ring and the baby momentarily stopped sucking. In a reflex, Ifeoma placed one of her fingers on the tip of her nipple to halt the flowing breast-milk. She was at the mercy of her body, and will continue to be for months to come.

When her husband picked up the phone, the lip-smacking sound started again. The baby had returned her mouth to the nipple, sucking with closed eyes.

"Hello, Mr. Odogwu speaking," Ugochukwu said into the receiver the moment he picked it up. "*Haaa! O tegokwa!*"—It has been long.

The quick switch to Igbo alerted her immediately. Who could it be? Of the few families and friends they had given their phone number to, she couldn't pinpoint who it was that would make her husband exclaim with such excitement. Her own mother had been calling every other day since her new grandchild arrived, but with the way her husband exclaimed, it had to be someone else. He would have greeted her mother first, out of respect, then exchanged pleasantries before waiting to hear why she was calling. And it was always about the new baby. There was nothing her mother hadn't advised since she was informed of the baby's birth.

Her mother wouldn't believe she was doing anything right where the new baby was concerned. She had an inkling that her mother still believed that she was still that little girl she raised. Wasn't that how all mothers thought? That their children haven't grown up yet. Her mother would be on the phone, repeating the exact things she had said earlier, as if trying to drum it into her ears. At one time, her mother had asked her to repeat what she had said about the dangers of breast-feeding the baby while lying down on the bed.

"*Kenelu m* mummy *o*,"—send my regards to mummy, Ugochukwu concluded. He placed the receiver back and turned to face his wife. "That was Ifeanyi."

Ifeanyi was Ugochukwu's younger brother.

"How is he? How is he faring at his new job?" Ifeoma asked.

"He's okay. He's happy about the baby and he sent his well wishes."

"I would have loved to speak to him. It's been long since I last heard from him." It was true. She hadn't spoken to her brother-in-law since she got to Mainz. She had been in the bathroom the first time he called the apartment the previous year. Amongst the three of her husband's siblings, it was Ifeanyi that she related most with, especially when the family gathered during the Christmas and New Year celebrations in the village.

"I told him you were busy with the baby, and he chose not to interrupt."

"Nice of him. Anyway, there is always a next time."

"He suggested that we name the baby Uwaoma, which is a beautiful name, but I told him we have named her and documented it already," Ugochukwu said. "In his opinion, the name would suit her since she came into the world in a better place with less challenges of life."

"I don't really get what he means. We name children based on birth circumstances because names have power and preserve legacies. That is why we named our son Ikenna. So, what does he mean by saying she was born in a better place?" she asked.

"He claims the name is befitting since having her here in Germany means that she came into a less-stressful part of the world," he answered.

"Is that his only reason?" Ifeoma asked as her eyeballs got bigger. "Is that the only reason he would want to name my precious daughter Uwaoma?" She spat the name out like it tasted foul in her mouth.

"Easy. You look like you want to jump on me and eat me raw. I did not suggest the name."

"Good thing you have already named her. I don't like the meaning in that name, though he couldn't have named her anyway. Why would he believe that everything in this part of the world is better than everything in our own country? Has he been here before?" She frowned as she spoke.

"You are funny," Ugochukwu laughed. "I knew this would be your reaction to his suggestion. You are so predictable."

"Let me be as predictable as you wish. Just look at us, locked inside this room as if we are some caged animals. We are here desperately trying to keep warm because of the climate outside. He is over there enjoying his life, free to go outside as he pleases and he thinks this is a better place?"

Ugochukwu went back to his newspapers. He knew better than to argue with his wife when she was starting to get worked up. He could end up taking the blade meant for someone else.

He had named his daughter Adaeze: the daughter of a king. He had also given her a German name, Lina, which means 'tender' or 'delicate'. He felt that she needed a link to her birth place, and what better way is there than to put it in a name? He had decided on the names the first time he carried her in his arms when they got home from the hospital which were direct expressions of his feelings for her at that moment. It had been under the same circumstances that Ikenna had gotten his name. He had looked at his son the first day he held him and seen his own father's replica.

Ifeoma looked at her husband. She could read him so well: he was trying to avoid an argument. As she finished speaking, she saw him raise the newspaper to his face as if something had caught his attention and suddenly glued him to it. They both kept silent, and for a while, only the sound made by the electrician repairing the refrigerator was heard in the apartment.

Three days earlier, she had prepared a spicy pepper soup and packed it in the freezer. She wouldn't want her mother to call and ask if she had done as she requested. Saying she hadn't done so would result to some scolding, as if she were a child not capable of handling her affairs. But the freezer had stopped working two days ago. A call had been placed to a refrigerator repair company and it had taken them two days to send someone.

She looked at the containers of food lined up just outside the window frame. Her husband had advised her to place the food containers on those frames, assuring her that they would remain frozen. He had claimed to have seen it done somewhere before, but couldn't quite remember where. It had been over twenty-four hours since she placed those containers there and each time she checked, they remained frozen. Winter surely had its benefits.

Adaeze laid on her mother's lap, warm and snug, with her tiny fingers curled up. Her chest rose and fell in a gentle rhythm as she slept, oblivious to anything around her. Ifeoma watched her with exhaustion, longing for long hours of sleep and some moments to herself. She wished her mother would somehow materialize into the apartment to help out with the baby. She sat very still, refusing to risk waking Adaeze.

Then, she shifted her weight slightly, trying to find a more comfortable position on the chair. Her back ached from the constant strain of holding and rocking the baby. She had barely had a good night's sleep since Adaeze's arrival and her body strained with fatigue. She closed her eyes and took a deep breath, trying to muster some energy to get up and place Ada in her cot.

The baby stirred as she made to stand up. Ifeoma froze, holding her breath and hoping beyond hope that Adaeze would settle back to sleep. After a while of waiting, desperate to get some rest herself, she stood up. As she straightened, she saw Adaeze's eyes open, wide and bright, staring at her. That was the way Adaeze mostly slept. Always on a shallow level as if she was trying to dispute the words: sleep like a baby. Then a shrill cry, loud enough to pierce through walls rang out.

She hissed. Ada's light sleep habits were annoying. Even more annoying was that her baby constantly wants to feel her mother. She cradled her close to her chest and began to sway back and forth.

The repairman's work continued to be a constant grating noise in the background, rising and falling depending on which tools he used. She had asked her husband to plead with the repairman in German, the moment he got to the apartment, to make as little noise as possible. She knew the repairman tried to accommodate them but he couldn't eliminate the noise completely. He definitely would not be able to screw open the freezer without making a sound, and he wouldn't be able to drill the screws back without making any noise. That was part of the reason Ada couldn't relax into her usual shallow sleep. She was bombarded by unfamiliar noise.

She began to sing in Igbo; a song that her own mother had often sung to Ikenna as a lullaby when he was still a baby. It was a soft, lifting melody from an Igbo folktale. She knew the song wasn't a lullaby *per se*, but the gentle melody could easily put any child to sleep in minutes. She had watched as the song performed its magic on Ikenna. It should do the same to his sister.

As she sang, she too felt herself begin to relax, with the tension in her body easing. The song weaving its magical spell on her...

O! Nwa mmuo, ka m kara gi. Inine—Oh! Child spirit, let me tell you a story.

I ma na nwunye di m di njo? Inine—Do you know that my co-wife is bad?

Nwunye di m, di njo. Inine—Yes, my co-wife is bad.

Ejere m kuru mmiri m ga-enye nwa. Inine—I went and took some water to give my baby.

O si m kwuo ya ugwo mmiri; mmiri nwa. Inine—But she asked me to fetch back the water I took; the one meant for the baby.

M si ya: "E chuo m Ogba." O si m: "Echuna Ogba." Inine—I asked to fetch water from Ogba stream, she refused.

M si ya: "E chuo m Iyi." O si m: "Echuna Iyi." Inine—I asked to fetch water from Iyi stream, she refused.

I siri gini? Inine—The child spirit replies: What did you say?

Nwaezeoba. Inine—She insisted I fetch water from Nwaezeoba stream.

Mmiri sere wam wam na n'elu igwe. Inine—The stream that flows very fast into Heaven.

Mmiri sere amuma ka onwa na-eti. Inine—The stream that sent lightening while the moon was still up.

Ewoo! Nne nwa, ndo. Inine—The child spirit replies out of pity: So sorry, mother.

Doo! Doo! —So sorry.

Adaeze whimpered softly as her sleepy eyes fixed on her mother's moving lips. Ifeoma's voice floated through the apartment. She had forgotten how melodious her voice could be. She knew Ada was enjoying what she produced, from the way she had her tiny, glistening eyes fixed on her face.

The song had calmed the baby even before it was finished, so she started singing the song a second time. When she neared the end, Ada was asleep in her arms.

Looking sideways, she saw Ikenna sprawled out on the floor beside his train tracks and sleeping as well. Singing had its hypnotic wonders. She pondered why it had never occurred to her to sing the song since she birthed Ada. She rocked her a few more times just to be certain she was asleep, then carefully lowered her into the cot. Adaeze snuggled into the blankets with her tiny hands curling around the fabric.

She stood for a moment watching her sleep, staring at the tiny human that dictated when she would engage in any activity. Then she moved closer to where her husband sat and saw the tiny smirk on his lips.

"This is not funny at all, why can't Ada stay on her own and just look around like other babies while she's awake?" Ifeoma asked him in whispers.

"I wish I could answer that. The doctor already said she is a normal baby and she would stop it with time," Ugochukwu answered.

"I really hope she stops very soon; she's wearing me out. I get confused with things most times because of her." Recently, she had gotten confused and forgetful about where some items were kept around the apartment.

Ugochukwu looked past her and smiled again.

"What is funny now?"

"Look under that door," he said, pointing at the adjoining door they shared with their next-door neighbour.

The next apartment was occupied by a Chinese woman who looked to be in her early forties. She lived there alone. She had been writing on sheets of paper in both English and German languages, passing it under their door for the past two weeks. Her request was always simple and straightforward: asking them to control their baby's cries. She had written many times, even in the middle of the night when Adaeze would choose to cry rather than sleep. On such nights when neither breast-milk nor soothing could placate her, the notes would show up always ending in the same way: that she needed peace and quiet to be able to sleep or do some other thing.

Ifeoma's eyes caught the paper lying close to the door. It was at the exact position as the earlier ones. She also knew it must have been slipped in when Ada was carrying on with those high-pitched sounds a three-week old baby shouldn't normally produce. "I honestly feel for her but there's nothing we can do. I cannot shut the baby's mouth, can I?" Ifeoma didn't bother to pick up the paper, she already knew what it would say.

"I pity her too. But then, it's not entirely our fault. I've often wondered why they build houses here with wood instead of the thick cement blocks fortified with concrete that we use back home," Ugochukwu lamented.

"That is true. The woods make it so easy to hear sounds coming from the next apartment, sometimes sounds you shouldn't even hear at all. If the walls were made of concrete, I don't think the lady would have much to complain about," she said.

"Exactly."

Ifeoma continued after a pause, "At least she didn't play her usual vengeful loud music this time around, trying to repel the baby's cries. I'm glad Ada has stopped crying at the moment, it was her prolonged cries that triggered her to put on her music and place the speaker close to that door we share with her. She wanted to revenge."

"Revenge? Maybe she played it to mask the noise so she could concentrate on whatever she wanted to do," Ugochukwu offered.

"Then why did she place the speaker very close to the door we share with her if she only wanted to drown Ada's crying? I doubt that was her intention. But whatever her reason was, I am a little glad that she puts on that music. It makes us even somehow."

"You have a good point. I won't call the police to complain about the cries now that we also have something to complain about."

"Yes. And then there's Julia. She was here two days ago trying to find out why the baby was always crying. I suspect our neighbour reported the matter to Julia who stated she had been getting complaints from other occupants of this building. I'm sure I know who that complaint came from. What do they want me to say is wrong with Ada? *Eh*? That she's not a normal baby like the others? They wouldn't hear that from me. I only told her what Ada's doctor said; that she would stop the constant crying with time," Ifeoma said.

"That's a good answer."

The freezer repairman approached them and started speaking to Ugochukwu in German, explaining what went wrong with the freezer and what he did to make it right. After the exchange, the repairman started to pack his tools into his toolkit.

"The freezer is fine now," Ugochukwu announced to Ifeoma.

"I can finally put back all the food inside," she rejoiced.

"Yes, but would it make much difference? Since the cold weather is doing the work of the freezer."

"Ha! It would, *biko*. I don't trust this weather to preserve my food as much as the freezer would."

When the repairman closed the apartment door behind him, it slammed shut with a loud bang, waking the baby. Ada's cries filled the room again, high-pitched and insistent. At that moment, Ifeoma saw red. If the repairman were still in their apartment, she might have lunged something heavy at him. It would have served him right for waking Ada.

She handed the baby to her husband; it was his turn to dance the dance of parenthood.

CHAPTER TWENTY-ONE

3rd February 1994

"Phew." Ifeoma eased her frame slowly into the cushion. Realizing she had made unnecessary noise, she waited with bated breath to be sure Ada didn't stir in her sleep. She stretched her tired muscles and rubbed the ache on her waist.

Taking care of the kids was taking a toll on her, the way she never suspected it would. The Christmas and New Year holidays were over and her husband had resumed his work. She couldn't say he didn't try. He did, in the ways that he could.

First, he had taken a week's leave from work. He had helped around the house; shopping when needed, cleaning, ensuring there was warm food, and taking Ikenna outdoors when the boy became fed up with the apartment. At the end of the week, she had asked him to extend his leave, but it wasn't possible. He couldn't get any more time off except he was sick or he had a family emergency. Having a new baby didn't count as an emergency, so he had to resume. Moreso, there was neither a replacement nor a substitute available that could cover for him.

Going back to work didn't mean her husband wasn't helping out. He still did the best he could. Before leaving in the mornings, he would bathe and feed Ikenna, making sure that the boy was okay before he left. He would sometimes take the list of items she put in the middle of the *Der Spiegel Magazine* on the table which contained what they needed at home. On his way back from work, he would stop at a store to pick those things up. As for Adaeze, he left the baby to her care which was understandable seeing as Ada's needs were many and most of them, she needed to see to herself. Adaeze was a child that could keep a parent busy all day, with barely some hours at intervals to spare. And she was struggling. In between caring for her new born and trying to manage her energetic son whilst also being a wife to her husband, she was coming to her wits end.

Now, she lay slumped in a chair with her eyes closed. As some mornings went, Ada had chosen today to be extra fussy. She had cried nonstop, which had turned her little face a shade darker than the red head warmer on her tiny head. It had been one of Ada's bad mornings where she required her mother to carry her and dance around. After she had eaten and burped, Ifeoma thought to leave her in her cot so that she would have her bath and put herself together but Ada had other ideas. She wailed her protest at being put down and so Ifeoma picked her up, placing her on her shoulders while bouncing around a little to hush her. Adaeze quieted. But when Ifeoma moved to put her back in the cot, she had made known her indignation. Indeed, she was carrying on as her name dictated: daughter of a king. Ada must think her mother was hers to order around as she pleased, but Ifeoma was tired. Maybe she should let Ada cry as much as she wished but she was not in the mood for any more notes to be passed under their door. She had torn and trashed the last one without sparing even a glance at what it said.

At the moment, Ada slept in her cot with tiny pillows around her. She had bought the pillows so that Ada could feel cuddled in her cot, to make her think that she was still in her mother's arms. Now that the baby was fast asleep, she needed to rest as well, to recharge for what was coming, in case she wakes up and decides to act up again.

"Mamaaaa!" A familiar voice rang out in her sub-consciousness. Was she dreaming? But the voice had sounded needy, sounded insistent. And she knew that voice. Only she could answer to that voice. She stirred and opened her eyes.

It came a second time. "Mamaaaa!"

This time it sounded desperate. She looked to the direction the cry came from. The apartment door was wide open. Just as the voice rang out again, she found herself racing to the open door, not bothering to put on her slippers. *Oh God*, she had left that door unlocked after her husband left for work that morning. Her mind had been so burdened with Adaeze that she had forgotten the simplest thing she could have done; locking the door.

Her heart thumped loudly in her chest. For Ikenna to have screamed the way he did, then something was not right. She took to the stairs, racing downstairs.

As she rounded the stairs to the ground floor, her worst fears were confirmed. Ikenna was under a huge, growling dog who bared its teeth at her son. The dog growled more and she saw her little boy shrink under it as though trying to make himself invisible.

"Hey! Hey!!" Ifeoma screamed. She was close to the scene, but not too close. She jumped and waved her hands to get the dog's attention. She needed the dog to look at her, to step away from her son and come for her instead. Maybe then, her son could escape. "Hey! Get away from him. Leave him alone."

She didn't know whether it was right to grab the dog from behind to push it away. What would it result to? The reaction could be unpredictable. The huge dog remained unmoving, the gaze unwavering on her son. The dog seemed to be daring Ikenna to move. It seemed to ask her son to stay just where he was till it decides on what to do with him.

She saw Ikenna's shivers. Her boy no longer screamed for her. He was too afraid to do that. He remained where he was, his eyes firmly closed. If she could sense his fear, so can the dog. Was that why the dog persisted? The 'smell' of fear? She saw the dog's spit drip on her son. Then she noticed she wasn't alone. The few apartment doors on the ground floor were opening and some of its occupants were coming out to the corridor.

Someone was desperately lifting a heavy door knocker and releasing it. The door knocker was very loud, and she knew it was only one apartment that had that knocker in the building. The Weavers' door knocker. The Weavers' dog: Bruno. She hadn't thought of that. She looked around and saw that people were doing all they could to lure the dog away from her son.

She saw Julia materialize. The old lady was in her house robe. She knew from her dishevelled hair that she must have been dragged out of bed. Julia joined in the commotion, ordering the dog, in German, to stop. Almost immediately, the dog became less menacing. It stopped baring its teeth as if the familiar voice had called it back from another world.

But it was still there, still standing over her child. Julia inched closer to Bruno, holding out her hands. She no longer gave commands. She spoke softly and reached out to Bruno's collar before brushing her hand down his fur. As she did that, she urged Bruno away from Ikenna.

As soon as the dog had gotten three inches away from her boy, she ran to him. There was no time to waste. Julia could lose her grasp of the dog's collar, and the insane dog could dash for him again. She wouldn't risk that. She carried him in her arms, his legs wrapping round her waist, his entire body trembling. She moved as far as she could from Bruno, up the stairs, to the first floor, and into the apartment.

Placing her son down on the couch, she ran back to the door. Ifeoma reached for the upper bolt and pulled it into its socket. Hearing it click into place felt satisfying and she exhaled deeply knowing that it was over. The ordeal was over and her son was with her, alive.

Her search began then. She started to check his body, starting from his head where the dog's eyes had fixated as it growled. She raised his shirt, pulled down his shorts as she looked him over. There were no visible bite marks on him. But the boy had a bruise on his left knee. It appeared to have been sustained when he fell down. Ikenna must have attempted to run from Bruno, it meant he must have known that the dog was after him.

But what could have made the dog come after her son? She had thought Bruno to be calm, never aggressive. What could have happened? The dog sometimes stayed in front of the Weavers' apartment, lying by their door and watching. Bruno rarely left that door when he was there. Why would it leave the door only to attack her son?

Something must have happened. Ikenna had obviously opened the apartment door, walked out of it, and down the stairs. He must have come across Bruno and decided to play with her because of the usual docile nature of the dog. But this time must have been different since the dog had growled at her child. Bruno had been angry, snarling, as if ready to attack the boy the next minute. She knew her son too well to know that he might have done something to the dog. The boy's playful, sometimes mischievous ways knew no bounds, and she wondered at what that something could have been. Since there was no way to validate her thoughts, she left it at that. It would forever remain a mystery.

She was relieved there was no major injury on her boy, except for the bruise on his left knee which she could take care of. Managing a baby and an injured child would have added to her stress. She couldn't bear to add more hospital trips to the routine ones she had already mapped out for Adaeze's vaccinations and appointments. Besides, her husband had spent enough money in recent times, they couldn't absorb any unplanned expenses at the moment. She looked at her son as he curled up on the chair. What happened had been her fault. She had forgotten to lock the door. She couldn't blame him.

Ikenna stayed unmoving on the couch. He seemed to be in shock. She couldn't bear to think about what he must have been feeling all the while he was under the huge, snarling dog.

She reached for the shelf in the inner part of the room where the first aid box was kept. That shelf had been nailed to the wall, far above Ikenna's reach after he once got hold of the cough syrup and overdosed himself with it.

As she grabbed the box, she saw that the baby was awake. The noise must have woken her up. That was normal. What wasn't normal was that she lay in her cot seemingly unperturbed by anything. This was a first because Ada usually cried herself to sleep and woke up with more cries. Right now, she wasn't crying but just laid there, moving her hands and feet in different directions as if trying to understand how they worked. She made cooing sounds, a sign that she was content and happy.

The doorbell rang.

The world stopped at that moment and Ifeoma froze. Adaeze began to cry. Why would the best moments in the world be interrupted? Why would such moments come to an end? She wasn't pleased with whoever was at the door. The doorbell sounded again as she lifted Adaeze, dropped the first aid box beside her son, and went to unlock the door.

The anxious face of Julia greeted her, followed by the smell of cherry and vanilla. Ifeoma knew that the aroma emanated from the covered dish Julia held which reminded her of how hungry she was. She had forgotten to eat that morning after settling Adaeze. As she stepped aside to let Julia come in, she knew for certain that whatever was inside that dish was more welcome than the lady.

"Got you some of the Black Forest cake I baked," Julia said as she walked in. "I came over to apologize for Bruno's actions. I am deeply sorry."

A flare of annoyance went through Ifeoma but she tamped it down. She mumbled her thanks and accepted the cake with her free hand.

It was the first time she was that close to Julia, and she noticed the eight lines of wrinkle on her eyes, with each four placed at the far ends of each eye. Julia had now changed out of her robes and into a long-sleeved brown shirt and slightly loose brown trousers of a darker shade.

Julia perched in a chair beside the table where Ifeoma and Ugochukwu usually ate their meals. Ifeoma set down the cake on the table and noticed Julia's hands trembling. That softened her a little but she hardened when she remembered how Bruno had stood over her son. That dog could have killed him! Julia's gaze was rested on Ikenna who was lying down with his two hands folded and used as a pillow under his head. The boy's eyes were open, and his gaze was fixed on Julia.

"Is he hurt? Are there any bites or scratch marks on him?" Julia asked. As she spoke, she stood up from the chair and walked to the couch where the boy lay.

Ikenna shied away from her as she sat down, moving his body to the end of the couch. Julia understood this and stepped away.

"I have checked him; there is a bruise on his leg. Though I can't be certain that there aren't others," Ifeoma said through gritted teeth. She now rummaged through the first aid box in search of the tube of antiseptic cream.

Julia sighed and hung her head. "I am deeply sorry. Bruno has never done anything like this before. I don't know what came over her today. But I promise you this will not happen again." She hoped the way she sounded would pass on as a sincere plea.

Ifeoma placed a warm towel on the affected area of the boy's knee. She didn't know what to say to the old lady. Yes, her son had been the victim, but she didn't know how to say she was angry that her child had been under a dog. Anything could have happened to him. On the other hand, she had left the door unlocked, so she had some blame to put on herself as well. In a calm voice, she said, "How can you be certain it wouldn't happen again?"

Julia breathed visibly. It wasn't the question she was expecting. It wasn't also the reaction she expected. She had thought this woman would shout and threaten to report the incident to the authorities. But she was taking things calmly. "Walter and I have just decided to permanently close the pet door at the entrance. Bruno wouldn't be able to leave the house unsupervised until further notice. She will also remain chained at a spot indoors since we can't trust her with visitors."

Ifeoma nodded. It was good that the dog would be kept indoors for the time being, she needed her son to feel safe around here. "I hope you're right. That dog is too big to be moving freely about within the building, anything can happen."

"We thought about that too, that is why we decided to keep her constantly indoors for added measure. She's an old dog now and we have noticed a lot of changes recently."

"What sort of changes?" Ifeoma asked, unscrewing the cap of the antiseptic cream and squeezing a small amount onto her fingertips. Slowly, carefully, she dabbed the cream onto the bruised area, watching as it faded from red to pink to pale yellow. Ikenna sniffled a few times but didn't make any other sound as she tended to his bruise.

"We noticed that the colour of the hairs on her body started to change in November last year. She used to have only brown and black hairs all over her body when she was younger, but it's now a mixture of black, brown, white, and golden grey. She is fifteen years of age."

"Fifteen? That must be old." Ifeoma wasn't sure of what she said. She was merely repeating what the old lady had confirmed. She didn't know how long dogs lived, not to talk of a German-shepherd.

Julia didn't miss the look on Ifeoma's face as she referred to her dog. It was a mixture of disdain and scepticism. She understood, given that her dog almost attacked this woman's son. She only hoped this didn't strain their relationship. "She is. Sadly, age comes with some changes. We highly suspect that the changes she's experiencing makes her aggressive."

"Really? You think so?"

"Sometimes, we wake up in the morning to see our foot wears have been torn apart by Bruno. At first, we thought she was playing with them, but we later realized her aging had a lot to do with her behaviour. It would hurt my husband and me to have to permanently restrain her but if this behaviour continues, it's likely the next course of action." Her voice cracked a bit but she sent a smile Ifeoma's way. "Even Susi, the cat, now avoids her."

Ifeoma saw herself genuinely smile since the attack on her son. "I don't blame the cat. I would do the same if I were her."

Julia was glad this woman was smiling. It was an indication that she would neither be pressing any charges against her, nor would she be calling the police to report the incident. Not that she was afraid of charges being pressed against her, but her dog had been out with neither a leash nor the owner, which could indict her. And the resulting consequences was what she didn't want.

She knew that if the roles were reversed, she may not have been as calm headed as this woman was at the moment. She would have raised hell if a dog attacked any of her children as a young mother, especially when the dog was still living within the building.

By now, she would have made phone calls to the authorities reporting the incident. Of course, that wouldn't be enough, she would have also started making arrangements to move from the place to erase the unfortunate memory from her child's mind, or to prevent the neighbourhood kids from mentioning the incident to her child in the future. Depending on the gravity of the attack, she might have sued the dog owner. For these, she was glad that this woman was smiling.

There was one fact she had noted about the immigrants renting her property; they liked to have nothing to do with the police. She had observed these many times. One man had sublet his one-bedroom apartment to another man without her permission. The act was directly in violation of the agreement he signed. When she confronted the man about it, his primary concern was that she wouldn't report him to the authorities, explaining that he had invested all his life savings into immigrating to the country. She knew they had a lot to lose. This woman was also an immigrant. The situation could likely not be different for her as well.

That aside, the last thing Julia wanted to be involved with at her age was a court case about her dog involving a little child. The law definitely ranks a child before a pet. She could even guess the outcome of the litigation without being told. Either she would be fined, or the dog would be taken away from her for public safety, or both. But that was not what bothered her the most, it was having a dent on her animal record. She would find it hard to keep pets if she was banned from that. Susi had been like family to her and the effect of this incident could extend to the poor cat. Thinking that through, she reached into her trouser pocket, bringing out some money. It was worth three months of the rent this apartment paid her. She extended it to the woman.

"What is the money for?"

"For your boy, just in case he needs a medical check-up or anything else. I'm glad it wasn't a very bad encounter."

Ifeoma stared at the money, unsure whether or not to accept it. As she considered this, she thought of the things the money could do. The relief it would be on her husband if he didn't have to bother about the next month's rent. Her husband's birthday was approaching and there were things she had thought of getting for him.

"I can't just take the money, Ikenna will be fine."

"Please, I insist. Use it to get anything for your boy," Julia pleaded.

Ifeoma hesitated again before reaching out to take the money. "Thank you."

"You don't have to thank me, I am just glad your son is not hurt," Julia said turning to look at the boy who quietly stared back at her. "And he has such lovely cat eyes."

Ifeoma shifted in some way, still facing Julia. Her eyes started asking the question before her lips moved. "My son looks like a cat?"

The question brought laughter to Julia's face, smoothing her wrinkles, but she didn't let it out. "Not like that. I meant that his eyes are lovely, just the way Susi's eyes look alluring. I give her anything she wants whenever she stares at me with those eyes."

It was a strange compliment. Cats were rarely used as pets back home. Some of them, especially black cats with striking eyes, were associated with witchcraft. But she decided to take it as a compliment since Julia's words made it appear so. "Oh! Thank you."

Ikenna was starting to drift off to sleep. Ifeoma looked at his peaceful face and hoped her boy was dreaming of a world where he could gain wings and fly into the stars. She hoped he was imagining himself soaring through space, looking down on different kinds of friendly dogs on earth and seeing them play with other children. That he could see the friendly faces of the dogs and fly down to join them and play. That when he finally wakes, the incident he just experienced would be far away from his mind.

Ifeoma heaved. "What a day!"

CHAPTER TWENTY-TWO

4th February 1994

Ifeoma opened the door the following afternoon to meet Julia's smiling face. Her brown eyes gleamed.

"I came to see how your boy is doing," Julia began, sitting on the same spot she had sat the previous day. She looked round the room, taking in the familiar space and the family photo the three took before the baby joined the family. It really adorned the wall. She liked the wall clock as well; designed like an Ostrich with the time placed at the centre.

"Ikenna is better today. His father took him to see a doctor yesterday and they confirmed nothing was wrong," Ifeoma said as she sat down, moving Adaeze from her shoulders and placing her to sit on her laps.

"I am glad to hear that." Julia extended her hands to Ifeoma. "Can I hold her?"

Ifeoma nodded, gently passing the baby to her.

"She's got such an alert look for a newborn. And that full head of hair, so impressive. Hard to believe she's the one crying in the middle of the night." Julia's voice was low in an effort not to wake Ikenna who is sleeping.

Julia could hear her baby cry? From the ground floor? That means it wasn't just her Chinese neighbour that Adaeze disturbed. "It is definitely her. She has a voice bigger than her size."

"Wow, it is almost unbelievable."

Ifeoma smiled.

"I also wanted to inform you. Your next-door neighbour moved out three days ago after her rent expired. She said she could no longer cope with the cries from your baby. It makes her unable to sleep and concentrate on anything. She made her annoyance quite clear the day she returned the keys."

"I'm so sorry for this, but the situation is beyond my control. Adaeze sometimes cries for no reason and nothing we do when she's in that mood can pacify her. We do try our best."

"If you say your baby is fine, I believe you. She certainly looks it. It's a shame that your neighbour had to leave, and she did mention that it was difficult to focus on her translation work with the noise."

"I wish we could have made amends. Although there have been some positive changes Ada, changes that would have put a stop to the notes she sent."

"She was sending notes?"

"We find them under the door, asking us to control the cries which we sometimes couldn't." There was a little pause. "Is anyone currently occupying the place?"

"Not yet. But we would have to inform the next occupant about the baby, just in case. I'm sure not many people would like to take up the apartment."

"That would not be a problem since we'll likely be taking the apartment. We have been discussing about getting a bigger place to have more room where we can receive our visitors. I will discuss it with my husband and then get back to you soon. You should have our feedback by tomorrow," Ifeoma said.

"In that case, once I get your reply, I will ask the property managers to take down the advert for the space. And taking the apartment will be cheaper for you both. That will mean reduced bills because the water bills and cleaning fees are calculated per occupant and not per apartment," Julia explained. "You will need to sign a few documents before taking the place so do let me know by tomorrow so the documents can be sent across."

"I will definitely do that. I will phone your apartment."

Adaeze was getting uncomfortable, and a low cry was starting to build from her little mouth. Her tiny hands were waving in the air, in a bid to grasp onto Julia's shirt. Julia chuckled at the baby's antics; grasping at, but failing to retain hold of her shirt with her tiny fists.

The cry became insistent.

"Thank you for carrying her," Ifeoma said, taking the baby from Julia.

Julia rose from the chair. "I believe I should take my leave so you can see to her."

Ifeoma nodded and walked the short distance to the door, opening it. Julia stepped out of the room and turned to face her. "I apologize once again for all the trouble Bruno caused."

"Everything is okay now that I'm sure Ikenna is fine."

"And I appreciate you letting me know what the doctor said concerning him. Bruno will not be seen outside after today so your boy shouldn't be afraid of going outside."

"That is good to know."

As Julia turned to go, Ifeoma took a step back and was about to shut the door when Julia turned back to her. "Is there anything else?" Ifeoma asked, a bit impatiently.

"It's about the water usage. I received the Water Bill for this building and it's been significantly higher. After reviewing the usage, I noticed that your apartment used almost double the amount of water compared to what you used in other months," Julia revealed.

"Really? I had no idea about this and we don't usually waste water here."

There was a brief pause. "The bills say otherwise, are you sure there's no new development or anything? A leakage? Maybe a tap in need of repairs."

"None that I can think of right now, but you're welcome to inspect the place."

Julia gave the inspection idea some thought, but her desire not to further upset the woman restrained her. "You know, it's very normal to get carried away with long showers but the result adds up with time. Everyone pays the same amount of bills here, so when an apartment uses more than it is supposed to, I end up bearing the extra expenses. It has the possibility of affecting the other occupants and it won't be fair to them if the water bill is increased. I hope you understand?"

"I do."

"I'm glad you do. But just out of curiosity, how often do you bathe?"

"Twice a day."

"Twice!" Julia exclaimed, widening her eyes and looking surprised. "That is a lot. That must be the exact reason the water bill is high."

"I don't understand. How many times are we supposed to bath in one day?"

"This is winter and it's usually very cold around this time of the year. In fact, people hardly bathe every day. We could manage to have our bath five times a week. That way, you reduce the possibility of catching a cold. That would tell you that bathing once every day is..."

Ifeoma could not hold in her laugh, but seeing the serious look on Julia's face made her stop. "Sorry, I never knew that. We bathe two times a day where I come from, no matter the weather."

"Bathing twice a day is a lot!" Julia maintained. "That's a waste of water resources."

Ifeoma said nothing.

"I can understand why you bathe that number of times. But since the weather here is totally different, try to conserve water as much as you can. Do you also bathe your baby that number of times?"

"Yes, twice."

"That must be the reason. You should talk with her doctor concerning her bathing, especially during winter. I don't think the doctor will approve how often you bathe her. She doesn't need to catch a cold at this tender stage."

There was an awkward pause before Julia spoke again. "Well, sorry for keeping you," she said and turned towards the stairs. Ifeoma waited to make sure she wasn't coming back before she closed the door with a soft click, sliding the bolt into place with a firm clang. She wasn't going to make the same mistake twice.

She went to the bed and sat down, as Ada latched on her breast and started feeding. She sighed, allowing the tension to drain from her. The room was quiet except for the soft sounds Ada made with her mouth. One of her hands was tucked under her mother's armpit while the free hand danced happily in the air. Ada's legs moved in the same rhythm as her free hand. Ifeoma ran her fingers through Ada's curly hair, then leaned her head back against the chair.

CHAPTER TWENTY-THREE

12th March 1994

I kenna ran around the park under the watchful eyes of his parents. His sister, Adaeze, laid in her covered carrier on the bench. She was staring up at the toys that hung above her head, swaying gently in circles. A soft tune emanated from the toys as they dangled.

"Does it snow forever in this place?" Ifeoma asked, not looking at her husband.

Ugochukwu was unsure whether the question needed an answer. "I am getting tired of it too."

"How can you be free and enjoy life when you're always hiding inside heavy clothes whenever you're outdoors?" She asked rhetorically. "How do these people do it? I mean having to put on all these layers of clothing for months is so exhausting, I don't think I can stand it much longer if this cold persists."

Ugochukwu stared at her. He knew he had to thread carefully, it was better to remain silent than to say the wrong thing. Most of the discussions they had had, had something to do with Ifeoma being uncomfortable with the country they were in, and he was always at fault.

"We are not any different from our village masquerade. I had to put on three layers of clothes. Three! Just to come outdoors, not to talk of how many clothes I had to put on Ada." Ifeoma seemed to be talking to herself. Recently, she found more reasons to complain. She came here expecting that life would be easier, more freeing. But that's not what she's getting. Instead, she was wrapped as thick as an Egyptian mummy. She hoped she didn't end up as dead as one from the cold or from suffocation.

"Do you want us to go back inside?" Ugochukwu asked, placing the bottle of hot tea he occasionally sipped on the bench and pulling her close to him. He was trying to play it safe. This month alone, they've had quite a number of disagreements. He preferred to have peace if it were possible; he didn't like being at odds with his wife. His question was met with silence. He sighed and tried to assure her. "Don't worry, spring is not too far away now. The weather should get better by next month."

"I hope you're right. The cold has lingered for far too long."

He had said something he wasn't very sure of and only hoped that the following month would prove him right. Even though scientists have observed and tried to predict weather patterns, nature still had a way of taking its own course. One example was when Zelda had told them to expect their first snowfall in late December, it had come in early December, proving Zelda wrong. He decided to move the topic to something about their home country. "You know, Nigeria is also cold at this time of the year."

"*Ah*! Ugom!" she exclaimed, pulling away from him. "How can you compare living inside this bone-chilling freezer with the good weather we have back home, *eh*? Besides, we are in March here and past the cold harmattan season, which means the weather at home is currently hot and dry. I will take it that you're joking. I just have to, for my sanity." She stared at his face, searching for the least sign to show that he was indeed joking. And it was there; that tiny smirk playing around his lips and eyes, trying hard to be suppressed.

"As a child, whenever I hear of winter, I usually likened it to our own harmattan. If only I knew." He was glad he had been able to shift the focus a little. "Dear harmattan, I am deeply sorry."

"I knew you were joking," she laughed. "But thinking about it now, I never knew that one day I would miss the harmattan season, this place has made me realize how mild a weather we have."

He looked around at the barren trees and at the white ground. "Exactly, I miss seeing the whole surroundings covered in golden brown, and breathing in dry air. At least the trees would have green leaves, and some with fruits on them."

"I miss all that too." Ifeoma sighed.

The harmattan usually started in December when the rains had ceased. The sun would scorch the ground, and turn green leaves golden. The winds would blow, bringing cold, dehydrating air, which dried the body and cracked the lips. There were also some good memories Ifeoma had as a child during each Christmas and New Year season. Her mother would go to the market two weeks before Christmas, buying various foodstuff which usually filled their storeroom. There would be bags of rice, beans, potatoes, tomatoes, onions, and all sorts of condiments. Some of these, her mother distributed to the many visitors who trooped into their home in the village; the visitors who had come to say *nno* to those who returned from the city. Ifeoma always suspected that the reason there was always an influx of women flocking into their home was because when one person received something, she would not fail to show off her gifts to another woman who in turn, would hurry to get her own share. That was how the news would keep spreading each day with women pouring in to get their own share under the guise of welcoming them back from the city.

As a young adult, she had once questioned her mother why she gave so much food away. Her mother had smiled and said that the foodstuffs worked behind the scenes for her. Her mother had remained the Vice President of the village Women's Association for two tenures. The foodstuff had probably aided her campaign.

That revelation changed how she thought of her mother, Ogechi. Her mother could only boast of basic schooling, but she was smart and resourceful. What heights would she have attained if she had gone further with her education?

Those days leading to the Christmas celebration were ones she looked forward to as a child. Their car was always filled with all the things her mother prepared to take to the village. Her mother usually said that she didn't want to leave anything behind in case she would later need it in the village. Her father, Okwesilieze, didn't begrudge his wife and would sometimes have to make a second trip with the car to bring whatever did not make it in the first trip. He could do this because the journey from the city to the village was just two hours long. The only downside to the excitement of going to the village was the stress that accompanied the preparations, even with the apprentices around to help. But in the end, she enjoyed the village experience.

The big, old house in the village contained lots of memories within and outside its walls. Her uncles, aunty, and cousins usually arrived in the next couple of days. She never met Papa Nnukwu and Mama Nnukwu whom her father had said died from a disease one month apart, all before she was born. Apart from the depressing chore of cleaning the old house which was usually uninhabited for months before their arrival and would be cloaked with dust, dirt, and cobwebs, everything else about the place was interesting. She could play with her cousins all day, and chores were few since they usually came with their house-helps.

She also remembered how cold the nights and early mornings were. Her mother would make sure she wore a sweater on top of her pyjamas and tuck her in with a thick woollen blanket. In the mornings, she would bathe with warm water and apply Vaseline on her skin and lips to keep warm and avoid dried skin and cracked lips. Then she was ready to play with her cousins.

Sometimes she noticed that the village children who played outside their house had skin made white from exposure to the harsh harmattan winds and dry, chapped lips which they licked to hydrate them but only made it worse as they played around in their scantily dressed bodies. Her mother once told her that the village children were used to the harmattan cold, so it wouldn't affect them so much. But she thought otherwise.

To her, they might have been used to the cold, but the effects of the harmattan still showed on their bodies.

Those memories made her smile now because the cold, harmattan season was child's play compared to the winter she was experiencing now in Mainz. Sweet old memories. To even think that she had been envied as she prepared to leave Nigeria seemed funny to her now.

"Ify!" her husband called her, snapping her from her thoughts. "Where did you go to? I've been calling you but it seems like you went somewhere else."

"I was thinking about my childhood." After a brief pause, she continued, "maybe we should move back to Nigeria."

This was what Ugochukwu had been trying to avoid. He had not wanted their discussion to get to the point where his wife would suggest they returned home. He knew that was what occupied her mind in recent days and each time they talked, he had tried to steer her away from voicing it out. However, his wife often managed to circle back to the topic he was now coming to dread. The outcome from there usually followed a pattern: once she voiced out her opinion, they would quarrel and he would take the blame. He couldn't ignore her words now that they were already out.

"Is everything alright, Ify? It's obvious from your recent actions that you're not comfortable here." He waited a little. "I have listened to the way you talk and seen the longing in your eyes. I am not saying going back home is not a good idea, but you already know we have better opportunities here. You know the kids would be better off here."

"I know all of those things, Ugom, but I prefer life back home. I am used to the life there. Lots of friends, lots of people

I can understand, lots of relatives to visit especially during Christmas, plus a lovely weather. I miss the whole life I had. Take a look at Ikenna, I can't even discipline him here whenever he misbehaves and it is getting on my nerves. You know your son and his excesses, he misbehaves a lot and all that I'm allowed to do here is to reprimand him without ever spanking him because the moment I do, the police will land on my doorstep. No-*o*, I won't spare the rod and spoil my child because of some greener pastures. I will not!"

He laughed. "Ify, my wonder woman, you are a good mother and I know you want what is best for our children. Your reasons are valid. But on a serious note, this here is what life is about, there will always be something we must sacrifice for a greater good. As for Ikenna, he would outgrow this stage, and there are other ways to correct him."

"Other ways that will mean less talking and less shouting?"

Ugochukwu had no answer and remained quiet.

They fell silent. Ifeoma stared into space as she wondered if Ikenna would repeat the incident of the previous week at the supermarket when both of them were out to do some shopping. Ikenna had dragged a particular giant toy car that was yellow in colour, with large tires, and adorned with blue strips. It was big enough for him to ride in. She tried to take his mind away from the car but gave up after failed attempts. She let him be since he would likely give it up when they got to the counter.

But Ikenna refused to let go of the car at the counter. He had dragged it along with him. Ifeoma had looked at the price tag again and begged the boy to leave the big car behind so they could leave. He still refused. She had gone back to the toy section to try and bribe him with a less expensive one, but it was no use. She remembered the looks and stares from the faces of the other shoppers. She got stares naturally, but to attract the stares through no fault of hers was embarrassing. A particular middle-aged woman had looked sympathetic and almost begged with her eyes to get Ikenna the car, but the look on some others' faces appeared to be annoyed at her. She could tell this from the brief eye-contacts and sharp frowns she saw thrown her way. She knew what could be going on in their minds; a mother that couldn't get a simple toy car for her son. The reprimand seemed to be screaming wordlessly from their faces. She recalled how she had struggled to keep her cool since she just couldn't afford to buy that particular car.

This wouldn't have been much of a fuss at all if they were back home. She could always spank her child the moment she saw he was misbehaving. She would have taken that option. In a bid to stop the drama, she had to drag Ikenna out of the place and paid deaf ears to his loud wails, screams, and the whispers she left behind. She had avoided shopping at that particular store since the incident.

The night of that same day, when it got a little dark, she had sneaked to the entrance of the building and plucked a branch from a coneflower. She locked the doors and gave Ikenna some spanking.

As the first stroke landed on his buttocks, she could read the confusion from her boy. What was happening? Was this supposed to be happening? But she didn't care. She had grown up with discipline and had to instil it in her own home. She was sure the boy wouldn't forget that incident in a hurry. Ikenna kept agreeing never to do all the things she had listed.

On her part, she was careful enough as she listed the dos and don'ts. She said those things, aware that sound could easily travel beyond the wooden walls. She only spoke in Igbo, in case someone was eavesdropping, trying to find out what could be going on. That way, the eavesdropper would be left with a wide guess.

Her husband never interfered. He knew better not to interrupt her when her mind was fixed on something. And the results were good. Ikenna seemed to be behaving relatively well since then.

Ugochukwu cleared his throat. "Guess who I came across at the university this week?"

"Someone I know?" She hardly knew her husband's friends at the university, except Zelda and Timo that had visited their place, and a few other names he had mentioned during their chats.

"Yes," he simply replied.

"Other than my mother, l don't know who else I would be interested in your coming across." She looked away.

He groaned softly. This was one side of his wife that stretched his patience. When she was consumed with a particular thought, she was usually like a dog with a bone, never letting go, but chewing on it for a long time, until she had made up her mind to either accept or change the circumstances as she deemed fit. He could, however, understand her feelings. It wasn't easy to be uprooted from all that was familiar and planted in the unfamiliar. In fact, he was proud of her for making the journey even in her condition. If only she would quickly adapt to her new surroundings. He didn't know how else he could help her; this was their home now. He shifted his focus back to his wife. "I know you miss her, we all do, but we're here now. This would be our home for a long time to come. Please let's try to make a go of it for the sake of our family, okay?" He saw her lips purse but he knew he had to let her internalize his words. After another pause, he went on. "You mean you won't try to guess who I saw?"

"Ugom, my mind is blank. Is it one of your colleagues?"

"Yes, I mean no."

"What are you saying?"

"I saw Olisa."

Her eyes grew bigger. "You mean Olisa! Your former colleague from Nnamdi Azikiwe University is here? What is he doing here?"

"He is pursuing his doctorate degree in our department."

"*Ahh*, I'm so happy for him. He always talked about leaving Nigeria and going to the United States."

"Exactly! You do remember him well. My best guess is that United States didn't work out for him. I couldn't ask him all about that. I still remember him jokingly saying he would leave Nigeria before me, like we were in a competition." He laughed and continued. "He's still his old funny self, except for one thing that surprised me."

"Which is?"

"He changed his name!"

"I don't understand."

"He changed his native first name to his English middle one. He dropped his Igbo name completely. People here know him as Albert."

"*Ah ah*! Does he think he is *Oyibo*?"

"I don't know, but I guess he had planned to do that long ago. It was one of the first things he did the moment he arrived here."

"Well, he can do whatever he likes with his name. Maybe you should invite him over one weekend. Just tell him your wife will be preparing one of our native dishes. He will likely be missing them in this foreign place."

"I will give him a call to invite him over. We should get back inside for the children's sake."

They soon headed towards the park's exit.

***

They were in the long corridor leading to their apartment when they saw a mailman in a navy-blue pants and blazer, with the German Postal Service sign emblazoned on his left breast pocket. He was standing with a large box in his hands in front of their door. The man pressed the doorbell and waited.

"*Suchen Sie jemanden?*"—Are you looking for someone? Ugochukwu asked as he approached the man. He noticed the mailbag the man carried had numerous pockets for sorting mail.

"*Ein Paket für diese Adresse,*"—A package for this address, the mailman said, turning towards the voice.

"*Das sind wir,*"—That is us, Ugochukwu said, gently lowering Ikenna down from his arms and accepting the box from the mailman.

"*Sie müssen hier unterschreiben,*"—You will have to sign here, the mailman said, handing a small book and a pen to Ugochukwu.

"*Natürlich.*"—Of course.

"What's in the box?" Ifeoma asked immediately the mailman left.

"Probably another set of baby items from the Welfare Department," Ugochukwu replied, reading the label. "The last package also came in a similar box."

"Another baby things? Are they for free again?" Ifeoma asked.

"Should be so. It seems they would be sending this monthly. This week made it a month since we received that last package from them," Ugochukwu said, unlocking the door.

"Hmm. They care so much about children here."

Once inside, Ifeoma started to unpack the contents from the box. It was the exact items they had received the previous month. It contained a few baby clothes which looked a little bigger than the last one they got, some diapers, baby bottles and formula, soap, wipes, toys, comb, and natural hair oil.

She had been surprised the first time the baby items arrived, and had thought that a family probably ordered them and wrongly gave their address. When she learnt that the items came from the government, she had still doubted it. How could the government send things to babies with the number of babies born every day in this country? But her husband had explained that the items weren't sent to everyone. It was just for those classified as low-income earners which they belonged to.

The baby napkins she had brought from Nigeria were still neatly packed inside her travelling bag. She had transferred them from there to the hospital bag, and back to the travelling bag when they got back from the hospital. The hospital where she gave birth to Ada had provided a bag containing diapers that she had used before the first package came from the government. At least one good thing could be said for this frozen and foreign land; they had welfare in place to cater for their people.

Ifeoma made her way into the kitchen. She needed to prepare dinner quickly before Adaeze started demanding hers.

CHAPTER TWENTY-FOUR

29th May 1994

Life was gradually returning to its comfortable warmth, with indications that summer wasn't so far away. The seasons had long changed from the sad, gloomy winter to a rainy, flowery spring. The days were getting longer, with the sun staying out later than usual. Rabbits, hares, squirrels, and birds ran and flew about without a care. How lucky they all were, with no one looking to hunt them for food or pleasure. The trees had leaves on them again after months of being bare. The late May morning air filled Ifeoma's ear with the sweet, melodious songs of birds that had long returned from their annual migration. They chirped and warbled and trilled, calling out greetings to one another. Ifeoma could hardly recognize most of the birds as they were different from the ones she knew.

Today, her hair fell freely over her shoulders, gleaming in the late sunlight. She pushed her permed, dark curls from her face as she tossed her head back. Now that the weather had turned, she took care to look good, revelling in the freedom of having to wear fewer clothes. She wore a flowing flowered dress that draped around her legs. The pink, white, and yellow flowers on her gown added a dash of colour to the already bright outlook of their neighbourhood. She held a handkerchief in her hand; a habit she formed long ago due to the hot climate back home. One was always handy so she could wipe sweat from her face and neck under the sun.

As she strolled along the street, pushing Ada in a stroller, a light breeze fluttered her dress, flattening it across her body, making her breasts seem bigger. The air carried the scent of water on it, the type that meant a river body was nearby. She knew this because it was the same scent she got when the wind blew across the stream in the village.

Ifeoma was indeed enjoying the weather, but her spirit was down. She had returned from church service that Sunday morning and had quarrelled with her husband when he got back from church, transferring the anger of an incident that took place at the church to him.

This morning, Ada's antics had delayed her and so she went late for church after Ugochukwu left with Ikenna. She entered the building after the service had started and taken a seat at the back of the pews since she had Ada with her. This would make it easy to go out and re-enter when Ada got hungry and needed to be breast-fed. Just as she sat down, the woman already seated beside her stood up and walked a few pews to the front and took another seat.

At first, she thought something might have been wrong with the space beside her, but the more she looked at that spot, the more she felt sure that there was another reason. Was it because of her? But she had been coming to this same church and no one had acted that way. No one had ever left their seat because she sat beside them. A bitter taste had filled her mouth and her stomach knotted. She stood up and walked out of the church, and didn't return.

Her husband returned later with Ikenna after the service while she still boiled from the incident. And she had poured her angst on her husband, somehow blaming him for what had transpired. She crossed her arms tightly across her chest while her husband tried to assure her that she might have interpreted it wrongly. She felt her temper rising, prompting her to take this walk to cool off. This stroll would do a lot to clear her head.

Looking around as she walked, the view gladdened her heart. It felt like everyone she saw outside was glad to leave behind the thick and padded clothes that were necessary for the winter and embrace the more freeing and lighter clothes for the late spring. It seemed like they were celebrating the end of the long winter. People were out and about. At the playground, kids were chasing each other around and laughing gaily. Even the adults seemed to be smiling for no particular reason.

She took a bend at the end of a street and spotted a little girl chasing a butterfly down the end of that street, her long hair dancing in the wind as she ran, almost colliding with a limping dog in front of her. It was the first time she saw a dog without its owner on the street. She clutched the stroller tightly at the thought of Bruno. But she soon loosened her grip when she reasoned that the poor dog wasn't attacking anyone, and it may have probably been abandoned by its owner.

The tunes from a nearby ice cream truck drew her attention. She had seen them last in October but they had disappeared as soon as the weather turned cold around November. The little girl chasing the butterfly had stopped now, dreamily staring at the truck. Gradually, kids started to appear from nowhere, drawn by the siren call of the ice cream truck. Parents and kids were buying ice-cream from the truck which had now packed across the street from where she was.

She looked at the little girl still standing and staring at the truck and thought of buying her some ice cream. But she quickly discarded the thought as soon as it came to mind. There might be dietary restrictions for the child, and she wouldn't want to put herself in a dire situation as a result of her generosity. Ifeoma looked on as the truck started to move again till it diverted at the end of a corner.

She took a bend at another corner and strolled on. There were indeed a lot she appreciated here. For one, the stroller made it easier to take her baby on these walks instead of carrying her tied to her back with a *lappa* like she had done with Ikenna at the airport and attracted stares, and the sidewalks were smooth enough to enable it. She took a deep breath and released it but not before catching the delicious smell of freshly baked bread in the air.

A quick scan down the lane revealed a sign hanging above a door just a little ahead of her - *Die Brotstube* - The Bread Room, with a picture of an oversized bread above the name. She couldn't resist.

The plump woman at the bakery had a wide smile plastered on her face which seemed like a welcoming gesture. Ifeoma smiled back and pointed to the bread she wanted, gesturing with her fingers for two loaves. The woman picked two loaves from the lot she had pointed at. But instead of wrapping the loaves up and handing them over, she heard the woman suddenly let out a laugh with a voice as sharp as the pointed nose in the middle of her face. The force of the laugh sounded like the woman had been trying too hard to hold it in. Was that what she had thought to be a wide and welcoming smile? Why was the woman holding in that laugh? And the sound had startled Adaeze who had started to cry. Without getting the answers to the questions pouring into her mind, she simply walked out, leaving the bread behind.

Outside, somewhere on one of the nearby trees, there was a sound of an alarmed bird; its wings fluttering rapidly as it started to take flight.

***

Ifeoma had just gotten to the entrance of her apartment when she noticed that two young women were at the end of the corridor moving from one apartment to another, knocking and handing out papers to the occupants. She opened her door and walked in, expecting them to get to the apartment door soon. It wasn't often that one saw anyone moving from door to door handing out something.

Before they could press the doorbell, she opened the door. The women standing at the door were dressed in revealing, tight-fitted clothing and had heavy makeup on their faces that could scare a child if they were to be seen at night. She could not place their age because of the makeup but she took a wild guess and estimated them to be between the ages of twenty-seven and thirty-five. Ifeoma didn't like the way they looked. She had always preferred light makeup. After all, the essence of makeup was to enhance a person's natural beauty, not to distort it. She wondered what they really looked like underneath the layers of makeup.

The first woman, a blonde, started to speak. "Hello. We are looking for a good-looking man who lives here. Is he around?" Her eyes darted past Ifeoma, trying to look into the apartment.

In her baffled state, Ifeoma thought about the question for a while. It even surprised her that they could speak English to a great extent. "I'm sorry, I really don't know whom you're speaking about," Ifeoma replied while shifting her body to block their view so they couldn't look inside.

The two exchanged looks before the second woman, a brunette, came forward. She demonstrated with her hands as she spoke. "He is tall and broad-shouldered. We just want to give him a message about our services."

She wondered what services these barely clothed women had to offer that would interest anyone. "No one with that description lives here at the moment but I can take your message," Ifeoma said.

Ifeoma saw them exchange another glance before handing a paper over to her, asking her to hand it over to the man when he returned.

It was a handbill. An advertisement for their services. As she read the handbill written in German and English, her eyes widened in surprise at the 'services' these women purportedly offered. Then she narrowed them and looked coldly towards them.

"You won't find anyone here who fits your description," Ifeoma said, as she backed into the apartment and started to close the door.

Ifeoma saw the disappointment on their faces, but she could care less. The brunette glared at her, her overly long eyelashes giving her a crazed look as they both turned to move to the next apartment. She quickly shut the door, putting the bolt into place and stared blankly at the handbill, wondering why they thought her husband would have any interest in prostitutes or sex workers. She had no idea that they could solicit for clients in the daytime, but to actually go from door to door in order to hand over their ads was so disgraceful. Where was their shame? She thought she had seen it all but this one beat everything. To say she was shocked was an understatement.

Ugochukwu soon emerged from the adjoining extra apartment they had rented months ago when their Chinese neighbour packed out. "I heard you come in, then I heard you talking." He was drying his hands with a towel.

"A couple of ladies brought this here, they said it's for you," she replied, handing the bill over to her husband and watching his face closely.

Ugochukwu looked at it and started to smile. "They actually came here?"

"Yes, looking for you," she replied, wondering why he found the situation funny. It wasn't funny to her at all.

"Those women have guts, the whole bunch. I have been disposing their ads each time I go to pick the mails, I didn't know they were bold enough to go to people's apartments. You must have seen some of the adverts in the streets. They post their services on notice boards, and some hand theirs out in the streets."

"But how did they know you? They even described you as if they knew you personally. Is there something I should know about?" Ifeoma asked, tapping her right foot on the floor.

Ugochukwu looked up sharply at her. "Ify, apart from their handbills, I haven't met any of those women personally. Besides, it's very easy to know people especially since I'm one of the very few Black men in this building."

Ifeoma stood silent the whole time he spoke. "So, nothing I should know?"

Ugochukwu raised his fingers in the air in the general scout's honour sign and said, "You have nothing to fear. Moreover, they're not as beautiful as you are," he said, winking mischievously.

Ifeoma stopped her toe tapping, relaxing a little. "But I still can't believe their boldness, you can get them arrested, right?"

"They can't get arrested. Prostitution is a legal business here. It's their job, they earn a living from it, and even pay taxes from the proceeds. There are laws protecting them, which is why they are free to advertise as they are doing. It's your choice whether you want to take them up on their offer or not, no one forces you to do anything you don't want to do."

"Really? They don't force themselves on anyone, yet they go from house to house. Not caring that some people could be married with wives and children. They could cause a lot of trouble for a man, like they almost did for you." Ifeoma raised her hands and dropped them in exasperation. "This place keeps getting more interesting by the day."

Ugochukwu chuckled under his breath. This was another culture shock that had been dealt to his wife, but he hoped that she didn't see this as one more reason to return to Nigeria.

214

"I can't believe this kind of job is allowed. It's actually disgusting. I don't like it at all. Raising my kids in this kind of environment will not really be easy," she said.

"This is one of the things with this place that you may never fully understand," he said, quickly turning to check what Ikenna was up to in the adjoining apartment, even though he knew he was using that as an excuse to avoid having to discuss the possibility of going back home.

"*Nawa o!*" Ifeoma exclaimed.

CHAPTER TWENTY-FIVE

7th August 1994

Stefan stood holding the phone receiver in his hand. His smile was wide as he called out, "Darling! Come downstairs, Hannah is on the phone." He heard his wife take the stairs two at a time as she came down. "Here, she wants to speak to you."

Zelda took the receiver, paused a little before breathing into it. "Hello, Hannah. How have you been? How's my grandson?"

He stood close to his wife smiling, listening as she jumbled over words and pausing in mid-sentences because she had probably started speaking at the same time as Hannah. He watched her as the tension built up, reached its crescendo, and began to lessen, before their conversation became more synchronized.

"I would appreciate if you could visit with the baby and husband," Stefan heard her plead at the end of their awkward conversation. He hadn't asked this of Hannah all the time they conversed on the phone because he knew Hannah would decline. He also knew it would be awkward with his wife around. He prayed silently for Hannah to accept the invitation. He was dying as much as his wife to meet their first grandchild. He watched as his wife's jaw clenched for a moment and knew that Hannah must have declined the request. Maybe the time wasn't yet ripe to ask that from their daughter. A little more time, surely, and she'd come around. He heard his wife ask Hannah to call again soon before placing the receiver in its place.

Zelda stood smiling, her face flushed, her burrow slightly wet, as she faced Stefan. "I guess Hannah is speaking to me again."

"I didn't ask that from her today, she just asked me to give you the phone on her own," Stefan explained.

"Well," Zelda breathed in deeply. "She says she's an adult now."

"She didn't agree to visit?

"She said she isn't ready for that yet, and she would speak to her husband first. My own daughter would need someone else's permission to visit me." Zelda laughed before continuing. "Anyway, I will ask her again when she calls next time."

"First things first, I'm just glad that you both are on speaking terms again," Stefan said, making his way to the front door. "I'm off to mow the lawn."

CHAPTER TWENTY-SIX

10th August 1994

The room was moderate. It had a table on one end, beside which two chairs were arranged for visitors. There were two other armchairs arranged at suitable places in the room. The walls were bare except for a painting of wildlife hanging close to a ticking wall clock. The blinds were drawn, casting a dim light over the office and blocking away the morning sunlight.

Ugochukwu was in his office at the university late in the morning. He had papers and books scattered across his desk. A trash can stood beside his desk on the floor, with crumpled papers scattered around it, the ones that missed the target. A bottle of an opened Fruchtsaftschorle which he got from the canteen vending machine sat on the table beside his computer. His mind was unsettled and he couldn't concentrate enough to do much work.

He sat there, staring intently at his computer screen and lost in thoughts. A deadline was on his neck. He had to submit the students' semester results soon, but lately he had been distracted and disturbed.

For several days, he'd had countless arguments with his wife, with Ifeoma deciding she couldn't cope any longer in this country. Just when he thought she had started to relax and gotten used to their new life, she wanted them to leave.

The tension at home wracked his mind, and his work suffered. But he understood his wife's demands as well, making it a very difficult situation. Yet, how could he agree to what she wanted when he had sacrificed so much and left much more behind to be where he was currently? He had resigned from Nnamdi Azikiwe University and bade his family and friends goodbye. If he returned now, where would he start from? Who would he go to? Of course, having an international experience would automatically boost his CV, but there were still so many uncertainties. He felt like a stranger of his own land.

They had better opportunities for growth here. Basic amenities were not lacking and he attributed his being more productive in his writings to that. He had already gotten used to the steady power supply, which went a long way towards making life easier. He didn't have to wait for the lights to come on to power his dead computer to be able to work or write, he only had to plug it in and do the work.

He entered a 'B+ grade' on his screen, noting that his students' general performance improved from the last semester. He was supposed to key in the results for the two courses he had taught that semester into the computer, but time was fast slipping away.

He thought of Lucas, the lanky young man who often disturbed his classes with endless questions and his endless requests for him to repeat himself. He would check his grade after finalizing the results. Although, given the way he usually appeared as though something weighed heavily on his mind, he wasn't expecting much from him. He asked too many questions during lectures, most of them quite unnecessary, breaking his thought flow and interrupting his classes with pointless shenanigans. From experience, he knew that such students weren't known to be overly bright. Last semester, Lucas had managed to get a 'C' grade, and though he didn't know how he scored on his other courses, he felt like the boy might be having some problems. Maybe girl problems.

He was having girl problems himself. The argument between him and his wife had consistently been about how fed up she was with 'this place'. He couldn't pinpoint any one thing that triggered her recent anger. His wife claimed it was a series of events that had been the proverbial straw that finally broke the camel's back. Their latest argument had taken place the previous evening. He had returned from work exhausted and ready for bed. His wife had asked him to look after Ada so she could do the dirty laundry in the laundry room. He had simply explained that he needed to rest for a while, but she flared up, accusing him of making life impossible for her. She reminded him that if they were in Nigeria, finding someone to look after the kids wouldn't have been a problem since there would be willing neighbours, friends, and grandparents to help at no cost. Here, she had to do it all alone.

He wasn't sure what had weighed him down more; his wife's angry outbursts that had stretched late into the night or his own mental and physical exhaustion. In the end, he had taken Ada with him to the laundry room and done the laundry.

As always, his wife had given him lots of reasons why Nigeria was better off for living and raising their kids, and it was as though she came up with a new reason every day, as though that was all she thought about all day. He even had to manufacture an event the previous weekend so that he could have a moment's rest and some peace. He had told her that Timo invited the lecturers from their department over to his house for a little get-together, but it was all a lie to get him out of the apartment. Still, he felt bad having to leave Ada and Ikenna in her care the whole day.

He hadn't known Ifeoma to be this moody and contentious. Living together as a married couple for those two years before they moved to Germany had been pure bliss. She had been a confident, warm, and optimistic woman who was quick to smile. But in less than a year of being in Mainz, she had become withdrawn, gloomy, and angry. She seemed to want to take out her frustrations on him.

He sighed.

Forcing himself to concentrate on what he was doing to avoid making any errors, he tried to key in more results, the deadline looming at the back of his mind. He had until tomorrow to finish and submit the results.

Not making any headway, he pushed back his office chair, stood up, and stretched his body. He walked towards the window and drew the blinds. Feeling the late morning sunlight felt soothing.

He peered outside the window, his eyes taking in the university grounds within his view and the buildings on it. He looked back at his table. How could something as simple as transferring records into a computer turn into such a chore?

He supposed life got that way sometimes. But one thing he knew was that when a man had a will in him, he could do whatever he wanted to do. He only needed to get his inner self together and the rest would follow suit.

A soft knock sounded on the door and he looked towards it. When the door opened and Zelda walked in, she was followed by a man he had never seen before. Zelda was the only person who opened his office door without first waiting to be asked in. He offered a smile that was hollow beneath the surface.

The man Zelda walked in with was tall; slightly taller than Zelda, even with her heels. Ugochukwu's eyes followed the man, studying him as he walked. The man moved with a certain level of confidence and his appearance seemed to speak of someone important. He held a folder under his arm and carried a bag.

He left the window and headed to his chair. "*Guten Morgen,*" he greeted them, smiling. "*Willkommen in meinem kleinen Büro.*"

- Good morning. Welcome to my little office.

The man smiled back. "*Guten Morgen. Es tut uns leid, Sie heute Morgen zu stören.*"

They were sorry to disturb him, that much was clear.

"No problem at all," Ugochukwu said, beckoning them to the two chairs across from his table. He sat, sweeping some scattered papers on his table into a pile.

Zelda turned to him, businesslike. "This is Mr. Schwarz. Not sure you've met him before."

He shook his head.

"We won't take much of your time, so I'll get straight to the point." Her eyes flicked over the desk and bin. "*Herr Schwarz wurde vom Universitätsvorstand entsandt, um herauszufinden, wie Sie sich im vergangenen Jahr, seit Sie bei uns sind, zurechtgefunden haben. Ich entschuldige mich meinerseits, ich hätte Sie früher über seinen bevorstehenden Besuch informieren können, aber es ist mir entfallen. Ich sah ihn warten, als ich in mein Büro kam und habe ihn sofort zu Ihnen gebracht.*"

She explained that Mr. Schwarz had been sent by the University Board to see how he had been adjusting over the past year and apologized for not informing him earlier about the visit: it had slipped her mind until she saw Schwarz waiting by her office.

Ugochukwu turned to the man. "*Schön, Sie kennenzulernen, Herr Schwarz.*"

- Nice to meet you, Mr. Schwarz.

"*Freut mich auch, Sie kennenzulernen.*" Schwarz smiled.

- Nice to meet you too. He leaned back in his chair.

"*Ja, ich wurde geschickt, um herauszufinden, welche Herausforderungen Sie möglicherweise erlebt haben oder noch erleben. Der Universitätsvorstand versteht, dass es nicht einfach ist, sich an eine neue Umgebung anzupassen. Aber da Sie jetzt seit einem ganzen akademischen Jahr hier sind, darf man wohl annehmen, dass Sie sich ziemlich gut eingewöhnen.*"

He had been sent, he explained, to find out what challenges Ugochukwu had faced, or was still facing. Adjusting to a new environment wasn't always easy, and now that he'd spent a full academic year here, the Board hoped he was settling in.

Ugochukwu nodded. "*Ja, ich bin jetzt vollständig eingelebt.*"

- Yes, I'm fully settled now.

Schwarz nodded. *"Die Universität würde gerne alles darüber wissen."*

- The university would like to know all about that.

"Okay. Es gibt mehrere Dinge, über die ich sprechen möchte. Zuerst geht es um meinen Akzent..."

- There are several things I'd like to talk about. First is my accent...

Ugochukwu stuttered to a stop as Schwarz raised a hand.

"Ich bin wirklich froh, dass du über die Schwierigkeiten sprichst, mit denen du konfrontiert bist. Das macht alles einfacher," Schwarz said.

He was glad Ugochukwu was opening up, it would make everything easier.

But Ugochukwu frowned. Wasn't that what he had just been trying to do?

"Danke, aber ich habe dir noch nicht von meinen Problemen erzählt," he said in a low voice.

- Thank you, but I haven't told you my problems yet.

Sensing the tension, Zelda stepped in. "He has some documents for you to write down your concerns. Though he's on the Board, he's only the messenger."

Ugochukwu nodded. Of course. That could have been said in fewer words.

"Natürlich, ich verstehe."

- Of course. I understand.

Schwarz retrieved the folder from his lap and placed it on the table. He drew out two sheets.

"Hier sind sie," he said, handing them over. *"Das einzelne Blatt ist ein Formular, das Sie ausfüllen müssen, während*

das zweite Dokument der Ort ist, an dem Sie detailliert alle Anliegen niederschreiben müssen, die Sie der Universität mitteilen möchten. Seien Sie versichert, dass sie eingehend geprüft werden."

He explained that the single sheet was a form to fill out, while the second was where he should write his concerns in detail. Everything would be carefully reviewed.

"*Danke, ich schätze die Fürsorge der Universität,*" Ugochukwu said, taking the pages.

- Thank you. I appreciate the university's concern.

"*Wir wissen, es war vielleicht nicht alles einfach,*" Schwarz went on.

- We know it hasn't all been easy.

"*Aber es ist wichtig, dass der Vorstand von allen Problemen erfährt, die Ihre Arbeit beeinträchtigen könnten. Und es ist auch wichtig, dass diese aufgeschrieben werden. Nur so können sie erkannt und möglicherweise behoben werden.*"

It was important, he added, that the Board learn of anything affecting his work. And that it be written down. That was the only way problems could be identified and, hopefully, resolved.

At this point, something clicked in his head. Was this about the problems affecting his work? That is, problems hindering him from discharging his job. Or was this about the expected problems he was facing in the course of discharging his job? They were both different now that Schwartz put it that way. The first could mean that he was allowing his personal problems to affect his job, and the second could mean there were natural problems expected to come his way. Both could have different outcomes. "*Ich werde sicherstellen, alle meine Anliegen aufzuschreiben,*" Ugochukwu said, - I will make sure to write all my concerns.

"*Gibt es eine Frist dafür?*" - Is there a deadline for this? He waved the papers in front of them.

Schwarz smiled.

"*Nicht wirklich, aber wir würden es schätzen, wenn Sie es vor der nächsten Vorstandssitzung einreichen könnten, die Ende nächsten Monats stattfindet.*"

- Not really, but we would appreciate it if you could submit it before the next Board meeting at the end of the month.

"*Entschuldigung, aber ich kann Ihnen bei dieser Anfrage nicht weiterhelfen,*" Ugochukwu said - All right, that wouldn't be a problem. He arranged the papers and tucked them into his desk drawer.

He'd give them careful thought before filling them out. He would speak to his wife first, she always had a sharp, strategic view of things. She would know how to help him respond without putting his position at risk.

Zelda shifted her chair back and stood.

"Well, Mr. Odogwu, we won't take up any more of your time. We have one more office to visit to do."

Schwarz stood up as well, a bundle of papers Ugochukwu guessed must be the same as the ones he had received neatly stacked in his folder.

"Is everything okay with you?" Zelda asked when they got to the door.

"Apart from the few things I will write down in my report, things are okay," he lied. His thoughts flooded again with images of his wife.

"Must be serious to give you this faraway look. You seem too taken this morning," Zelda stated.

"Oh, it must be something from home, not work-related."

"Are you sure?"

"I am sure."

"If it is something I can help you with, do let me know."

He nodded and watched her catch up with Mr. Schwartz in the corridor.

He sat back in his chair, reaching for the documents from his drawer and glancing over them. He laughed to himself. It was a delight that the University checked up on their staff and concerned itself with their well-being. First, Zelda had been assigned to see to their settling down, now, they were asking to know the concerns he had. That is, if this was about his well-being, instead of the well-being of the university. Or maybe it was both. He smiled again and slid the papers into his bag so that he wouldn't forget them.

Now, his head was clearer than it was before his visitors came. He started clicking away on his keyboard.

Finally, some progress.

CHAPTER TWENTY-SEVEN

10th August 1994

U gochukwu checked his wrist watch to see it was 2:15 p.m., just enough time to get the results to the computer laboratory for printing before heading home. He saved his work and burned it on a CD for record purposes just after he checked and saw that Lukas made a 'B-'. This was an improvement from his previous grade. He was glad to be done with this particular set of students. He hoped someone like Lucas wouldn't be sitting in his class, amongst other students the next academic year.

Locking his office door behind him, he pocketed the keys and headed for the lab, with the CD in his bag.

Once he was done printing the results, he gathered the papers and placed them in his bag before heading to his departmental office to submit the printed copy.

He glanced at his wrist watch again and noted that the next bus would be at the bus stop by 3:30 p.m. It was 3:15 now but what was the use of hurrying back home? He knew he would likely regret it.

He started walking again when he realized he'd been standing at a spot, lost in thoughts. Worrying made him restless and disorganized.

The sound of a taxi horn jolted him to reality. He hailed the taxi which had the words JOHANNES GUTENBERG UNIVERSITY, MAINZ boldly painted in white against the backdrop of the maroon car like the other taxis in the university. It would cost him more than a bus ride, but he wanted to head to a store first which was outside the bus route.

"*Bringen Sie mich bitte zum Geschenkeladen,*" - Please take me to the gift shop, he said the moment he was seated at the backseat. He had been to the University's gift shop in the past and was certain he would see something interesting there to buy for his wife. She loved it whenever he bought her a gift even though it had been a while he did so. Maybe that could be part of the problem.

"*In Ordnung, mein Herr,*" - All right, sir, the driver accepted. He only looked at his passenger from the rearview mirror without turning.

Ugochukwu ducked into the gift shop as soon as the taxi stopped in front of it. He wanted to hurry as the taxi's meter was still running. He reappeared fifteen minutes later holding a hamper that was filled with different things he knew his wife couldn't resist.

He had a set of jewellery with amber gemstones, a sleek gown with animal print he was sure Ifeoma would love. He filled the basket with a few other items he thought she might appreciate: feminine perfume with oriental fragrance, a woollen sweater, a box of chocolate, luxury bath oils, and lotions.

The wind blew hard on his face as the taxi sped towards the apartment. He needed the breeze to keep alert. He knew they had to talk and resolve things, but the outcome of that talk scared him silly. His wife had made it clear that resolving things meant moving back to Nigeria. His stance that his job would give him more exposure and reward was not received well as she countered by giving him reasons why their kids should not grow up in his ideal 'developed' country. But since family comes first, there was a greater need to end the fight. He would talk things over with her. At least that would be a step forward.

He began to rehearse in his head how to begin the conversation in a way that would not ignite Ifeoma's ire.

The feeling of dread and uncertainty became almost overwhelming as the tyres of the cab rolled to a halt in front of the apartment building. He was sitting silently looking towards the building when the driver's voice came.

"*Hier ist die Adresse, die Sie angegeben haben, mein Herr.*" - This is the address you provided, sir.

"*Natürlich, danke schön,*" - Of course, thank you so much, Ugochukwu said as he shook off the apprehension that was starting to creep in. He paid the taxi fare and began to walk slowly, still trying to rehearse his opening statement, but those words seemed to have been relegated to the back of his head. Trying to calm himself, he began to repeatedly talk in his mind – *It will eventually turn out well. Life has its good and bad times; it is the way of the world. Everything will be all right*. The more he repeated the words, the more they felt like prayers rather than the solo conversation it was supposed to be.

He was close to the lamppost outside the building when he heard Ikenna's voice.

"Daddy! Daddy!!" The boy was running to him. He extended his hands and lifted him up the moment his boy got close enough.

There were three other kids running around the front of the building. Toys were littered around.

Julia approached him. "Your son and my grandkids were playing before he saw you." She pointed to the corner where the toys were littered and her grandkids still played.

"What about his mother?" Ugochukwu asked.

"Inside. I only took Ikenna. She said she had something to do and couldn't stay out and enjoy the sun with us," Julia explained, beckoning to Ikenna to come over and continue playing.

"What about Bruno?"

"Bruno is always indoors, no reason to worry. We are also planning to put her down soon since the vet diagnosed her with chronic pain and respiratory issues which explains her recent difficulty in lying down and getting up," Julia said.

"I'm so sorry for Bruno," he said.

"It's okay. A dog's lifespan is a short one."

He nodded. "Can you watch Ikenna a little while longer? I will come back for him in a short while."

"Of course," Julia said, leading Ikenna away.

***

He climbed the stairs and stopped in front of the apartment door. Holding his breath, he pressed the doorbell, a little longer than needed.

When the door opened, they both looked at each other and as he was about to open his mouth, Ifeoma left him at the door and headed to the adjoining apartment they'd rented. The reality he was avoiding finally faced him and a feeling of dread caught up with him.

Music from the radio was coming from the apartment. He followed closely behind her, struggling to remember the line he had planned to start the conversation with.

"Ify."

Silence.

He turned off the radio and waited for her reaction but none came. "Ify, please can we talk?" He almost slipped from Ikenna's Lego scattered on the floor of the room as he tried to go to where she was. He gathered the toys together with his feet, leaving the pile close to the couch. Then he carried Ada up from the Baby Walker she was playing in, kissed her forehead before placing her back in it.

"Please talk to me."

More silence.

Ifeoma lay still on the couch looking up at the ceiling, as if there was something fascinating about the white stained ceiling. He watched as she stared and used one of her hands to rock Ada's walker.

He sat beside her. "We need to talk." He knew she would ignore him again. "Please."

"I've been talking for days! Did you hear me? Did you listen?" Her voice was low but angry. "What else is there to talk about?"

"I'm sorry, Ify. I just didn't know what to say."

"And you suddenly know what to say now? After days of making me look like a mad woman! Please leave me alone, I'm resting."

He was aware that the pitch of her voice was rising. "Ify, I'm sorry." He took her hand in his but she pulled away. "Sorry for all the things I've done wrong. At least, let's talk it over."

She stood up and made to walk away but his hand held her back, pulling her gradually back to the couch.

"Please, let's just talk. *Biko,*" he pleaded.

"I'm listening." Her eyes looked upward as she pled silently for patience, before she returned her gaze to the man she married. She watched his Adam's apple bob up and down as though he swallowed a fish bone. She waited, thinking about how time and time again she had flared up, cajoled, shouted, screamed, and even kept silent, all to make him budge and understand her. Yet, this man before her kept pretending everything would get better with time. She was looking at him now, willing him to say something, to assure her, though not fully convinced, that whatever he was going to say would resolve anything.

Ugochukwu paused. Everything he had planned to say was gone, so he reached for the basket instead. "I got you these," handing the basket over to her.

She didn't make a move to accept it. "You only buy me things on my birthdays and on special occasions. What are the gifts for?"

"Just thought to buy something for you, there's no occasion."

Ifeoma took the basket and looked into it, bringing out the gifts and placing them with nonchalance on her laps. He looked at her closely, watching for a change in her attitude. Then he saw her lips move, *Oh, Ugom! I love these gifts. You always know what I want!* He moved his gaze to her eyes expecting to see delight there but was shocked to find her glaring at him. The voice had been in his head.

She spread out the animal patterned gown on her laps. "So, you buy me one dress and jewellery and whatever else you have in this basket and think that all will be well just like that!" Ifeoma snapped her fingers. "I can see you don't rate me at all, you don't value me or my opinion, or even my feelings! Do you think I am Ikenna that you can bribe with gifts?"

By now Ifeoma was standing, breathing hard, and the basket with all the goodies in it lay overturned somewhere on the floor.

"I didn't get them to bribe you, Ify. I just want us to talk things out. Please, let us resolve this problem." While he talked, he gathered the gift items and arranged them back in the basket before setting it beside the couch.

Seeing the extent of her husband's pitiful face, Ifeoma softened. "Okay, let's talk."

"Sit down, please," he gestured beside him. When she hesitated, he grabbed her from the waist and pulled her down. "I'd better hit the nail on the head. You've said many times that you don't like it here anymore, right?"

"I want us to go back home. This whole place is not for me and the kids. I have said this countless times. Do you not see? Do you not feel the things I feel?" She shifted from him and faced him. "Why do you like it here? Why did you choose to come here, of all places?"

"Would you believe it if I said I became as surprised as you about the things bothering you here only when I got here? Would you? I didn't know everything about Germany before choosing it." His eyes seemed to be challenging now, trying to match hers. But his expression soon softened as he realized he was getting into what he was trying to avoid. "Never mind my question. Can you think back, back to when this journey started? You remember we had been happy when this opportunity came?"

"That was in the past when I didn't understand everything. When I didn't know that I was coming to a place I wasn't wanted. A place I am not even seen."

"Okay. But have you thought about this well? Have you compared it with what we had back home?"

"I don't look at life that way, Ugom. It seems you're viewing life differently from the way I view it."

"How then do you view it?" he asked.

"You have friends here, I don't. You can speak their language, I cannot. I feel odd each time I step out, like the rejected cornerstone. The stigma too is something you also experience, or don't you?"

He ignored the question. "The language is something you can learn if you put your mind to it. Within months of putting in the effort, you can speak German to some extent, Ify. The opportunities here are much more. The quality of education is higher. Have you also considered the quality of life generally? The country has a very strong economy. Let's be practical, you remember how the ambulance was prompt in coming to take you to the hospital and the difference in the healthcare system? Aren't these the things we considered before coming here?"

"I'm not saying that this place does not afford all the things you mentioned, but it's about the things they offer that I didn't know about before coming. For one, I didn't know we would, or rather, I would be this lonely with no friends to talk to. Look at our daughter. Ada is not even a citizen of this place even though she was born here. She is still an outsider to the system. What's the benefit then?"

"We can't have it all." There were signs of resignation in his demeanour.

"I left my comfort to come here to be stigmatized, to put my life on hold." With the back of her fingers, she wiped a tear from her cheek. "I'm sure you have conscience, Ugom, you understand what I'm saying. Look at me and tell me you don't."

Many questions without clear answers filled Ifeoma's mind like a fog. She felt as though her husband wasn't in the same ship as she. He seemed to have set sail while she remained at the harbour. She had to admit she was trapped because she couldn't just get up and leave Germany with a toddler and an infant. The saying that whoever brings the money made the decisions rang true in her situation. Tears came to her eyes.

He knew that the tears were a sign that she was letting off; opening up to bottled pain. "I understand you perfectly, Ify. But I don't know if you understand me."

Her eyes flashed to him. "I understand you, really, I do. But I've been so miserable here. I miss Mama, I miss Papa, I miss my friends back home, I miss having people to talk to who would understand me and not make faces at me when I speak." Ifeoma was crying in earnest now as she listed off more things that she missed back home when suddenly he held her as her sobs shook her whole body and then began to subside.

"It's okay," he consoled her. "It wasn't meant to be easy, but I believe that things will get better the more we get used to being here."

After sometime, Ifeoma raised her face in a mock glare at him. "I just wish that in my next life, I'll be a man and make the decisions and I will definitely decide to not have to leave my homeland for some place where people speak funny with noses long enough to poke my eye."

He was laughing before she even finished. "This is proof that my wife is getting back to her usual self."

She smiled. "Well, there's something I've been thinking about for a while. I know you would not want to leave what you have here but I cannot stay. Life is short to waste it when there are other options. What if I take the kids with me back to Nigeria?" she asked, fixing her gaze on his face to see his first reaction. "That way, you can visit us and we can also visit you here."

Without his response forthcoming, Ifeoma wondered if she had said the words at the wrong time. Or maybe she hadn't thought of phrasing it well. She had thought about this all day and she believed he would like the idea. She watched his forehead crease into many rows, which she had never noticed before. She suspected she might have said something that hit him hard, maybe too hard.

But what was he expecting? He had seen her complain almost every day. What solution was he expecting her to proffer? Surely, he should have known she was fed up with this arrangement and wanted out.

The room was silent. Even Adaeze seemed to feel it as she stopped her solo play and fixed her eyes on her father with great seriousness. Ugochukwu was not sure he heard his wife correctly but as he replayed the words in his head, his whole body turned cold as the implications of what his wife said sank in, words his mind was not ready to process its implications.

His head started to pound and he blinked several times, trying to stop the tears that were threatening to fall. He tried to run his hand across his face in an attempt to wipe something from it. Instead, his eye glasses slipped down to the end of his nose and he pushed them back. He closed his eyes and placed his two hands on his bent head.

Ifeoma watched him go through the process of internalizing her request, she had never seen him seem so stressed in the space of two minutes.

Finally, he sighed. "You want to take the kids with you? That means we would be living apart. We would not live together as one family. Did you think of that?" His words came out slow and painful.

"That's what it implies. That way, I would be certain the kids imbibe our culture while growing up. But with time, we can finally decide the country all of us can live in together."

A pause.

"Let's not make any hasty decisions now, Ify. Let us sleep on this because what you just asked of me, of us, is quite difficult." He continued almost immediately when an idea came to his mind, "And before you think of other ways to resolve this, I have a surprise for you."

"What surprise?"

"Get ready with the kids, we are going out to see the city next weekend."

"Can we afford that?" she asked.

"We should. You've been stuck in here for too long, it's time to see the outside."

Ikenna pushed the entrance door open and ran into the room, panting. When they heard the door open, they both emerged from the adjoining apartment to see who it was.

Ugochukwu forced a smile to his face, "Whoa, young man, you're all sweaty. You must have really enjoyed yourself," he said, holding the boy still so he could catch his breath.

Ifeoma walked hastily to the bathroom to dry her tears and clean her face. She knew that Julia wouldn't be far behind Ikenna, and she wouldn't want her to suspect anything from her face.

Julia soon walked in. "Ugh, your son is so full of energy," she announced. "Had to walk faster to make sure he doesn't miss his way."

Ugochukwu feigned a laugh just as his wife got back from the bathroom. "That's Ikenna for you."

"I should thank you again for letting him go out to play with your grandkids. It surely kept him occupied," Ifeoma said, addressing Julia.

"Not a problem. He's so much fun to have around," Julia replied. "It's good that they're all getting along, especially with the last one who should be your son's age," Julia said, then continued. "Just to be sure, how old is he?"

"Two, he turned two in March," Ifeoma said.

Julia's eyebrows raised in surprise. "Wow, I could never have guessed that he is only two. He looks bigger than two and I simply assumed he was three years old as my last grandchild."

"Kids grow differently," Ugochukwu said.

"They surely do. Anyway, I should take my leave now. I would come get your boy another day to play with my grandkids."

"I would appreciate that," Ifeoma said, genuinely smiling.

When Julia left, the atmosphere in the apartment became sober again.

***

The news of Walter Weaver's death spread in the building the next evening with the arrival of an ambulance. Walter had been found sitting on his cane chair in his usual position outside, appearing very relaxed with his newspaper lying on his laps and his eyes closed shut. His wife had waited for him to come into the house for dinner and when he didn't show up, had gone outside to meet him.

Julia had called out Walter's name several times before proceeding to nudge him over and over. She started to panic when Walter's head tilted sideways from her shoves and he still didn't respond. That was when she rushed to the phone and called for an ambulance. Walter was pronounced dead when the team arrived. He had been dead for over an hour from heart failure before Julia found him.

It was a devastating news when Ifeoma heard about it and she blamed herself for it. Walter had been nice to her. If that incident with Bruno hadn't occurred, maybe Walter would still be alive. If only the dog had not been left indoors. Maybe

Bruno would have raised an alarm at the early stage of the heart failure and saved Walter's life.

She mourned the old man in her heart. He would never be vertical again. Death was a debt all living mortals owed and must repay. There were no exceptions.

"But the man was lively," she said that night as she lay on the bed beside her husband. "Always playful and accommodating. Even though he witnessed the Second World War, I never sensed any hatred in him. God rest his soul."

"Amen," Ugochukwu whispered.

Her sleep was filled with disturbing dreams that night.

CHAPTER TWENTY-EIGHT

20th August 1994

"Don't you love this place?" Ugochukwu asked. They both lay in beach lounge chairs sipping their drinks and watching the people traffic on the Rhine Promenade. Ugochukwu had researched places they could go out to relax this weekend and was glad to find that the city had a big river. His friend, Timo, had been the first to suggest the place and he suddenly remembered reading about the river in one of the magazines he had stacked on the table. He had gone through the magazines, searching for details about the Rhine. Now, beside him, Ada's four-wheeled baby bassinet rocked and she seemed happy with the sound the wind made as it rocked her bassinet.

Ikenna wasn't being his usual self. It was one of those rare days when he had been asked to do something and he was actually doing it. His father had warned him sternly to play on the sand with his toys, and not to go near the water. In an attempt to keep the boy in check, Ugochukwu had spiced it up by telling him that masquerades would emerge from the river and carry him off if he ventured into it. To their surprise, the boy ran from the water each time it seemed the tides were coming close. And it was a delight to watch him run from the river.

Ifeoma lay down, looking up to the sky through the sunshades perched on her nose and thought of telling her husband that today seemed to be one of her best days in months. She had laughed more and enjoyed nature. The wind was refreshing. In just one day, she had felt a lot of sand under her feet as though she were back home. "The end will have to justify the means", she answered in reply to her husband's question. "Let's just say that if I knew this place existed before now, you wouldn't be seeing me at home some of the time. I'm already considering coming here again next weekend, it's a good way to unwind after a full week with the kids."

He chuckled, adjusting his sunglasses. "That means you love this place but don't want to admit it. All the same, we can't come back here next weekend. Remember Zelda called last night to invite us to her place again for dinner."

"That is true, I almost forgot that. Just so you know, I won't miss her invitation for anything. That apple tree at her place produces such sweet succulent fruits." She unconsciously licked her lower lips. "And I would love to see jovial Stefan again." To Ifeoma, there were lots of things endearing about Stefan. His pleasant nature, his easy laughter, and his jokes made him warm to be around. All these made his funny features insignificant. It must be, for how else could Zelda have fallen for him? How else if not that Zelda must have been swept off her feet by his charming manners, and agreed to marry him before the scales had the chance to fall from her eyes. At some point in their marriage, those scales must have fallen off. But it would have been too late. "Any specific reason why she invited us again, apart from having dinner?"

"She mentioned that her daughter, son-in-law, and grandson will be visiting next weekend. So, she just wants us to be there," Ugochukwu revealed.

"Interesting! I didn't know she has a grandchild. And they both never mentioned that any of her kids were married when I was going through their family photos. But why would she need us to be there?" Ifeoma was looking at her husband now, blinking rapidly as if to dislodge any scales in her eyes. She needed to be sure she hadn't been blinded to the true features of her own husband when she had agreed to marry him. She watched a little smile appear on her husband's face and considered if it was attractive enough, especially to others. She watched his nose as it took in and exhaled air. That is what a normal nose should look like, she thought. Her husband's not-so-pointed nose looked sexy now. Her eyes went to his ears; those were good-looking as well. His ears had the right shape and size. They wouldn't flap if the wind blows too hard. Ifeoma's mind was accessing her husband's lips when his voice came.

"Her son-in-law is Black like us. She wants us to be there to keep the conversation going. I didn't want to ask her too many questions, but it seemed she doesn't want the man's visit to end up being awkward between them. It's the least we can do, considering all her help. Did something get into your eyes, Ify?" He saw how she kept her eyes fixed on his face, and the more she stared at him, the more she blinked.

"No, my eyes are fine, just clearing them," she smiled.

Ifeoma remembered that first day she met Zelda, how awkward the conversation had been. Zelda had seemed lost that day. She was beginning to understand now. "I don't think Zelda likes Black people that much. She found it difficult talking to me the first time I met her, she also wasn't very relaxed the day we honoured their first invitation at their house. And she never mentioned her daughter being married. Now, I have many questions about this invitation. And I guess whatever happens next weekend will answer them. I am going there to see things for myself." She knew she might have been tempted to ask some questions if she were the one that had picked the phone when Zelda called the house, but she can as well wait. Patience required time and time revealed things that were hidden.

"You might be right. She said she'd send a cab so the baby wouldn't be stressed."

"She really needs us to be there, and we're definitely going." She looked at her man. "Enough about Zelda. Let's talk about you. You can be romantic in an old-fashioned way when you want to be."

"What is it now, Ify?"

"I should be giving you more trouble and keeping you on your toes. That's the only way you would think outside the box on how to make me happy. See how peaceful this place is, and you've been caging me inside that small apartment."

He laughed. "Please no more trouble, I beg of you."

***

The scenery around the river was magnificent. Ifeoma had expected to see a river similar to the stream they had in the village: brown and sometimes muddy. But the River Rhine was clear, even soothing to her eyes. This was why she had stood on its shorelines earlier as the breeze went past her. She had found a pebble on the sand and thrown it into the water. How beautiful nature was. She stood there, admiring the blue reflection of the sky in the water.

At the moment, she felt very relaxed in her mid-thigh shorts and a singlet, having refused to wear the two-piece swim suit her husband had bought her. She let her eyes roam around the beach and saw other women in their bikinis. So very indecent, she thought to herself.

She had first seen the women in their swimsuits when they got to the beach that late morning, and her eyes had popped wide open, shocked by how much flesh was on display. But what did her husband do? He'd laughed at her reaction. He and Ikenna wore singlets and similar beach shorts with palm trees and beach balls printed across them, looking like people on holiday.

But a few minutes later, when one of the almost-naked women walked past them with a kind of confident sway, she caught her husband's eyes lingering a bit longer. Just a second too long. She had said his name slowly, "Ugo-o-mm," dragging it out like a warning bell.

He had blinked and turned to her with the guilty smile of a child caught sneaking biscuits.

She didn't say another word. She didn't need to.

***

Not far away, a robin was chattering at another bird, and the sound, coupled with the crash of the waves, made a soothing rhythm.

They had spent the day talking about the families they missed, how different things were in Mainz, friends they hadn't spoken to and the other things the peace of River Rhine allowed them to, until the chatter and excitement of people started to die down.

"We should grab something to eat and head home now that we've eaten all the snacks we came with. I'm famished," Ifeoma suggested.

"Good idea. Those restaurants lined up over there should have something for us, let's check it out."

"They definitely should," she concurred.

"Have you forgotten you have refused to eat most food here, even when they smell nice?"

"This could be different."

She watched as her husband packed a notebook and pen he had come with into the bag before he moved to pack up Ikenna's toys. When she had asked him what he was writing, he had simply mentioned that the atmosphere on the beach gave him inspiration. While she had read a book, every now and then as birds flew by, as the waves rolled in, as kids ran around playing tag, and as couples walked hand in hand on the beach, her husband had jotted down things into his notebook. If she were to be completely honest with herself, she couldn't say she understood the man she married.

But now that she thought about it, her husband had said something about a poetry collection he was working on that would soon be ready for publication. She guessed that must be it. She would wait until then as that would be proof that his efforts were worthwhile.

CHAPTER TWENTY-NINE

20th August 1994

They settled for a restaurant situated in the perfect spot. The windows were wide, giving a breathtaking panoramic view of the river and allowed for the sea breeze to waft in unhindered. It gave those sitting inside the feeling of being outdoors.

The restaurant was painted beige to resemble the beach, seashells were affixed to the walls, and a wood carving of a tuna hung from the ceiling. The aroma of freshly cooked food and the smell of beer permeated the air.

They chose a small square table, and tucked the large bag containing the children's toys and other items from their time at the beach, under the table. While they waited to order, Ifeoma took in the artwork scattered around the restaurant. She could tell that the people here loved art because she had also noticed a painting at the entrance: a family dining by the river with food spread before them. It reminded her of her own, and she wondered if the painting was based on a real family. Would someone else sit where she sat now in twenty years, staring at the same artwork, thinking the same thoughts?

That was what art should be, more than ordinary life. At first glance, it might seem simple, but with a closer look, it stirred something deep: laughter, wonder, dreams, emotion. That was its magic. She understood this.

Across from where she sat, a stuffed bull stared down from the wall.

Her husband lifted the menu list placed on their table. After scanning it, they decided on pasta, and a waiter was called to take their order. It was safer to have something they were familiar with.

Not long after, the waiter returned with fruit salad placed in small soup bowls as appetizers. She glanced up at the waiter as he set the bowls down and the bull's horns behind him stood just above his head, making it look like he had sprouted horns.

Soft music from the back of the counter filled the air. But the music was swallowed by the din of voices all around the place. Somewhere in the middle of the room, a high-pitched laughter rang out, followed by a loud sound of cutlery on a glass cup. Someone was trying to raise a toast.

There were all kinds of people. Some still in their bikinis waiting for their orders, some already eating or having a drink. Then she caught some looks directed towards them. Were they being stared at again? But maybe she was mistaken. She stole a look to confirm her suspicions, and sure enough, some people were staring. She was certain her husband noticed the stares as well. That he was not bothered by the attention, disturbed her even more.

"How do you cope with all of these? All the peering eyes? As if we are a mystery to be solved."

He started, not expecting to have this issue mar the perfect day they had had. "Ify, we've had this talk before, let's just enjoy our food and forget these things. They don't matter that much."

"Just answer me. People are stealing glances at us here, and it's getting on my nerves. How do you cope with all of these?" she persisted.

"That is a difficult question and it's not something we can get to right now. We are in a public place, let's just eat first."

"If you brought me out to show me this city, then I need to know. These people staring are a part of the city you're showing to me." As she spoke, she looked up and met the bold stare of a woman who was sitting on a chair at the counter. She held a mug of beer in her hand. Ifeoma felt a sense of familiarity, like she had seen the woman before but she couldn't remember where. The woman in question soon moved her gaze from them, her eyes scanning the restaurant for something. Her makeup was exaggerated, and after a while, she got up and walked away, swaying her thin waist. Ifeoma returned her attention to her husband who was still speaking.

"This is simple, Ify. If a white man comes to my village, people will stare at him. They will stare and stare hard because it is not something they are used to seeing every day. People might even gather together just to stare at the fellow. It is the same with us here. Many don't get to see people like us here all the time. So, it isn't out of place to get this reaction from them. It's not like this place does not bother me; it does. But I simply focus on the good part rather than on what I can't control. You know there are many good reasons to be where we are. You know what our people mean when we say *kwechiri*? - We Igbos are known to stand strong in the face of adversity. We stand our ground and persist no matter what is facing us. We always look to the prize; to the reason we started in the first place and focus on it. Why do you think we are able to do that?"

"I don't know."

"Because of our mindset. That is the long and short of it. We have a strong will to persist and persevere in whatever we set our minds to do. Sometimes try to see the good in things around, it works like magic."

As he spoke, she became more transfixed, her eyes fixing on him longer than usual. "I've never heard you sound so philosophical, do I even know you?"

He smiled. "That is why I ask that you look beyond everything you see. A lot of potential is hidden from us when we are close-minded and not open to discovering new things. It's all about our mindset, Ify. As for your question about how I cope, I would say I just have a thick skin."

She put her hand across the table and pinched him. "Your skin is not that thick."

He winced. "You know what I mean. I don't allow myself to be disturbed by certain realities beyond my control. In fact, I could smile through them like they don't exist. I am more focused on why we are here, every other thing is a distraction. That is how to survive life."

"You sound like you're a survivor." Ifeoma knew he was telling the truth. That truth was what she consciously hid at the back of her mind, not willing to admit it to her husband. Not even to herself. How could she? The moment she does that, she ceases to have any argument. She knew that a lot had to be foregone for some other things to be achieved, but she wasn't prepared to do that. At least not yet.

"We all are survivors," said Ugochukwu, echoing her.

She looked around the room: most of the attention was no longer on them. It seemed as though those who were staring had found better things to look at. But the question remained, could she really give up what she held dear for the sake of survival? It was easier said than done. "That is not a good way to live this short life, pretending that what is staring right at you is not there." She shifted her eyes to Ikenna who was still scooping the fruit salad into his mouth, some of which missed their aim and landed on the table.

Her husband set his empty salad bowl aside. "Not everyone here is staring at us, a greater part of the people here is not."

Her eyes swayed to one of the tables closer to the counter and there she was again; the lady who had caught her eyes earlier. She seemed to be everywhere and nowhere at the same time. It wasn't her suspicious movements that worried her, but the fact that she felt sure she had seen her somewhere, and it felt significant. But she couldn't recollect, for the life of her, where it had been, and that was what worried her.

"You know racism here was worse ten years ago. That means it will get better in another ten years. By the time our kids would be grown, things would have changed significantly," Ugochukwu said.

"So, when they start school and two or three of their classmates see them as lesser humans, what do you think would happen to their psyche?" She looked at Ada sleeping peacefully inside the bassinet and wondered if they had made the right decision in bringing their kids here. Pity clouded her eyes for her, for all the things her little girl could possibly face in the future. Ikenna might develop a thick skin like his father when he gets older, she could even see the toughness in the boy already. But she understood the way the minds of females worked. Women do not deal well with rejection. They loved to be appreciated, wanted to be desired, to belong. Would Ada stand it all? Would her little innocent baby cope? Then she felt guilt. If her baby wouldn't cope well, it would be her fault. Yes, she was the one that decided to come here when she was still pregnant with Ada and birth her here. She caused it.

"It won't be that bad," Ugochukwu's voice rang out.

"Ugom!" she said firmly. "I'm talking about my kids here, not some games." As she spoke, she noticed that the familiar face was now seated across from a man, speaking in a low insistent voice as if she were bargaining for something.

She thought hard, glancing towards the lady again until it clicked. She covered her mouth with her hands and gasped. It was one of those two women that had been to the apartment handing out bills! Bills advertising their prostitution services! The blonde one, to be precise.

Her husband was saying something in reply to what she had said earlier, but she didn't hear him. She was no longer interested in what he was saying. Then she noticed it. There were women looking to be in the same trade as the blonde, searching for customers, though discreetly. Why hadn't she noticed this earlier?

She saw the blonde stand up from the table with the man and started walking towards the exit. This wasn't a good place to bring kids to.

"You know you're an interesting woman," Ugochukwu said.

She eyed him, then held his gaze for a few seconds. "You always say that. Do you mean it in a positive or negative way?"

A crooked smile appeared on his face. "Both ways. You know the level of ethnic stigma we face back home. You know that very well. Yet, you don't want to swallow the attitude of a few intolerant people here. Is racism worse than ethnic bigotry? They are all the same. Even the effects of the Nigeria-Biafra War we fought when we were kids is still heavy on everyone's heart. We are still fighting that war individually and systematically. Don't ask me to explain that, please. But have you forgotten that was part of the reasons we left home? For a place where no one looks at your ethnic group and religion before giving you what you deserve?"

Her face gave the impression of trying not to laugh. "Are you not getting a worse treatment here, Ugom? Back home, at least, we have neighbours who are the same with us. People with the same ideas, understanding, and beliefs as we do. Does that not matter?" Ifeoma felt the unbelievable look of disbelief on her husband's face as the waiter returned with their order, setting it out before them.

Three women who sat at the table next to them started to speak softly in German. Ifeoma had noticed them initially because they were quite loud. Now they spoke softly. Occasionally, they laughed. Ifeoma could tell from their padded looks that they were mothers hanging out, possibly with teenage children at home. They didn't look that young to pass for new mothers.

"Es sind inzwischen einfach zu viele Fremde in dieser Stadt. Haben sie nicht ihre eigenen Länder?"

- There are just too many foreigners in this city now. Don't they have their own countries? One of the women said, directing her voice to the waiter who had brought the food to Ifeoma's table. One of them, the one closest to Ifeoma's table had said this out loud.

There were stares from tables nearby, a few chuckled.

"Wir waren zuerst hier. Wir haben unsere Bestellung vor ihnen aufgegeben. Warum werden sie vor uns bedient?"

- We were here first. We made our order before they did. Why would they get served before us? The second woman said, directing her question to the waiter as well.

"Es tut mir sehr leid wegen der Verzögerung, Ihre Bestellung kommt gleich. Die andere war einfach schneller zuzubereiten und ist deshalb zuerst herausgekommen,"

- I'm so sorry for the delay, your order will be out soon. Theirs was simply easier to prepare, so it came out first, the waiter answered them and continued arranging the cutlery near the plates.

The stares that exchange attracted, and the harsh tone with which the second woman had spoken in made Ifeoma believe they were the subject of that exchange. It was unmistakable. Those women had turned from the waiter to them, and back to the waiter as they spoke. "Those women were talking about us, weren't they? What did they say?" Ifeoma asked her husband. "They looked annoyed."

"Nothing that should bother us."

The waiter, done with setting down the dishes and cutleries, started to walk away.

"Ugom! What did they say about us?"

He hesitated. But with the level of firmness in her voice, he knew he had to tell her. "They were just being silly. They were angry with the waiter for serving us first..."

The muscles in her neck tensed and her eyebrows drew together. The anger flooded her entire system, filling her with heat. She felt her hands clench in fists. Her heart was beating fast as she rose, her chair flew backwards as she stood up abruptly, her face was twisted, and her body trembled with a fierce force unlike anything she had ever felt. She pointed at the women now, her pointed finger encompassing the three of them. "You are crazy! All of you! What gave you the right to talk about us like that? *Eh*?"

Ifeoma wiped the spit that appeared on her lips with her palm and continued, "You think you are something? You are not! You are just empty barrels wasting space and time. You look at us and think you all are better, *eh*? It is a shame that you think that. You all look very stupid. See your faces! The face of devils!"

One of the women began to laugh while she spoke, and the other two joined.

One of them, sitting closest to Ifeoma, was not having this strange woman talk to them in that manner. She jumped to her feet as German curses poured from her mouth. But the woman had barely straightened up when Ifeoma grabbed her hair, yanking it sideways with so much force that the woman lost her balance and fell, hitting the floor hard with her buttocks. Ifeoma did not stop in her fury. She kept pulling and yanking the woman's hair, incoherent words escaping her mouth.

The woman's face was bent now. Ifeoma had her placed in between her legs as she pulled at the hair hard. The woman kept swearing in German as she held Ifeoma's leg in an attempt to shake her off-balance. That was the only possible thing she could do in her position. Ifeoma knew this and planted herself firmly, cursing as she kept yanking at the hair. From her position, she could see that her opponent's forehead had turned red, shining under the dull light. She was getting what she deserved.

Ugochukwu was surprised at how fast things had unfolded. One second his wife was in front of him asking him what the women had said, the next moment she was in a scuffle, right in front of him. He sat there dazed at first, watching his wife raging. He waited. Ifeoma would let go of her grip on the hair in no time. It wasn't really a fight; it was his wife gripping and pulling on that woman's hair. She would let the hair alone soon, he thought. He said something to that effect to his wife but he wasn't sure she heard him.

He should act. He should do something, at least. He suddenly remembered that he had Ikenna on his laps. The boy shouldn't be seeing his mother reacting this way. He stood up, placed the boy on the chair and made him face the opposite direction, away from the scene. He instantly regretted telling his wife what those women had said. That was not a wise thing to have done. He should have known she would react. Yes, he should have suspected that. How could he not? He knew she was getting fed up, and had been working up her anger for a while. He should have fabricated some sweet lies instead.

He himself had been a little annoyed when the meaning of the things those women said got to him, but he pretended not to have heard them. Ifeoma wasn't like him. A part of him wanted her to deal with that woman, she needed to learn a lesson, but another part of him abhorred it. It wasn't civil in the least. It wasn't a proper way to act.

Ifeoma had the woman under her grip and so had the upper hand. She had taken her by surprise. She had grabbed her before the woman was prepared for a full defence. The woman could be stronger but she wasn't ready to find out. She felt the head under her legs slipping out of her laps and she pushed it back there firmly and kept pulling at the hair. She just pulled, and pulled. She pulled with the built-up anger she had stored in her blood stream. As an Igbo proverb says: if you could not wrestle the machete out of the hand of a man when he was on the ground, was it when he got to his feet that you would do it? There was so much sense in that proverb, she thought of it now. She could see that the two remaining women were standing away from their chairs, away from their friend, offering only words in support.

She felt satisfied with the sound of pain coming from her opponent's mouth. That was good enough. She should feel that pain, it was the pain she too felt when they spoke and laughed at them. She swirled the woman from right to left, then left to right, and watched her vain efforts as she tried to free her head. She wondered if her opponent was making any efforts at all, even with the encouragement coming from her friends. To act. To do something in return. To fight back.

Then she heard a high-pitched male voice scream, "*Rufen Sie die Polizei!*" - Call the police!

It has been a little over a minute since the scuffle started. Yet, his wife still held to that hair. She didn't appear like she would let go any minute. Once he heard someone shout to call the police, he left Ikenna's side in a flash, after giving the boy a stern warning not to turn around.

Ifeoma was about to swirl the woman again when she felt a strong grip behind her. "Ify, stop! You have to stop!"

"Leave me alone, Ugom! Just leave me! She has to learn her manners today." Her grip on the hair started to loosen as Ugochukwu pulled her.

"Let us leave! We have to leave now! We have kids with us!" He kept dragging her till they were both outside the restaurant. He left her in a dimmed corner outside with a warning not to leave there. Then he dashed back into the restaurant, paid for the meal they hadn't eaten before grabbing Ikenna and the baby.

Ifeoma was still breathing hard when they got into a taxi. She could still feel the weakness from the woman's body. What surprised her was how the woman couldn't fight back, she had been there like a powerless bag of potatoes lying in a corner, waiting for anyone to do with it as they pleased. Yet, that woman had been so bitter and hateful. She had no physical strength to add to it.

A feeling of fulfilment enveloped her as the scene unfolded again in her mind. She had pulled the hair so hard. She was certain that a chronic headache would result from all that hair pulling. Those friends! Those people her opponent call friends. Were they worth the friendship? None of them had attempted to help their friend. They obviously didn't want to be involved. They had left their friend to her fate, offering only words. Her people called such persons *oji onu* - the one with only mouth but no strength.

259

She liked the silence of her husband throughout the ride home. Such a sensible man, to know she couldn't handle any form of talking in her current state of mind.

She shut her eyes and pressed both palms over them, mimicking the ancient Japanese monkey that refused to see evil. She remembered spotting the figurine, carved in bronze, in a glass case at the antique shop where she'd once bought a silverware set. The image of the other two monkeys that heard no evil and spoke no evil, all placed together, filled her head. Today, she had seen evil, heard evil, and acted evil. But why would those monkeys refuse to see, hear, and speak of any evil? There was so much evil happening in the world. Who would bear witness to all of them if those monkeys refused to see, hear, and speak of any?

Why were her thoughts filled with these ancient Japanese monkeys? She stared at Adaeze and tried to focus her mind on the baby to keep the monkey thoughts away.

She straightened herself. Today was the first time she was comfortable with pairs of eyes staring at her. She had finally given people a good reason to justify the stares.

CHAPTER THIRTY

27th August 1994

The taxi Zelda sent to pick them up arrived at the Wolf's residence a little past four p.m. This time, Zelda ushered them into the house carrying a toddler of mixed race.

"Welcome dearies," Zelda beamed as she caressed Ada's cheeks with her free hand. Ada smiled at the touch. Behind her, Stefan said his welcome and shook Ugochukwu's hand.

After the pleasantries, they entered a tastefully decorated living room. It was as beautifully arranged as the exterior of the house Zelda had taken them around during their last visit. A large grey sofa was placed in the middle of two navy-blue cushions, with four single wooden chairs arranged at both ends, all set up in a semi-circle before a sturdy wooden coffee table. The white walls had the family photographs and a few artworks. Not far from the door, there was a bookshelf, with the top well above anyone's reach.

"Meet my daughter, Hannah," Stefan said immediately Hannah came into view. Hannah was busy putting baby items into a bag placed on a wooden side table. "And her husband,

Marcus. They flew in this morning, and will be going back to America tomorrow afternoon."

"Good to see you both," Hannah said as she turned to their guests. "Mama told me she helped you settle in our city."

"That is true," Ifeoma acknowledged, walking towards her. At the same time, she noted that Hannah possessed more of her mother's features which made her appear more beautiful than she had noted from the family photo album she had seen on their first visit. "Thanks to her, we settled quickly."

Ugochukwu approached Marcus and shook his hand, "Nice to meet you, Marcus."

"Now that we are done with the introductions, we should get ready for dinner," Stefan announced and gestured towards the dining table which already had drinks and glasses arranged on it. "Please, settle down while I go help my wife grab the food."

As soon as they were seated, Zelda appeared carrying a large bowl of potatoes on her right hand while holding her grandchild in the other.

"Mama, you know Alexander can walk around by himself. He started walking even before he turned one," Hannah stated.

"Let her do it her way," Stefan said to Hannah and laughed before placing a bowl of roasted pork and vegetables beside the potatoes. "She is in love with him. Alexander has replaced me in my own home." This caused some laughter.

Ifeoma smiled uneasily. She wasn't sure she had slept for three full hours at a stretch in the past seven days. Tension overwhelmed her. Each time her apartment doorbell sounded, she jumped thinking that the incident at the River Rhine had caught up with her. Her husband had told her to worry less so that the creases developing on her forehead could flatten out, but how could she? Not when she was scared of getting arrested any day. It was why she had applied some make-up that afternoon to hide the eye-bags under her eyes. She had longed to come to the Wolf's residence because she needed a distraction, she needed something else to occupy her thoughts at the moment.

She smiled again as Stefan cracked another joke at his wife's expense. Looking up from her plate, Ifeoma saw the reason. Zelda was too occupied with Alexander, spooning mashed potatoes into his eager mouth while barely touching her own meal. It was clear she was smitten with the boy.

"So, Marcus, how's the teaching job going?" Stefan asked, turning towards him after everyone had spooned some portion of the food into their plates.

Marcus straightened slightly, catching Hannah's eye before responding. "It's going well, Mr. Wolf. The students keep me on my toes, but I enjoy it."

"Too busy for my daughter, I hope not?" Stefan asked. He sounded half-teasing, but there was a sharpness in his tone.

"Papa..." Hannah said, gently warning. "Marcus does what he has to do. He's not too busy for us. Not for me or Alexander."

Stefan nodded and continued, his gaze never wavering from Marcus. "Hannah has always been the softest of my children. I want to believe she is in good hands."

"Hannah and Alexander are my world. I believe in being there for my family. Always," Marcus said.

That seemed to land well because Stefan's expression softened, and Ifeoma caught the quick glance he shared with Zelda.

"And you, Ugochukwu?" Stefan continued, shifting the spotlight. "Settled in now? I hope those early hurdles are behind you?"

Ugochukwu stopped the food halfway into his mouth. "Mostly. Germany is cold for much of the year, but I've adjusted." He smiled, deliberately avoiding his wife's gaze, though hoping she might take the hint and do some adjusting of her own. "I have even started craving *sauerkraut*, which I never thought I would say."

Marcus turned to him, grinning. "That is how you know you're getting in deep."

A wave of laughter passed around the table, though Ifeoma noticed it came mostly from the men.

"So, where are you from?" Marcus asked.

"I was born and raised in Nigeria." Ugochukwu answered. "What about you?"

"My grandparents were from Liberia. I was told that in the late 1930s, my grandfather was posted to America on a diplomatic assignment, and that's how I came to be born there."

"So, you cannot be classified as still finding your feet, like those of us who left our home country."

"Nothing like that," Marcus said, shaking his head sideways. "I consider myself an American. I don't even know anyone in Liberia from my grandparents' families."

Ifeoma didn't miss the way Zelda occasionally stole a glance at Marcus whenever he talked about himself, her face seeming to analyse briefly before turning her attention back to Alexander.

Not long after, Hannah turned to her, and the conversation drifted to parenting stories. She and Hannah swapped tales of sleepless nights, toddler tantrums, and the joy that came with it all. For a while, as the table warmed with conversations, Ifeoma forgot about the episode at the River Rhine.

Zelda, done with spooning the food into Alexander's mouth, finally looked up, her gaze lingering on her daughter longer than it had all evening. As if on cue, the conversations began to die down and she spoke when Hannah returned the gaze. "You've become a wonderful mother," she said softly.

Hannah blinked. "Thank you, Mama." There was a short pause. But then, something seemed to loosen in Hannah. "You know, I used to worry if I could do this. Not just being a mother to Alexander. Everything. Choosing Marcus, and living with how you reacted at first."

With this revelation, Ifeoma sat very still, wanting to connect the meaning behind the spoken and unspoken words. She had suspected that a brick wall lay between Zelda and her daughter even before accepting Zelda's invitation to this dinner. But witnessing its confirmation hit differently. She didn't want to miss out on any of this. She noticed Zelda's body go very still and the table stilled with her, until Hannah spoke again.

"I didn't expect you to understand my decisions fully," Hannah continued. "I had really hoped you would at least try. Or maybe just trust me a bit. Support me. I didn't just give myself to Marcus. Not at all. I love him because he truly sees me. He is always there, and he cares. He listens, even when I don't know how to say things. With him, I don't feel like I am too much, or not enough. He understands me in ways I cannot express."

Ifeoma could see how uncomfortable this was making Marcus. He wasn't looking at anyone in particular, just staring blankly at his almost empty wine glass. She thought back to all her past encounter with Zelda and finally understood why some things had happened the way they did. She could see that Zelda wanted to have this conversation with her daughter, but she didn't want it to happen before her and Ugochukwu's presence. Or maybe she did. She had actively invited them here, and even sent a taxi to ensure they made it. She saw Zelda exhale slowly when Hannah finished speaking.

"I have come to understand all of that, and I have been sorry for a long time. Longer than you can imagine. All my concerns were because I want the best for you. I wanted you to experience something familiar. But I can see now that you have the best," Zelda said, stealing a glance towards Marcus before continuing, "have you met his family?"

"They welcomed me well, Mama. His parents call me 'our wife' in a way that makes me feel like I belong with them," she said with a smile.

"I suppose I didn't make you feel that way," Zelda said, something close to a smile perching on her face.

"No," Hannah replied quietly. "You didn't, Mama. You made me feel like I was doing something I shouldn't be doing. Like I was still a child."

Zelda reached across the table and touched her daughter's hand. "I admit I was wrong. I can see that now."

For the first time that evening, Hannah smiled without reservation. "And I accept the apology. By the way, *Oma* really suits you. You do it so well."

It was then, when Stefan cleared his voice, that the table came alive again. It had seemed like mother and daughter were lost in their conversation, oblivious to anyone at the table.

Stefan glanced briefly at everyone before stopping at Marcus. "Well, since you have survived this dinner, you are officially part of the family now, Marcus. Let's all put the past behind us. We should raise our glasses to this. Welcome to the family!"

The empty and near-empty glasses clicked together, and a welcome chorus sounded. Marcus promised to put his wife and child before anything else.

"Let's have the dessert now, darling," Stefan said to his wife.

When it arrived, Zelda made a little speech.

"This dessert is a special one to me," she said as bowls of apple strudel were passed around. "It used to be Hannah's favourite when she was little. Making it today reminded me of her childhood. And I still remember Ifeoma's delight with apples on her first visit. I hope it brings back good memories for all of us."

And the table toasted to good memories.

Even the strudel, Ifeoma thought, tasted warmer than it had any right to be.

"Thank you, Mama," Hannah said.

Zelda held her daughter's gaze. And for a long beat, nothing moved, until Ikenna screamed when he sighted a cat on one of the cushions, and the room filled with soft laughter.

It was almost seven p.m. by the time Ifeoma left with her family, and the River Rhine details slowly crept back into her mind.

CHAPTER THIRTY-ONE

2nd September, 1994

Ifeoma ran her hand over her hair, further worsening her dishevelled look. Her scalp has started to itch and it needed washing, except that fixing it to look and feel good was the last thing on her mind. She had woken up this morning and rushed to take her bath the moment she realized she had forgotten to do so the previous day. Was there ever a day in her life when she hadn't taken a bath? Yet, somehow, she had forgotten to take her bath yesterday.

A knock sounded somewhere close and she startled, almost knocking over Ada who was playing beside her. She then let her shoulders drop, after realizing the knock wasn't from their door.

Ugochukwu had gone out with Ikenna immediately he returned from work and eaten. He claimed the boy needed to play outdoors, but she knew better. He didn't want to stay indoors with her these days and she didn't blame him. There was little about her that she could control now. Most times, she would suddenly realize she was shouting at her husband in a simple argument without meaning to. She was sure her husband was only trying to avoid further quarrels by offering to take their son to the playground on a Friday evening when Fridays was his time to unwind and relax at home from the week at work.

No. She didn't blame him.

The police were looking for her. It was only a matter of time before that dreaded doorbell or knock would sound, and she would be whisked away from the life she had come to know and was familiar with in the past year.

So much for seeking greener pastures.

So much for being in a better place.

Her hand ran over her hair again.

Nearly two weeks had gone by and she was sure the investigations would be complete; the investigation to track and arrest her for the River Rhine episode. She should have controlled herself, she thought for the nth time. What if she hadn't sprung up and responded to the anger as it welled up in her? What if her husband hadn't told her the truth about what those dreadful women had said?

What if they hadn't come here in the first place?

She had asked herself for the past two weeks what really was the point of remaining in Mainz. What remained for her children if she became a shadow of herself, while she waited for and dreaded the unknown?

Her fretting added to the already strained relations with her husband, leading to more arguments. No matter how much he tried to allay her fears, telling her that she wasn't only to blame, and that the police would take all things into account, she didn't believe him.

Wouldn't the system naturally favour their own?

Wouldn't the police think the worst of her should the episode at the River Rhine be modified, considering that she was not one of them?

She was a stranger here. The stares alone were enough to make her feel unwelcome.

Her head ached as she thought of how differently things would have turned out in the same scenario. If only she had acted differently. There was that word 'if' again. She was tired of the 'what ifs'. Her head pounded harder. She would need to take another painkiller soon.

As a breastfeeding mother, would the police allow her to take Ada with her during her arrest? What conditions would her sweet baby be kept in? But she stopped herself from going further with this line of thought. She would allow things unfold as they will, rather than imagining the worst-case scenario.

She desperately longed to be far away from here; from the dreadful anticipation of what the unknown might bring.

She wished the waiting would end so that her heart could stop beating erratically and resume its natural rhythm.

But again, wishes were not horses.

CHAPTER THIRTY-TWO

17th September 1994

Ada sat on the bed, laughing at something her brother was doing. Her laughter came as frequent as her sporadic crawls. She would laugh, crawl a little, before sitting again. Now, she was clapping and moving her body up and down in dance moves, watching as her brother ran around the bed. The entrance door of the apartment opened and Ugochukwu walked in.

"A taxi is waiting outside," he announced, panting slightly.

"Was there a problem?" Ifeoma asked. She had been sitting on a chair waiting for her husband to return. She was done with the final preparations. Everything was ready. "You are sweating a little."

"It must be the sun. I'm surprised at the intensity today. And this is early fall," he replied. "Traffic is a little congested today so it took some time to get a taxi."

Ugochukwu picked up the heavier luggage. "We should get going, the taxi is waiting."

Standing now, Ifeoma looked round the apartment she had lived and called home for close to a year before taking the handle of the second box. It was only a year but she felt like she had lived longer than that in this apartment. It had witnessed more memories than she could count. She would miss this familiar space, but there were other places she would rather be.

She took a deep breath and released it slowly as the four of them left the apartment, to the direction of the waiting taxi. Outside, the warmth of the afternoon sun brought back memories of home: the home she was heading to.

Minutes later, after settling Ada and Ikenna beside her at the back, while her husband sat in front, the taxi raced down the familiar street, out of the city of Mainz, towards Frankfurt airport. It was the same road they had taken when they first arrived in the city. They also passed by the stores where she had done her shopping. She wouldn't be seeing them in a long time, or, perhaps, in forever.

The watch on her wrist read 2:02 p.m. indicating that they were still within time. She looked out of the window of the taxi, inching her head closer to it to feel more of the breeze that blew in. She wanted to get as much air as she could before she boarded the plane.

Her mind circled back to the fight (if that was what one would call it) that occurred at the River Rhine restaurant a month ago.

Agbacha egwu, ola na ukwu - After the dance, the waist bears the brunt of it. Ifeoma had anticipated an arrest, an assault charge, or something similar to be brought against her, but none came. She wasn't sure how the law worked here, but she had been apprehensive about being made to face the consequences of her actions. Why had nothing happened after that incident at the River Rhine? Why had the *polizei* not followed it up?

Someone had shouted to call the police as she held that woman in-between her legs. She knew the meaning of those words as they were shouted. She had heard the word *polizei*, just before she felt her husband disentangle her from the woman she held. So, it was likely that the police arrived the restaurant in minutes after they left it. There was no way she could ascertain if that call was placed, but it had to have been.

Police cars were stationed all around the city, especially in the evenings. She had seen a few of them patrol her neighbourhood, so it was safe to assume that the River Rhine has a patrol car somewhere nearby. A place littered with restaurants, possibly pubs, and night clubs, would be a haven for prostitutes and gangsters. Fights could easily break out in such settings, especially when people get drunk.

She had worried for the past month. Creating different scenarios, comparing, and ruling out the odds.

Why the silence? Why were the authorities not involved yet? She wouldn't know. Something seemed off to her. If she recalled the events well, the woman had made an attempt to charge at her first, as she stood screaming at them. Or was it her that charged first? She wasn't sure anymore. She could hardly remember with clarity the details of that day with all the anger she had felt at that moment. Could the episode be called self-defence? She would have pleaded that if a case was filed against her.

Or maybe her identity wasn't discovered, Ifeoma reasoned. Maybe neither the woman, her friends, the eye-witnesses, nor the restaurant owners could describe her well. But she had laughed at this absurd thought. How possible was that? In a city where people like her were in the minority, it wasn't just about being in the minority, people like her were few. Seeking out a Black couple with a two-year-old boy and a baby wouldn't be difficult, would it? Of course not. Not many families would fit that description.

She hadn't also entirely dismissed the possibility that investigations could still be ongoing, but what kind of investigation would linger for a month without the police paying her a visit? They would have visited and questioned her, probably even warned her not to leave the city. After waiting for the law to take its course for weeks, she and her husband started to believe that no officer would eventually come knocking at their door. That was when they started to relax.

All those things were behind her now.

***

Frankfurt International Airport looked busier than the last time. There were more people and more movements.

After the check-in process, she and Ugochukwu sat in the waiting area of the airport, waiting for their flight to be announced. Words needed to be said, but neither knew how to begin. The memory of their last disagreement after the River Rhine episode, before they took this decision filled their tired minds. They just sat, both minding the kids.

The announcement finally came and they both stood at once, as if something had pricked their bottoms. There was deep sadness in her husband's eyes, she could understand his emotions by just looking at him. A tear escaped her eyes as he hugged her, and quickly, she wiped it away before he could notice.

Her husband made a move to break away from her but she held onto the hug. She needed to steady her emotions so the tears wouldn't flow. She was the one that had insisted she had to leave Germany with the kids, so there was no need showing him that she was very pained. He could misinterpret the tears as a desire to stay back.

The day they had both rejoiced and celebrated the Humboldt Scholarship came back to her as if it were yesterday. Life indeed had lots of twists, you wouldn't know until you lived through it. Only a push from Ikenna made her untangle from him.

"I will be back before Christmas," he whispered into her ears. His voice wasn't steady and he seemed to be fighting tears as well.

She looked away so he would not read her mind from her face. This decision she had taken, knowing it couldn't be undone weighed on her. She had taken a long look at their apartment before it was locked this afternoon, she wished she could get back inside now. "Christmas is not so far, we will be waiting for you," Ifeoma said.

"Ify, let's part now or go back home. I wish you will agree to the second option."

She smiled as she worked to steady her nerves. "You know there's no going back now, so we must part company."

"Don't say I didn't try." He framed her face with his hands and started to kiss her lightly, then he deepened the kiss, becoming more passionate.

Stunned, Ifeoma pushed him slightly away when she noticed he had gone way past caring. She looked around before speaking. "I never knew I could be kissed in public."

He gulped in air and replied after letting it out. "It is normal here, Ify. It is not a big deal."

"I have a feeling that if it were up to you, you would drag us back to the apartment," she teased.

"You got that right." Ugochukwu said, noting that the lines that had developed on his wife's forehead after the incident at the River Rhine were gone now. He hadn't noticed the exact moment the light returned to her face, but now, it was unmistakable. Her eyes were clear and she no longer had that faraway look. She was returning to her old self.

***

Ifeoma carried Ugochukwu's kiss with her to her window seat in the plane. Her mind was a whirlwind of confused thoughts. She glanced out of the window, and her gaze followed another departing plane as it picked up speed, lifting into the sky with an easy grace that lifted her heart. Before she came to Germany, she had desired to be here, she had longed for it, even dreamt of it. And now, that dream has fizzled out into the energy-sapping struggle of living here as an African.

Now that she was leaving, was there a possibility she would miss this place? It is said that the value of something is usually high when you don't have it, and its value decreases when you finally have it. But she didn't think that was all there was to it. What then happens if you discard what you've wanted after having it, would it be more valuable or less valuable? That was something she would find out only when she was gone from here.

She knew that her mother would be at the Murtala Mohammed Airport waiting for them. She had informed her of their expected time of arrival and her mother had promised to meet them at the airport. She had asked her mother to arrange for a private cab to take them all the way back to the east from Lagos. A day's rest in a Lagos hotel would be enough. She wanted to be back in her old city as soon as possible and she was not ready to go through the stress of public transportation again for any long distance. Once bitten, twice shy.

She knew what her mother would do first once she sets her eyes on them. She would snatch Adaeze from her and begin to examine the baby, she would accuse her of underfeeding her grandchild even if Ada looked plump enough, she would accuse her of giving her the wrong food, and in fact, doing every other thing wrongly. But all those accusations wouldn't matter. She will only be glad for her mother to take over from where she stopped. She would do the *omugwo* she always wanted. It wasn't too late to do a thing as long as it got done.

And then there was something else on her mind. Something she swore needed to be done. Something that would at least help deter a future occurrence.

After reuniting with her mother, she was going to look out for those custom officers who had taken her through the luggage check the first time. She hoped to find the woman first. She would remind her of what happened a year ago and watch her face.

The thought of the woman deeply displeased her. Whatever happened to women supporting women? The officer looked plump, with that padded look that middle aged mothers got - a fellow mother cheating a pregnant woman out of her money. They'd asked her to hand her money over, saying she wouldn't need it where she was going. At first, she thought it was standard airport procedure, until her husband told her she'd been extorted. She knew extortion was common. People often went along with it to avoid trouble. Some even landed in problems that didn't exist prior to refusing to be extorted. But being tricked without realizing it, that is what stung the most.

Her mother would be the perfect person to deal with the officer; she would see to that. She was already imagining what her mother would do: point out the woman among her colleagues, announce her extortion offence loud enough for everyone nearby to hear, and demand that the officer return at least double the amount they had taken from her a year ago. She guessed the officers would try to quieten her mother to save their jobs and faces.

Drama would likely unfold, and she would be beside her mother watching it all. She trusted her mother with this kind of drama.

She adjusted Ada on her laps and strapped Ikenna firmly on his seat before realizing she was smiling in anticipation. She couldn't wait to get to business with those custom officers.

A teenage girl sitting by the window in front of her caught her attention. The girl was reading a book, which she could tell was a novel by its length and cover design. She wondered what kind of story the young girl was lost in, huddled as serenely over the book as she was. To be able to escape from reality into a world inside a book was something she had missed. She'd neither found the time nor the energy to read a novel since becoming pregnant with Ikenna. She would start reading again soon.

There were things she would miss about Mainz, if she told herself the truth. Her husband was top on the list. It would be three months before he would return to Nigeria to spend Christmas with them.

Her thoughts were still in Mainz; the town she had called home for so many months. The people she had met. She hadn't made any real friends, though she had met some nice people. She would miss Zelda. She had enjoyed that last dinner her family had with Zelda and her son-in-law's family. Even though the atmosphere during the dinner was a little awkward, everyone had had a good time. The men had thoroughly enjoyed themselves, talking and laughing and it smoothed things over. It was the men that made that day worth it. Stefan had kept the table lively.

Hannah had proved to be as friendly as her father and they had had an interesting chat.

Then the widowed Mrs. Julia. There was a big age difference between them, but she had been friendly enough, even after the dog incident. Late Walter had been friendly too. She would miss them. She didn't want to think about Bruno. Since she hadn't seen the dog after Walter's death, she might have been euthanized as Julia hinted.

As for the city itself, she thought about the beauty of the land, about the infrastructure, and the amenities that were readily available to the citizens. She thought back to the prompt emergency response when she was in labour and the baby supplies that she received after she had given birth to Ada.

She remembered the cold winter and how she thought she would never be warm again. She shivered a little in the airplane as she remembered those long winter period when they had to stay in the apartment for days when the weather was particularly cold.

She was also glad to have escaped the stinging bites of mosquitoes while she was in Mainz, but she could use mosquito repellents and net back home.

She shifted a little in her seat and adjusted Ada as well, checking to see that Ikenna was buckled in his seat.

Resuming her musings, she thought about the things she wouldn't miss.

At first, she hadn't been too worried about the food. She'd brought along foodstuff and ingredients from home. But after those had dwindled, the only things she found edible were spaghetti, potatoes, bread, and a German delicacy called *Leberkäse*: a kind of meatloaf that somewhat reminded her of *suya*, though softer and without the spice. Other foods had made her want to throw up, with their funny smells and weird tastes, unlike the local dishes she could prepare at home with ingredients that were within reach. She wondered how Ugochukwu was going to survive now that she was no longer there, although he seemed to have adapted to the food and didn't have a problem with how they tasted. She would make it up to him when he came home for Christmas.

She thought of the language barrier and the different way of life from the one she knew while growing up. Her parents had instilled discipline in her by use of corporal punishment, but the system in Germany did not allow for that. Her own children would not grow up to be wayward because she spared the rod, *mba nu*! Especially Ikenna who needed a taste of the rod every now and then.

Last but not least was the lack of communal life. Everyone had minded their business and most only interacted with their fellow countrymen. She had been lonely and had wanted to have conversations with people other than her husband. Hannah would have been a good choice but she was not based in Germany.

She determined not to narrate all her experiences to her mother because what was the point? She would only tell her the beautiful stories, knowing how dramatic her mother could be. She didn't want her mother to develop bad feelings toward her husband or berate her for choosing to stay when she was going through such difficulties. Her mother might also try to oppose any attempt on their part to visit Germany again and she wasn't prepared for the drama that would ensue.

Ikenna tugged at her gown and interrupted her thoughts. He had finished the biscuits she had given him and wanted water. Ada had fallen asleep while she mused, a soggy half-eaten biscuit in her fist. As she searched her handbag for the water bottle, the safety announcements came over the loudspeaker. She leaned back in her seat as the plane took off on the runway. She felt the unsteadiness, her heart lurching as it did once upon a time.

Her eyes were closed now as they ascended and she could almost see herself walking the familiar dusty streets, passing by women vigorously fanning *oka* and *ube* on the locally made grill as they called to customers to come and buy. This is home. This is where she wants to be above any other place in the world.

She felt lighter as the plane rose higher, leaving behind the burdens of yesterday, and sailing into a tomorrow filled with promise and hope.

ACKNOWLEDGEMENTS

I owe the existence of this book to many minds that shaped it along the way.

My deepest gratitude goes to my mother, Ngozi Ezenwa-Ohaeto, whose life and experiences in 1993/94 Mainz inspired the heart of this novel. She gave me her time on the two nights I interviewed her, and she answered every phone call and message I sent along the way. I have dedicated this book to her, for this story could not have existed without her.

I owe so much to my late father, Ezenwa-Ohaeto, who sparked my love for reading and creative writing. I grew up watching him read every evening, which inspired me to pick up books myself and ignited so many imaginations, and that habit stayed with me. This story would never have been written without him.

To Chinua Ezenwa-Ohaeto, who was the first to read the early draft in 2023 and noted that there was still much work to be done, thank you. His input set the standard that shaped this book.

My thanks also to Chidimma Nwokocha, who read the manuscript in its earliest stages and offered careful grammatical guidance.

And to Chinaza Okoli, for taking time from her busy life to read this story, I am grateful for her generosity.

To Glory Ejike (Dr. in incubator), thank you for giving so generously of your doctorate time to make the corrections you did.

I appreciate all who offered encouragement in one way or another: Nnamdi Elekwachi, Onyedika Ezenwa-Ohaeto, Uche

Ezenwa-Ohaeto, Chinelo Adilih, and Chito Modeme. I truly appreciate you.

I am especially indebted to my two principal editors.

To Chidera Onyebinama, whose dedication carried this book through every stage, from developmental editing to line editing, copyediting, proofreading, and fact-checking. Her sharp eye, patience, and multiple reads made this work far stronger than it began.

And to Chimezie Chika, for your developmental editing, proofreading, line editing, insight, and literary wisdom, I am deeply grateful.

I am surprisingly grateful to Dodger, the German Shepherd my family had when I was a teenager, who became the inspiration for Bruno. At around four years old, perhaps her version of a midlife crisis, she started tearing up every shoe she could find, and we soon learned to keep all footwear safely out of her reach.

To Chioma Umeanaeto, who was unable to read the manuscript because she was expecting a baby, yet still cheered me on throughout the process. I am deeply grateful. I must also note that she is a genius. She wrote a children's storybook when she was in primary two, at an age when most children were still learning to write.

To my husband, Chidozie, whose support granted me the time and quiet to bring this story to life. And to Chiagoziem and Arinze, whose laughter and love made the long days and nights worthwhile, thank you.

ABOUT THE AUTHOR

Nnedimma was born in Germany, grew up in Nigeria, and lives in Canada. Her short stories have appeared in the International Human Rights Art Movement Magazine, Parcham Magazine, Rathalla Review, CultureCult Magazine, Helix Magazine, and Storyhouse.org. One of her stories was selected as a finalist for the Barry Hannah Prize in Fiction. Torn Between Homes is her debut novel.

Let's connect! Find me on:

Facebook: Nnedimma Ifechukwu

Instagram: @nnedimmaifechukwu